Nine Florida Stories by
Marjory Stoneman Douglas

A Florida Sand Dollar Book

Nine Florida Stories by
MARJORY STONEMAN DOUGLAS

Edited by Kevin M. McCarthy

University of North Florida Press
Jacksonville

Copyright 1990 by the Board of Regents of the State of Florida
Printed in the United States of America on acid-free paper

21 20   19 18   17 16   P   11   10   9   8   7   6
95 94   93 92   91 90   C   7   6   5   4   3   2

Library of Congress Cataloging-in-Publication Data
Douglas, Marjory Stoneman.
Nine Florida Stories / by Marjory Stoneman Douglas: Edited by Kevin McCarthy.
p. cm.
Contents: Introduction—Pineland—A bird dog in the hand—He man—Twenty minutes late
for dinner—Plumes—By violence—Bees in the mango bloom—September—remember—
The road to the horizon.
ISBN 0–8130-0988–X (alk. paper) —ISBN 0–8130–0994–4 (pbk. : alk. paper)
1. Florida—Fiction. I. McCarthy, Kevin. II. Title. III. Title: 9 Florida stories.
PS3554.08275N56 1990
813'.54—dc20   89-29037

The University of North Florida Press is a member of University Presses of Florida, the scholarly
publishing agency of the State University System of Florida. Books are selected for publication
by faculty editorial committees at each of Florida's nine public universities: Florida A&M
University (Tallahassee), Florida Atlantic University (Boca Raton), Florida International
University (Miami), Florida State University (Tallahassee), University of Central Florida
(Orlando), University of Florida (Gainesville), University of North Florida (Jacksonville),
University of South Florida (Tampa), and University of West Florida (Pensacola).

University Press of Florida
15 Northwest 15th Street
Gainesville, Florida 32611
http://www.upf.com

CONTENTS

Positions of numbers on the map below correspond to the settings of the stories in this book.

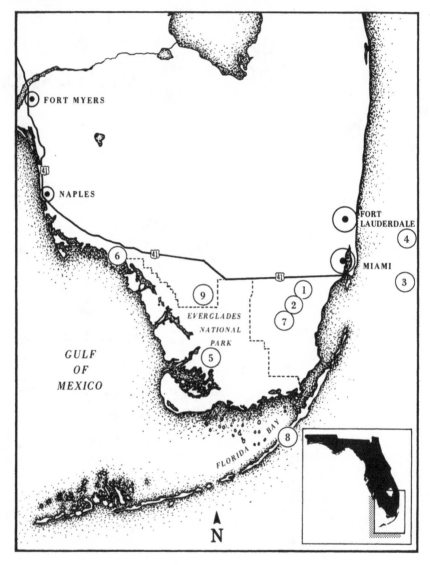

INTRODUCTION

Ms. *MAGAZINE* named Marjory Stoneman Douglas one of its six Women of the Year for 1988, saluting her for "continuing to battle for a safer, more beautiful environment. Her 60-year fight to save the Everglades is a testament to the tenacious energy older women offer today's world." That acclamation was just one of many that Ms. Douglas has received for her life-long dedication to the environmental problems of her beloved state.

Hers has been a long, productive life. In her thirties and forties she wrote more than three dozen short stories and a play. In her fifties, she wrote the definitive book on the Everglades. In her sixties, she produced three novels and two nonfiction works. In her seventies, she directed the University of Miami Press. In her eighties she founded the Friends of the Everglades, now with more than 4,000 members, and led the fight to restore the Okeechobee-Kissimmee-Everglades basin that the U.S. Army Corps of Engineers had tampered with. In her nineties she finished her autobiography and continued the fight to save the water resources of South Florida, especially the Biscayne Aquifer, which supplies Florida's southeastern coast. One shudders to think what the state would be like without her tireless pen and her perseverance. Now, in her hundredth year, she is engaged in writing a biography of W. H. Hudson, whom she considers the first deliberate environmentalist.

Marjory Stoneman was born in Minnesota on 7 April 1890, brought up in Massachusetts, and graduated from Wellesley College in 1912. After the death of her mother she married Kenneth Douglas.

In 1915, when she realized the marriage would not work, she moved to Florida to get a divorce and to be with her father, Frank Stoneman, who founded Miami's first morning paper, The News-Record, which later became the Miami Herald. She then served overseas with the American Red Cross with its publicity department in Paris in 1918 and 1919. After World War I, she returned to Miami to resume working for the Miami Herald. In 1922, she interested the newspaper in establishing the Baby Milk Fund, the first charity in Miami not run by a church and one that raised money to buy milk for local, impoverished children.

After becoming disenchanted with the constant pressure of writing for deadlines, she left the Herald to write short stories, articles, and longer works. She has also written novels—Road to the Sun (1951) about the real estate boom in Miami, Freedom River (1953) about three boys who grew up around the Everglades, and Alligator Crossing (1959) about a Miami boy who matches wits with an alligator poacher. Her nonfiction work includes Hurricane (1958) and Florida: The Long Frontier (1967), the first nontextbook history of the state.

Her most influential book has been The Everglades: River of Grass (1947). Up to that time, most people had considered the Everglades to be a swamp, but Ms. Douglas pointed out that the Everglades is actually a river. "That was my contribution to our knowledge of Florida," she said. "Before then everybody thought it was just swamps, but it's not; it's running water, moving several miles an hour. A river is a body of fresh water moving more in one direction than another."

She was already familiar with the area, having served on the 1927 committee to establish the Everglades National Park. The fact that she could write about birds and Indians and the Everglades and hurricanes fit in with her notion that the area's ecosystem is interrelated, that one part will affect the others, and that human beings had better try to live in harmony with the water, the weather, and the wildlife.

Part of the reason for Ms. Douglas's political power is her ability to organize concerned citizens, part is the great deal of public attention she can garner. She is a powerful public speaker. People may not expect much from the frail lady with the big hat and thick spectacles, but she has the facts and data to support her positions, as well as the passion to arouse supporters. As she liked to say, "I studied elocution at Wellesley more than fifty years ago and have been going around elocuting ever since." She has also maintained friendships with powerful politicians like Senator Bob Graham, formerly the governor of Florida. It has helped that Bob Graham is from South Florida and that his mother worked with Ms. Douglas many years ago.

In the 1980s she spent much time working on the problems of the Kissimmee River and Lake Okeechobee. She and the Friends of the Everglades fought to restore the course of the Kissimmee River, straightened under the guise of "flood control." The group also worked on cleaning up Lake Okeechobee, which had become polluted by the dumping of untreated cow manure into the lake by dairy farmers and by the back-pumping of irrigation water full of pesticides into the lake by sugar growers. Her group saw some success when the South Florida Water Management District voted in 1988 to severely decrease farm runoff in an effort to reduce the pollution of the lake, the nation's largest freshwater lake outside the Great Lakes.

Ms. Douglas has watched Miami grow from a small town of fewer than 5,000 people in 1915 into the huge international city it is today. She worries that many of the approximately 900 people who move to Florida every day are unaware of the fragile balance between nature and humans, that many of them come from more environmentally sound locations, and that too many look on the Everglades as a swamp to be drained for more homes. She has made people aware of the fragility of nature, to ensure that developers safeguard the area's water— clearly the issue of the nineties.

The nine stories in this collection represent some of her best fiction and deal with issues that she would write about in her longer works of nonfiction and fiction. All nine stories, which are presented in the order in which they were published, are set in Florida and were originally published in the *Saturday Evening Post*. Ms. Douglas referred to her Coconut Grove house near Miami as the house that the *Post* built.

PINELAND

When Ms. Douglas decided to leave the hectic life of a *Miami Herald* reporter in 1924, she began writing short stories for the *Saturday Evening Post*, thus joining the ranks of many other American writers, like F. Scott Fitzgerald and Ernest Hemingway. She reached an audience of millions and earned enough money to write free lance, full time. She studied many short stories in the *Post* and decided that the editor liked success stories about a noble protagonist, with a little sex and a few cuss words thrown in. Her first short stories in the magazine followed that formula, but with "Pineland," published 15 August 1925, she broke away from the formula and wrote in her own style.

She often based her stories on her own experiences and travels, placing them in France, the Balkans, Cuba, and Florida. The Florida stories were particularly popular because they dealt with an area that was relatively new in fiction. So many people wanted to know more about the state, from real estate investing to crops to vacations, that Ms. Douglas's stories found a ready market.

"Pineland" has some autobiographical elements in it, including the fact that it deals with a New England woman who married an unsuitable man and came to South Florida to begin a new life. Sarah McDevitt, the protagonist of "Pineland," clearly had the independence and perseverance that marked Ms. Douglas's life. The image in the story of "the white brilliance of the Florida noon" was one that Ms. Douglas had of Miami from her first visit to the city.

What drove Sarah McDevitt south was the great Florida freeze of 1894–95. Legend has it that during that freeze Miami's Julia Tuttle sent Henry Flagler some orange blossoms to show the railroad builder that the freeze had not affected South Florida. Whether the story is true or not, Flagler decided to extend his Florida East Coast Railway from Palm Beach to Biscayne Bay. The railroad reached Miami in 1896 and eventually Key West in 1912.

A BIRD DOG IN THE HAND

Published 12 September 1925, this story deals with two issues of great importance in Florida's history: the real estate boom of the 1920s and the drainage of the Everglades. The first issue concerned the wild speculation over land prices around Miami. "Binder boys" placed options or deposits on land and sold them over and over again for profit. The boom ended when the 1926 hurricane scared many northerners away from Miami, and hundreds of people defaulted on their land contracts, halting the development of South Florida for many years. This story revolves around dreamers, the short-sighted ones who wanted to make a quick profit and the far-sighted ones who envisioned what the land might look like after engineers got through with it.

The second issue deals with a drastic measure for making dry land: draining the Everglades. In 1881, Hamilton Disston, a tool-making millionaire from Philadelphia, bought four million acres of South Florida for 25 cents an acre and began draining the land. The lowering of the water level made the land suitable for crops and houses. Much of the land around Miami that is now inhabited by people was drained, thanks also to the efforts in 1906 of Governor Napoleon Bonaparte Broward, who ran for office on the slogan of draining the Everglades. Dredges converted two million acres of wet land into dry and habitable land and enabled towns like Hialeah and Miami Springs to expand westward.

In *The Everglades: River of Grass*, Ms. Douglas wrote that dredging the Everglades "was an idea more explosive than dynamite, which would change this lower Florida world as nothing had so changed it since the melting of the glacial ice four thousand years ago." Today environmentalists follow Ms. Douglas's lead in opposing drainage of the Everglades, pointing out that the vast wetland provides most of South Florida's precious water supply. We now know that much rain comes from the evaporation of the wet Everglades, and that draining the wetlands will curtail the rain that the land so desperately needs.

HE MAN

If you secretly despise sports or being around naturally athletic people, you will empathize with this story of a 19-year-old boy who prefers the quiet life to that of his extroverted, athletic father. If you have a fear of heights or of flying, you too may get white knuckles as you ride with Ronny on his ill-fated flight east of Miami Beach. Published 30 July 1927 and named one of the O'Henry Memorial Award Prize Stories of 1927, this story deals with the perils of the sea and treats two themes of Ms. Douglas's own life: endurance and fortitude. How one adapts to unexpected challenges, especially if one seems physically frail, is the theme of the story and of the writer's career.

This story mirrored Ms. Douglas's interest in young people, both real and fictional. While working as a reporter for the *Herald*, for example, she learned the tragic story of a young man, Martin Tabert, who had recently come to Florida. Authorities picked him up for vagabonding, placed him in a work camp, and beat him to death. Angered at his senseless, tragic murder, Ms. Douglas wrote an impassioned poem, "Martin Tabert of North Dakota Is Walking Florida Now," that deeply affected others and became what she calls "the single most outstanding thing I was ever able to accomplish."

Martin Tabert of North Dakota Is Walking Florida Now

Martin Tabert of North Dakota is walking Florida now.
O children, hark to his footsteps coming, for he's walking soft and slow.
Through the piney woods and the cypress hollows.
A wind creeps up and it's him it follows.
Martin Tabert of North Dakota is walking Florida now.
They took him out to the convict camp, and he's walking Florida now.
O children, the tall pines stood and heard him when he was moaning low.
The other convicts, they stood around him,
When the length of the black strap cracked and found him.
Martin Tabert of North Dakota. And he's walking Florida now.
O children, the dark night saw where they buried him, buried him, buried him low.
And the tall pines heard where they went to hide him.
And the wind crept up to moan beside him.
Martin Tabert of North Dakota. And he's walking Florida now.
The whip is still in the convict camps, for Florida's stirring now.
Children, from Key West to Pensacola you can hear the great wind go.
The wind that he roused when he lay dying.
The angry voice of Florida crying,
"Martin Tabert of North Dakota,
Martin Tabert of North Dakota,
Martin Tabert of North Dakota,
You can rest from your walking now."

The poem aroused the public, who in turn persuaded the legislature to pass laws that stopped prisoner beatings in the work camps. Using her pen to right wrongs was something she would do for the rest of her career.

In addition to that poem and to this short story, Ms. Douglas wrote two novels about boys. *Freedom River* (1953) explores the interrelationships among three boys before the Civil War: a white boy whose father was a Quaker abolitionist, a Miccosukee Indian boy, and an escaped slave. *Alligator Crossing* (1959) is about a boy in the Everglades National Park and how he coped with men killing the wildlife there. The short story describes how a young man faced a life-and-death situation as well as commenting on the unreliability of early airplanes. Its dramatic tension made it popular with the reading public.

TWENTY MINUTES LATE FOR DINNER

When America entered World War I, the Miami Herald sent Ms. Douglas to cover the story of the first woman in Florida to enlist in the Naval Reserve. When Ms. Douglas heard the Navy spiel, she found that she was raising her hand and swearing to defend the United States from all its enemies, both domestic and foreign. She later telephoned her father at the newspaper and said, "I got the story on the first woman to enlist. It turned out to be me."

If she thought serving in the Armed Services would include some of the daring, dangerous work described in this short story, she was disappointed. The Navy assigned her to secretarial tasks, for which she was overqualified and led to her resignation after which she, joined the American Red Cross and went to Paris to help in the war effort. Her work in Europe provided her with material that she later used in her short stories.

"Twenty Minutes Late for Dinner" concerns a problem we still have today: smuggling. Florida's long coastline, with its many inlets and secluded bays, plus the nearness of the Bahamas and Caribbean islands, along with the public's indifference to the enforcement of Prohibition, encouraged liquor smuggling by well-organized professionals in the 1920s. Because the Bahamas allowed the sale of liquor during that time, smugglers stocked up on supplies in Nassau before dashing to the Florida coast at night by boat or plane. Speedboats could make the trip to Florida in about two hours. Smugglers, as in this story, usually packed six bottles of liquor at a time in burlap bags called "burlocks" or "hams." Each bag weighed 20 pounds, took up little space, and easily survived the rough bouncing of the trip. Authorities concerned with stopping the drug smuggling into Florida today can appreciate the difficulties that the Coast Guard had during the years of Prohibition.

Ten months before the appearance of this story, first published 30 June 1928, authorities at the Coast Guard base in Fort Lauderdale hanged a rumrunner for the murder of two Coast Guardsmen and a Secret Service agent. Ms. Douglas alluded to the "rummy that got killed" early in the story. A judge had ordered that he be hanged in Dade County, but officials there were spared the duty when they claimed they did not know how to hang anyone. Coast Guard officials in Fort Lauderdale then reluctantly carried out the sentence.

PLUMES

A monument at Flamingo in Everglades National Park commemorates Guy Bradley, a game warden killed by plume hunters in 1905. The son of Palm Beach's first barefoot mailman, Guy Bradley grew up in the lawless town of Flamingo and shot the many birds that nested in the vicinity, just as his neighbors did. Plume hunters could sell the beautiful feathers of snowy egrets for $35 an ounce, the same price as gold. Milliners used these feathers to make large plumed hats for European and American women, hats beautiful to look at but which caused the slaughter of thousands of egrets. In 1902, Bradley had a change of heart and switched sides to become a game warden to stop the wanton slaughter of the birds.

Two kinds of egret, which are of the heron family, make their home in the Everglades. The Great Egret, also called the long white, stands more than three feet tall and has foot-long, straight plumes; a smaller bird, called the snowy egret, has 6-inch, curved plumes. As Ms. Douglas's story indicates, the latter's plumes are most beautiful just after the young are hatched, at a time when the parent birds will not leave the rookery, even when hunters are shooting at them.

On 8 July 1905, plume hunters shot and killed Bradley as he attempted to arrest a poacher. After plume hunters killed three more game wardens, the Audubon Society succeeded in having plume hunting outlawed, and the fad of wearing the large, feathered hats died, especially in this country. In 1947, the Everglades National Park was established, and that helped the preservation of the habitat suitable for the egrets.

Ms. Douglas has wielded her pen and her voice for more than 60 years to save the beautiful birds of Florida. She published this story in the *Post* (14 June 1930), the nonfiction "Wings" about plume hunters (*Post*, 14 March 1931), and *The Joys of Bird Watching in Florida*

(1969) about Florida birds and the harm that humans can do to birds with pesticides and poisons. She pointed out that egrets, flamingos, limpkins, and ibis are an integral part of the Everglades and must be protected.

BY VIOLENCE

This story, published 22 November 1930, takes place near Chokoloskee Island below Everglades City in Collier County. The name Chokoloskee, pronounced "Chuckaluskee" by long-time residents, means 'old house' in Seminole. The surrounding bay, ten miles long and about two miles wide, is very shallow, as the men in the story found out. Part of the Ten Thousand Islands protect the bay from the Gulf of Mexico.

Chokoloskee Island, which is only about 150 acres in size, rises to 20 feet, making it one of the highest points in the area. Ted Smallwood, whose store is mentioned in the story, tapped an underground source of water in 1918 that provided a good supply of water and thus enabled people to live there. Smallwood (1873–1943) settled on Chokoloskee around 1900, set up a post office/trading post there, and dredged a channel from his dock to the deep-water channel several hundred yards offshore. Life on the island centered on the sea, which produced subsistence to a dozen families in the early part of this century.

The boy in the story probably attended the island elementary school, although the lack of teachers sometimes kept it closed. Spartan conditions on the island dissuaded the squeamish from settling there. One settler wrote in 1924: "We have no preaching at all and no school. We heard of a he-teacher who started down here and got as far as Marco and found out he did not have his fighting spirit along; so he went back up the coast." The next year the same settler wrote: "Our school teacher, we understand, is going to give up her school today; it is too much for her nerves. She seems to be a nice refined body and we are sorry for her. She had a trying time here, but we can give her praise for her endurance." Conditions on the island would not change very much until the Tamiami Trail opened in 1928 and a causeway connected the island to the mainland in 1955.

BEES IN THE MANGO BLOOM

First published 12 December 1931, this story is about a fruit that many South Floridians grow in their yards but which has never enjoyed the favorable press that the grapefruit and avocado have received. Fruit growers in Dade County, Florida, concentrated on grapefruit growing in the early part of this century, with a few farmers growing avocados. Very few farmers grew mangoes because the fruit had too much fiber attached to the large seed and seemed unpromising for commercial ventures.

Near West Palm Beach, the U.S. Department of Agriculture had a researcher plant three small trees of the Mulgoba variety from India, but the 1895 freeze killed two of the trees. From the third tree has sprung much of the mango crop of South Florida, greatly helped by the area's dry winters and wet summers.

Two men had a major impact on the area's mango crop. Dr. David Fairchild, a friend of Ms. Douglas, introduced several varieties of mango into the Miami area, beginning in 1901; Captain John Haden of the Eighth U.S. Infantry retired to Miami with his wife and began collecting tropical plants and fruits. Captain Haden saw the Mulgoba tree in Palm Beach County, brought several large fruits to his home in Coconut Grove, and planted the seeds. The resulting fruit, which was a combination of several mango varieties, is called the Haden mango, which is mentioned in this story. The other mango mentioned, the Saigon mango, comes from the Far East.

The reason planters grow mangos for a windbreak, as in the story, is that the trees grow fast and tall and strong and also produce fruit before the hurricane season. However, the mango tree is subject to a fungus disease called anthracnose, which manifests itself in leaf spot, blossom blight, and fruit staining and rotting. Freezes, like the terrible one of 1894–95, seldom affect South Florida, so mangoes have done well there.

SEPTEMBER—REMEMBER

This story was published 7 December 1935, three months after the terrible hurricane that hit the Keys on Labor Day, 2 September 1935. Ms. Douglas mentioned in her story the train that was backing down the Overseas Railroad Extension to pick up 683 World War I veterans who were building bridges in the Keys. That hurricane, a force-5 storm and the worst in the recorded history of the western hemisphere, had winds of 250 m.p.h. and a barometer reading of 26.35, the lowest ever recorded by the U.S. Weather Service.

The hurricane pitched the veterans' relief train off the tracks, destroyed hundreds of structures, and killed between 500 and 1,000 people. Flagler's railroad would never again run to Key West. Instead, his company sold all the embankments and line to the U.S. government, which built U.S. Highway 1 to Key West.

Ms. Douglas covered that hurricane and others in *Hurricane* (1958), a 393-page book that describes in dramatic detail the many storms that have changed the history of the world. When the book was reissued in paperback in 1976, the publisher took out all the descriptions of hurricanes, keeping only the scientific parts, a fact that hurt its sales. Her original book may have had some influence on the establishment in Miami of what may be the most stringent building regulations of any city in America, regulations that are meant to minimize the damage caused by hurricanes.

Hurricanes have played a major role in the history of Florida, from the one that wrecked the French fleet in 1565 to the one that ended the Florida real estate boom in 1926 to more recent ones. Ms. Douglas has done much in her writings to alert Floridians and other coastal state residents to the potential devastation of these storms.

THE ROAD TO THE HORIZON

The two dominant images in this story, which was published 22 February 1941, are saw grass and mosquitoes. As a boy and a man slowly make their way across the Everglades through muck and swamp from west to east, the saw grass repeatedly cuts them. Saw grass is not like that of our ordinary lawns but is more of a cutting sedge. Reaching heights of 10–15 feet, it withstands everything except fire, and even fire will only slow its growth temporarily. Cutting it down leaves a stubble that can pierce a canvas boat, as in this story. Ms. Douglas wrote in *The Everglades:* "It may be that the mystery of the Everglades is the saw grass, so simple, so enduring, so hostile. It was the saw grass and the water which divided east coast from west coast and made the central solitudes that held in them the secrets of time, which has moved here so long unmarked."

The boy in the story dreams about building a road across the Everglades, clearly anticipating the Tamiami Trail, which was completed in 1928. The 274-mile road allowed motorists to speed from coast to coast, oblivious of the tremendous obstacles engineers had to overcome, especially in the 143-mile stretch from Miami to Fort Myers.

A man who made the trek across the Everglades in 1891 wrote the following: "If a man is a dude, a trip through the 'Glades is the thing to cure him. A day's journey in slimy, decaying vegetable matter which coats and permeates everything it touches, and no water with which to wash it off, will be good for him, but his chief medicine will be his morning toilet. He must rise with the sun when the grass and leaves are wet with dew and put on his shrinking body his clothes heavy and wet with slime and scrape out of each shoe a cup full of black and odorous mud—it is enough to make a man swear to be contented ever afterwards with a board for a bed and a clean shirt once a week."

The nine stories have been selected not only for their excellence but also for the picture of life in South Florida during the first half of this century. They are told by a woman who has lived in Miami for the last 70 years and has spent her career writing about the area's problems and scoundrels and its beauty and heroes. For her writing and her contribution to the state's environmental concerns she might very well be Florida's Woman of the Century.

1
PINELAND

*L*ARRY GIBBS was thankful that the roughness of the road took all his attention, because he had no idea what to say to a woman whose son has just been hanged. She sat like a stone beside him in the front seat of the car. Out of the corner of his eye he could see her cheap black skirt covering her bony knees and the worn toes of her shoes to which still clung some particles of sand from around Joe McDevitt's grave. The heavy black veil which muffled her hat and her face gave off the acid smell of black dye. Her hands in black cotton gloves with flabby tips that were too long for her fumbled with a clean folded handkerchief in her lap.

All around them the white brilliance of the Florida noon poured down upon the uneven road from the burial place, caught on the bright spear points of palmettos and struck into nakedness the shabby houses among stumps of pine trees of this outskirt of Miami. The light and the hot wind seemed whiter and hotter for the figure of Sarah McDevitt in her mourning.

It was Jack Kelley, the man who had turned state's evidence on the Pardee gang case, who had told Larry he would loan him an automobile if he would take Sarah McDevitt home. It was the same Jack Kelley who had started the fund to provide Joe McDevitt's body with decent burial. He had seen to it that his own figure had a prominent place in the newspaper photographs of the grave, which next morning would assure all Dade County that the Pardee gang, including the McDevitts, was at last broken up, either by being driven from Florida or doing endless terms in prison camps, like George McDevitt; or like

Joe here, made safe for Southern progress with a stretch of rope, a pine coffin and a few feet of Florida marl.

"Go on now," Jack Kelley had said, pushing at Larry with large, firm pushes. "There's a story in Sarah McDevitt yet. The last of her boys gone and she going home to sit and listen to her pine trees, see? A nice little front-page story, see? And you might just mention the canned goods I've put in the back of the car for her. Enough to last her a month. Here you are, Sarah McDevitt. Larry Gibbs will take you home, see?"

Larry wondered miserably if she were crying in behind that stuffy veil. He had not seen her face yet. He had never seen her before.

She had not come to the trial, although he wondered a little why Joe McDevitt's lawyer had not brought her in for her effect on the jury. He thought of Joe McDevitt as he had been then, lounging, copper-haired, a sleek reddish animal, his veins crammed with healthy life. He had not shown much interest even when the facts about the bank robbery and the cashier's death were made damningly evident.

Now Joe McDevitt was dead. It had made a tremendous impression on Larry. It was his first big court case since he had been on the paper. He had written home to his mother that he was seeing the real bedrock of life at last. He pictured his mother reading it in her breakfast room in Brookline, turning the pages of his letter with that little look of amused horror on her distinguished face. She would hope he would not be obliged to come in close contact with miserable creatures in jails.

He had written with affected carelessness about interviewing McDevitt the man-killer, but secretly he was thankful that he had not had to cover the hanging this morning. The other court reporter had done that. But this business of taking home the mother was almost as bad. It made him feel perfectly rotten. She was so quiet.

"That road," she said to him suddenly, and he flushed and jerked the car around on the way she had pointed. He was taken completely by surprise that her voice could be so clear and firm.

"This is—this is the Larkins Road, isn't it?" he asked hastily to prevent the silence from forming again. "I didn't know it was surfaced yet."

But she said nothing, and he continued to stare forward at the road paralleling the shine of tracks, the shine and glitter of palmettos on the other side. The sky ahead was steely and remote, and it made his eyes ache. A corner of her veil snapped outside the car. Every once in so often her hat joggled forward over her forehead and she pushed it back and wiped her face with the wad of her handkerchief. He was somehow sure that it was not tears she wiped.

He turned to ask her if she would not like to have him stop somewhere and get her a glass of water, and saw for the first time that her skin was pale and clammy with heat. Her mouth, with the deep soft wrinkles on it of an old woman, was half open and panting. But as he spoke she closed her lips in a tight line and looked at him straight out of faded gray eyes within faded lashes. There was nothing feeble in her glance. She pulled off her hat abruptly and her thin gray hair blew against the brown skin of her forehead.

When they had passed by the stores and railway station of Larkins she began slowly to take off her black gloves. She rolled them into hard balls, working and working at them sightlessly until he thought she would never let them alone. Her hands were curiously like the look in her eyes, vigorous in spite of the blotched brown skin stretched over the large-boned knuckles.

"What did Jack Kelley think he was going to get out of sending me home with a lot of canned goods?" she asked suddenly.

"Why—I don't know," Larry said. "He—I think he was just—I mean I imagine he wanted to show you he was sorry that you—that your——"

"Huh!" she said, and her voice was dryly deliberate. "Any time Jack Kelley spends money you can bet he knows right well where he's going to get something for it. I guess maybe he figured you'd put something in the paper about it."

Larry was always sharply conscious when his fair skin reddened. "But, Mrs. McDevitt, I wouldn't write anything you wouldn't want me to write. I——"

"I could tell you to write something Jack Kelley wouldn't want you to write, about the time he tried to do me out of my homestead. I guess he wouldn't relish that much."

"When was that?" Larry leaped eagerly to the question. He felt easier, now that she was talking. The only sense of strain of which he was aware was the slow dry way she talked, as if her tongue were swollen and sticky. "Tell me about that, won't you?"

"Oh—it wasn't much. Nothing to put in the paper. He just wasn't so smart's he thought he was. It was one time about two years after I come down on my land here. McDevitt's mother up in Vermont wrote me that George was awful sick. I'd been working in Miami, waiting on table like I did in the six months they let you live off your homestead, and it was time I went back on it, but I got permission from the land agent to leave long enough to go north and look after my children.

"In Jacksonville I met this Jack Kelley between trains, that I'd seen coming into the restaurant time and again, and the minute he saw me he knew I was supposed to be on my land. 'Well, Sarah McDevitt,' he says to me. 'So the pineland was too much for you, was it?'

"'When you see me giving up my pineland you can have it yourself, Jack Kelley,' I says to him, and thought no more of it. But don't you believe it but that man turned right around and come back to Miami and started to file a counterclaim against my property. And now he thinks he can fool me with canned goods. Jack Kelley. Huh!"

"But he didn't get your land, did he?"

"Of course he didn't, the big fool. He didn't have a chance. I had my permission right enough, and the day after he'd filed the claim he come down to look at my house, and a good neighbor of mine that see him coming fired off a six-shooter in the air, and he said Jack Kelley ran like a whitehead. And up in Miami Mr. Barnes that owned the restaurant told me he'd go to court himself to see I kept my place. He said Jack Kelley'd ought to be run out of the county for trying to take a woman's land from her. I don't mean you should put that in the paper, though."

Larry pondered regretfully the news value of that story. But she was quite right that he couldn't print it. The paper wouldn't stand for it, and besides it was libel.

They were running past pineland now, and he turned and stared at the passing ranks. They were like no pine trees he had ever seen in his life, these Caribbean pine. Their high bare trunks, set among palmetto fans that softened all the ground beneath them, rose up so near the road that he could see the soft flakes of color of their scaly bark, red and brown and cream, as if patted on with a thick brush. Their high tops mingled gray-green branches, twisted and distorted

4

as if by great winds or something stern and implacable in their own natures. Their long green needles were scant, letting the sky through. They were strange trees, strange but beautiful. The brilliance of the sun penetrated through their endless ranks in a swimming mist of light. They were endlessly alike, endlessly monotonous, and yet with an endless charm and variety.

Every tree held its own twist and pattern; every tree, even to the distant intermingled brown of trunks too far away to distinguish, was infinitely itself. Sometimes the pine woods came so near the road he could smell their sunny resinous breath. Sometimes they retreated like a long, smoky, green-frothed wall beyond house lots and grapefruit groves or open swales of sawgrass or beyond cleared fields where raw stumps of those already destroyed stood amid the blackness of a recent burning. Against the horizon their ranks rushed cometlike and immobile into the untouched west. He felt the comprehension of them growing upon him—the silence of their trunks, the loveliness of their tossed branches, the virginity of their hushed places, in retreat before the surfaced roads and filling stations, the barbecue stands and signboards of the new Florida.

"They're wonderful, aren't they, the pines?" he said abruptly. "There's something beautiful and fresh about them, different from any trees I've ever seen."

The woman beside him took a great deep breath, as if what he said had released something in her.

"I remember the first time I went to see my place," she said. "Twenty years ago. In those days the nearest road was six miles away. You could take a horse and carriage from Miami to a place near Goulds where the road branched. Then you'd have to walk across country to where my land began. It wasn't my land then, though. The land agent had it surveyed and told me where the boundary stob was. The palmetto was deeper than it is now, but I was younger and nothing was too much for me. When I'd walked a ways through the palmetto under those pines and come to the place where they said would be good for a clearing, I just stood still and listened, I don't know how long. It was so still you could hear little noises a long ways off, like a bird rustling up on a branch or an insect buzzing.

"The tops of the trees were higher up than these here, and they didn't move any. The light was all soft and kind of bright, and yet green and dim too. Those trees were the quietest things I ever see. It did you good just to feel them so quiet, as if you'd come to the place where everything began. I couldn't hardly believe there was places outside where people were afraid and worried. I just—I tell you I just started crying, but not to hurt. I never was one for crying, but this was just good easy tears, the way you cry when you're so happy you don't believe it's true."

Larry hardly dared to speak, keeping his hands tight on the wheel and his eyes on the road. Yet when she continued to maintain the silence into which she had fallen he ventured, "What made you come down here homesteading in the first place, Mrs. McDevitt?"

"I was in the freeze years ago, up in Orange County." Her reply came with a little effort, as if she had lost her present self in a sturdy dark-haired woman, wiping her eyes all alone among silent acres of pineland. "Eh, law!" she sighed. "That was a long time. McDevitt bought an orange grove and we were froze out."

"Tell me about that," Larry insisted. Presently she went on speaking, with her chin on her breast and her eyes staring forward at the road racing and racing toward them, between the straight gleaming rails and the dusty palmettos, the few pines, half dying, with patent-medicine signs tacked to them, that followed this part of the road. She talked as if it were as easy as thinking—easier. McDevitt would have it that we mustn't sell the oranges until the season was later and the prices better, although I told him to sell. The fruit was coloring wonderful that winter. 'Ninety-four and five. In those days in Orange County the orange trees were tall and dark and glossy, on strong thick trunks. When you walked in an orange grove the dark leaves met overhead and you walked on bare brown earth in a kind of solid shadow, not like the pines that strain the light through clear and airy. Up in the dark branches you could see the oranges in clusters, growing gold color like there was sun on them. I never saw fruit like ours that winter. It seemed like the branches would break with it. Then came the big freeze. There never was one like it before and there never has been since.

"That was about the last difference McDevitt and I had." Larry felt a pricking in the back of his neck at the even depth of hatred in her voice, the first naked emotion she had shown. "He was a smooth one, a smooth, smiling, hateful man, with easy ways and eyes

6

boring in for the weak place in you. It was what made him furious, not finding mine. 'll be stronger than you are,' I'd say to myself often and often. 'And stiller and more of a man. You see if I won't.' That was even as soon as after George was born. I'd grit my teeth and bear that look in his eyes until he'd fling off and leave me a week or two for spite. We come down to Orange County from Vermont state, where his mother was. He got this orange grove with money my own mother left me, but I knew he'd never be one for holding it. So I held it."

The car dipped and rose on the swinging levels of the road. The sun was beginning to crawl down from its zenith and the burning white of the sky was turning a faint flower-petal blue. The wind from the invisible sea to eastward came to them in steady, freshening gusts.

"Turn here," she said. "That winter he had a great beard that was the color of the oranges, and he'd sit around barefooted on the porch of the shack we had and comb it. Joe was—Joe was a year old then." Her tongue thickened as she spoke the name for the first time. Larry heard the sticky parting of her lips. The car was running almost silently on a dirt road in the shadow of pines that seemed stronger and more dense than those by the main highway.

"I was a thick stumpy woman then, and the heat behind all those trees there in the middle of Florida was like a tight hand over your lungs. But I'd leave the baby and little George on a mattress in the breeze-way between the two rooms of the house and go out to see that the nigras were working. McDevitt wouldn't ever. He'd sit there smiling, with those eyes over his beard and never sweated. The heat was terrible. That's what made the fruit ripen early. I was wild with nerves at it, but I wouldn't let McDevitt know. Only when he come home from Orlando and said he'd got an offer to sell the crop on the trees for ten thousand, only he'd decided not to, that night I had to go out and walk up and down the road that had a place where there wasn't any orange trees. That night I thought I'd choke with orange trees.

"Up around the house the shadow of them was black and thick, and the smell of the new bloom that was coming here and there up among the yellowing fruit sickened you. There was a starlight that fell wet and glittery like knives on the leaf edges. The next day McDevitt went off somewhere to spite me because I wanted him to sell, and left me alone. I'd never let him guess how afraid I was to be alone. I guess that's why I married him when he come along when ma died. Or maybe he guessed and thought I'd beg him to take me away.

"He would have liked me to beg him to. But I never let on that my knees were like string to see him go. He turned at the gate and smiled at me over that orange-colored beard with his stone-white teeth and his eyes that were like wires boring into you, and I shut my mouth tight and let him look. So he stopped smiling and went, and I was there with the two children and four nigras living down a ways in a shack in the grove, and the days got hotter. I would of sold the crop, only I couldn't find the man that made the offer. But everybody in Orlando, at the bank and everywhere, said to hold on, because prices were going up. Then one day it begun to get cold.

"It came on in the morning, and by afternoon it was so cold the children shivered, and I had to put two-three extra shirts on them. In all the groves up and down the road they began to light fire pots and start bonfires to keep the oranges from feeling it. You could smell the smoke and the blossoms in the chilly air. The sky was heavy and gray-looking and there wasn't any wind, and the smoke drifted and hung between the long dark rows of trees. But still it kept getting colder. Late that afternoon I went out and stopped the nigras from lighting any more fire pots. I could see it wasn't going to do any good. I told them to cut down a couple of old trees to keep themselves warm in their houses that night and had them bring me some of the wood too.

"Then it got dark sudden and I gave the children some bread and milk and put them to bed with all the bedclothes over them, and I put a shawl around my knees and one over my shoulders and sat close to the stove and fed it with orange wood. All night long I sat there and it kept getting colder. About midnight I could tell it was freezing outside, because the trees begun to crack and snap. Then pretty soon you could hear thumps on the ground where the oranges were freezing and falling off. I set there and heard them and knew that every cent I had in the world but two dollars was being frozen up. Then some more oranges would thump down.

"Next morning when I unbolted my front door and looked out the ground was all covered with frost that was melting in the sun, and everywhere you looked the edges of the leaves were blackened, and on the ground carloads and carloads of oranges were scattered. The crop was ruined. Every orange was hurt. And all the way into Orlando and all over Orange County and all the way up to Jacksonville it was the same way. It wasn't just me that was ruined. The whole state was. I've often wondered why we had to get caught in the one big freeze Orange County ever had.

"Well, when McDevitt heard how things were, he told a man that was coming to Orlando to tell me that I could have the grove. He said he was tired of oranges anyway and thought he would go to Texas and I prob'ly wouldn't see him any more. So there I was. I was scared so when the crop went I didn't hardly know what to do, but what McDevitt did, put the ginger in me I needed.

"Maybe he thought he'd find the weak place in me that way, but it made me mad enough to do anything. So then I found that the trees weren't dead, only the fruit. There was maybe a chance to save next year's bloom. So I went into the bank at Orlando and borrowed some money to keep going on, and almost everybody else that wasn't too discouraged done the same thing. Things looked bad, but they weren't too bad.

"Until along in February when the second freeze came. The sap had begun to come back with the heat that shut down again and the bloom was forced beyond its time. People were getting real cheerful, like people get in a fruit country, living on next year's promise, and Orlando looked prosperous. And then the second freeze came. I sat up all night again and listened to the crackling of the boughs. There wasn't any oranges to thump down, but somehow now it made it all the worse. You couldn't hear anything but the crackling and snapping of wood, but you could feel the chill that meant that next year's hopes were dying.

"My fire went out and I was chilled through, and yet even when it come daylight and the sun straggled in the window I kept sitting there by the stove, not daring to go and look. There wasn't a sound outside, nobody going by in the road, and the nigras not making any noise at all. I just sat there all huddled up until little George woke up and ran and opened the door and told me to look.

"You never saw anything like it in your life. It was the abomination of desolation. It wasn't only that the leaves were black and shriveled and fallen and the new bloom gone. The trees themselves were frozen stiff and the sap had frozen and then split the trees down to the roots; and there they lay, looking like an earthquake or a tornado had hit them. Every tree was killed, every one of them, down to the roots. And when the sun was hot and the warmth was coming back all the country smelled of rottenness. People went around with mouths that spoke but couldn't smile, and they could look with their eyes, but it was like they weren't looking at anything.

"It was like death. Business was stopped. All the banks were ruined. Then the people begun to go away. They could have stood it without money, but they couldn't stand it without the hope of their trees that they'd worked so hard over and put their last cent in. They went away from the blackened rotting groves and they left their houses wide open and maybe food on the table and bread in the oven, and in a week it was like everybody had died. Some went back to places they'd come from in the North or the old South, and some went to Texas and Oklahoma.

"But some of the young men that didn't have all the spirit taken out of them were talking about going farther south, way down in South Florida that nobody thought was fit to live in on account of swamps, down to this new place Miami on the coast where they were bringing the railroad. These men said that maybe down there they could start new orange groves, and there was gov'ment land you could homestead. "If I hadn't been so mad with McDevitt I don't see how I could have done it, but I begun to think if a man could take up a homestead maybe I could, and then I'd put a grove in and show him I was a smarter man than he was, if I was a woman. So I wrote to his mother that lived in Vermont state and told her just how it was, and she wrote back she was sorry McDevitt had been so mean and she'd take the children for a while. She was a good, kind woman and I guess McDevitt took after his father. There was some people going back to Vermont state from Orlando that could take the children to her. So that's how I took up the land. Perhaps I made a mistake. There's plenty of people has made good money growing oranges in Orange County since then. Go slow here. We're coming to my gate."

There was a straggling grove of grapefruit at the left, which presently revealed a road more like a path. Up this, in answer to her hand, Larry turned. The weeds were long under the trees. Beyond that was unused cleared land that may have been used to grow vegetables. But beyond that still the pines began again, pressing down almost into the faint roadway, rising endlessly to each side and ahead, larger and more stately than any Larry had yet noticed. The palmetto around their roots was all untouched. Between their ranks the distance was smoky with crowding trunks. Superb trees, they seemed to be the very ancestors and originals of all the others they had passed. The house stood in a small clearing, perhaps the half acre prescribed by the Government for homesteaders. It was made of pine logs and there was a well beside it and a small garden. When he stopped the car Larry found himself listening intently. It was as she had said. You could hear only little noises faint and far away. When she was walking from the car to the house steps, stiffly, with her black hat and veil trailing from her hand and her heavy black skirt bunched up as she had been sitting on it, Larry asked, "Where do you want me to put these canned goods, Mrs. McDevitt?"

At first he thought she had not heard him, but at the top step she turned and looked back at him and her thin lips stretched in a mirthless smile. "You take those things back to Jack Kelley," she said, and stood eying him. Something in the flush on his face must have reached to her, for she said, "Come and set down, don't you want to? I'm going to have me a cup of coffee. You've been—you're a right kind young man and it's a long ways back."

When she came out again with a pot of coffee in her hand, and cups, Larry had been sitting on the porch steps, thinking of the pine trees. Their airy quiet was a healing and a blessing. He had had a moment of feeling sure that if he could only be still enough himself, hands still, eyes still, heart still, perhaps he would enter into the knowledge of something deep and hidden and wonderful, as if he were standing on the threshold of a slow moment of revelation, a moment for which being had been created. The feeling went when he heard her behind him, and he stretched and looked about him with a feeling of good happiness. The long light of afternoon slanted through brown trunks across the grass of the clearing. Beyond the tossing green of pine tops the sky was glowing with a blue at once misty and intense, and a great cloud mass, as if carved from a soft creamy marble, was lifting up and up into unimaginable free heights, where the great clean wind ran westward from the sea.

She gave him a cup of coffee, and he took it absently, noticing that she had changed her heavy black for a shapeless dress of some gray cotton stuff that made her look thinner and smaller. She sat in a rocking-chair at his shoulder and creaked it softly now and then.

"But you must have had a terrible time clearing all this, Mrs. McDevitt. And living here all by yourself. How did you ever do it?"

She creaked reflectively. "I had a six-shooter," she said, and then stopped again. "And it's wonderful how you toughen up to using a grubbing hoe. I grubbed all that out myself, after the men cut the trees. I made them leave all those pine trees, though. I didn't mind being alone here. It got so I didn't like to be anywhere else. Once when the rains were bad I waded in from Goulds with water up to my waist and a sack of Irish potatoes on my shoulder. Mr. Barnes didn't want me to go.

"I was up in Miami, waiting on table to make enough money to put grapefruit in. A man come in and said all this part of the country was swept away with a cloudburst, and I couldn't rest until I'd come to see. My house hadn't been finished long. But when I got here, sopping wet to my armpits, the house was all high and dry. This land is higher'n anything around here. So I stayed here for a week until the water went down, and worked around and lived on Irish potatoes. I was glad to get back here from town. It was getting too crowded to like it. I finished clearing my half acre and an old nigra that was around here then showed me how to put in sweet potatoes."

The chair creaked, "That was kind of funny. I wasn't afraid of much of anything by that time but snakes and McDevitt. Staying out here by myself nights somehow I got to hating him worse and worse, and every once in a while if I'd hear somebody coming up that road I'd think what I'd do if it was him. Well, this morning—just about when my house was finished and the well was dug, it was early in the morning. I always got up at the peak of day, and it wasn't hardly light when I thought I heard McDevitt stumbling around the well. I don't know what got into me. I was all of a-tremble, and I went to the door and fired all six shots up in the air over the man I could see down by the well.

"All he did was kind of crouch down, and when I went over to look, it was this old nigra, and he was so scared he was as white as I was. 'Law, Miss Sarah,' he says to me. 'No man's goin' to ever steal up on you in the nighttime,' and he would of run when he got his breath, but I started laughing and I told him he needn't to be scared. All he wanted was a drink of water, anyway. Uncle Joseph, they used to call him, and when he showed me about the sweet potatoes I put a lot in just over there where the soil's good, and I sold them to Mr. Barnes in Miami. Then I put in tomatoes for a while, and did right well with them, so I didn't have to work in town the six months they allow you off your land. I did all the work myself, so it didn't cost much."

Larry had leaned back against the post so that he could look up at her and at the soft sky too. The morning and what had happened to Joe McDevitt seemed very far off to him. He thought perhaps they began to seem so to her, too, for suddenly her face wrinkled into a network of silent laughter. Her narrowed eyes were brightly vigorous and all the lines of her face were pleasantly relaxed. Her hands were relaxed on her knee.

"Talk about funny, though. I have to laugh every time I think of it. It shows what a fool I was in those days. When I'd made enough money in Miami to get my house built down here I was crazy to get into it. I wanted my own roof and my own pine trees. Well, it was all done but the front door, and that had to come down from Miami special on a wagon. I'd been sleeping over to the Marshs', those good neighbors I told you about ten miles up the road, and I'd got my furniture in, a stove and a bedstead and one-two things McDevitt's mother sent down to me, and I made up my mind I wasn't going to wait any longer for that front door.

"I was just going ahead and live in my house, anyway. So when night come I put on my six-shooter, with the belt over my nightgown, and I shoved the headboard of the bed right up against the open door. It's one of those high wooden headboards. I went to sleep and slept like a log, not thinking of anything. Well, 'long about three-four o'clock in the morning I woke up with a jump and lay there listening to how still it was and thinking how far I was from anything and how dark it was, and me all alone in the middle of it. Well, it come over me all of a sudden that anybody could crawl right through that door in the space under the bed. I never thought of that before. And while I was laying there thinking that, something screamed way out in the woods.

"Well, say—scared? I was so scared I was cold and stiff, and I could see things moving in the dark all around me and things crawling and creeping out of the dark under that bed. I didn't dare to move or creak the bed springs, and there was my six-shooter that had worked around under my hip and was boring a hole right through me. When that thing screamed I thought I'd just die right there. You could hear wild cats sometimes in those days, only then I didn't know what it was. And the next morning I went over to Marshs' and stayed there until that door got there, and I had three bolts put on, and you bet I used them. But I can laugh over that now any time I think of it.

"And two days later was the time I shot all the snakes I ever see around here. That was another funny thing. I can't bear snakes. I was sitting in this chair inside my door, with the door open—that was before this porch was built. I was sewing something and I had my six-shooter in my lap. And all of a sudden I just kind of saw something on the floor out of the tail of my eye, and before I ever turned to see what it was, a kind of cold feeling went all over me and, thinks I, 'That's a snake.' Before I knew exactly what I was doing I grabbed my gun and I shot all six shots at that thing I saw, and it was a rattlesnake as thick as your wrist, and not two feet from my foot.

"The first time I got a good look at it, it was as dead as a piece of string, and there was bullet holes through it and around it right into my new floor. You can go in and see where they are right now. And that afternoon there was a man here and we were planting some orange trees, for I thought I'd see how they'd do here. He says, 'Look, there's a snake,' and I turned around, and sure enough there was another one. I guess maybe two snakes in one day was too much for me, for everything went all kind of black and I didn't know what I was doing until I see the man looking and laughing at me. I was killing that snake with a stick and then stamping and dancing on its head like I was crazy, with my six-shooter bumping on my hip. He says he never see anything so funny in his life the way I looked, but I didn't remember much of anything, I was so blind mad. I always did hate a snake. But that was about all I ever saw on my place. Though that time I told you about when it rained so hard and I waded in from

14

Goulds there were moccasins on some of the stumps. You don't see them hardly any now, except out in the deep Glades."

The chair creaked. The high great pillar of cloud was turning a soft pink. A mocking bird, tail and wings all a-cock, landed on the ground before the steps with a flirt and stared at them first out of one eye and then the other, and flew off as suddenly as he had come, with a flash of white wing bars and three or four notes of song like sweet impertinent words.

Larry fumbled in his mind for the right question. "Were you—did you stay here all alone, always?" he asked cautiously. "You were very brave, I think."

Her profile in the softening light was bold and bony, he saw as he stared up at her. The gray hair blew straight back from her forehead and the scanty knob of it behind hardly altered the shape of her head. The skin over the cheek bones was smooth in spite of the soft wrinkles about the mouth and eyes. Her body was a bony shapelessness under the cotton dress, but her head, from the angle at which he gazed, seemed fine and distinguished. There was about it that sexless look which approaching age sometimes takes on, in which men seem like old women and old women like delicate, bony old men. She looked like a worn old statesman, wise, weary, patient.

He found himself thrilling to all this she had been telling him, as if the courage and drama of it had stirred deeply his sensitive imagination. She was indeed a better man than McDevitt, this shapeless old woman. She was unique, she was magnificent. Staring at her he saw what it was really to be a pioneer, a woman, lonely, afraid of snakes, sustained by no dream of empire, but only by a six-shooter and the enduring force of her own will. He felt at once humbled and exalted at this glimpse of the dumb, inevitable thrust forward of the human spirit. Her name was Sarah McDevitt and her sons were——

As if in the brooding into which she had fallen she had come to a similar place in her thoughts, she turned her bright gray eyes on him slowly, and he remembered that he had asked her a question.

"I sent for the boys as soon as I could," she said. "George was big for his age and Joe was—Joe wasn't a baby any more. They come down with some people that were coming to Miami, and I met them there. I was afraid they wouldn't recognize me. I was sunburned more than they had ever seen me and I guess I was a lot heavier. George said I was taller, and maybe I was. Carrying boxes of tomatoes makes you stand straight, and grubbing palmettos and planting and hoeing and picking kind of stretches your spine. I couldn't seem to sleep much the night the boys got here. I'd have to keep getting up and light the lamp to look at them all over again. Sleeping that heavy way children have, they looked beautiful. George was black-haired and heavy, like my father, and Joe was all kind of gold color then. He used to—he used to wrinkle up his nose and laugh right out loud in his sleep."

Larry studied carefully the nearest knot hole. He felt a stinging behind his eyes at the careful monotony of her voice. Her words were labored. And yet when he looked up again there was only on her eyelids that look of a worn, distinguished old statesman with silence lying heavy upon her mouth.

"It didn't seem—I guess it was pretty lonely here for the boys after a while," she went on slowly, "They'd been to school in Vermont state and there wasn't any school here nearer than Coconut Grove. They were used to playing with children, and I was busy from daylight to dark. George liked to help with the tomatoes sometimes, but Joe was too little at first. They got to like to roam around the pine woods. Once George shot a wild cat. I gave them the orange trees if they'd take care of them, but they didn't take to that much, and anyway, oranges aren't so good here as in Orange County. I saw that right off, and besides, I didn't want to bother with them.

"Times when my tomatoes failed or the crop was short I could always go over to Goulds or Peters and work in the tomato-packing house. It was easier money than waiting on table in Miami, and I could walk home nights. Sometimes the boys liked to pack a little when the season was good and I saved up money for them. I knew they'd have to go to school sometime, but I kind of kept putting it off. There's a lot of company in a couple of kids fighting and hollering and yoo-hooing around. I'd got used to baking big batches of bread and pies and having to patch trousers. And besides, I was afraid of McDevitt.

"It didn't seem any time at all before they was big. Time goes fast down here, with the pine trees. There isn't much difference, summer or winter. In the winter the warm dark comes early and there's maybe cool nights, and once in two-three years maybe a slight touch of frost, and there isn't any rain, and the grass and leaves are yellow-green and brittle. In the summer you can hear the rains come booming and hissing in from the sea way out beyond and trampling down the dry grass. And afterward everything springs up juicy and green and the palmetto blossoms are sweeter than orange bloom, and little yellow and purple wild flowers grow up around the pines, and on a west wind the mosquitoes come. The nights are like pieces of black-and-white velvet laid on the earth, and the mockers go crazy, and all kinds of little birds that come from hot countries farther south sing all night in the moonlight.

"The old leaves fall off the trees and the next day the new leaves are rich and glossy and the young pine trees carry long white candles on their tips. But summer and winter smooth into each other so you don't notice how time goes creeping, except by watching young trees grow taller and boys grow big and try to act like men. Springs they would get excited to see the fires that start in the dry time leaping and roaring off in the pines. Falls, when the big rains filled up the roads, and the swales and all low places and everything was sopping, they'd run around splashing in it and having fun with plank boats. But all the time I knew they ought to be in school.

"The country around here was changing too. When they'd put the railroad through, gangs of men camped out not ten miles from here, and the boys liked to hang around the camps. That was what started me to send them to school. I was afraid they'd learn things that wouldn't be good for them, and I guess they did. Then the railroad was being finished way to Key West and the roads were better and people begun to come through and buy up land and talk of grapefruit groves and the tomato prairies.

"So I sold some of my land nearest to the main highway and sent the boys to Miami, where a woman I knew that used to cook for Mr. Barnes promised she'd board and room them and darn their stockings and look out for them. Sometimes Saturdays and Sundays they'd come down here or I'd go in and see them there. But they didn't like school so well as they thought they would and George was crazy to go to work. I didn't like him to. All my people in Massachusetts were educated and I wanted my boys to have all the learning they could. But the next two years my tomato crop failed, once with too much wet and the next year with nail-head rust, and I had to get a job cooking for a woman over to Perrine.

"So George worked awhile and then Joe wanted to go to work too. They worked around at different things, so I could give up cooking and next year put in another crop of tomatoes. That was about all we thought about raising down here then. And that crop was fine. It was a big year and I got George and Joe down here to help me picking and carrying to the packing house, and I paid them the same wages as anybody, and it was real nice. They were big strapping boys then and it seemed like everything was coming all right at last. We'd get home and light the lamp and I'd cook them a good hot supper and see them lean over the table and eat hearty.

"Then McDevitt come back. I can see it just as plain as if it was yesterday. After supper the boys were setting on the porch with their shoes off and smoking and I come to the door after the dishes was done, and just as I stood there McDevitt walked out of the dark into the patch of lamplight by the steps. I knew it was him even before he looked up at me and smiled with his teeth shining under a long red mustache and his eyes gleaming like hot wires. His beard was gone and he had a good suit of clothes on and a white collar. He put a leather bag on the step and stood looking at me, and then the house and at the big boys staring at him, and my knees begun to shake with the cold that come over me.

"'Well, Sarah McDevitt,' he said, 'I see you've done pretty well here,' and he started to come up the steps.

"I couldn't say anything at all at first, and then all of a sudden I called out to him, 'Don't you dare to set foot on this porch, Peter McDevitt, or I'll shoot off my gun at you. This is my land and my house, and I got made a free dealer right and proper under the Florida law so's you couldn't get any of it. You've got no more right here than a dog has, and you can just go back the way you came.'

"He stood there and looked at me, with his nose coming down over his mustache and the veins standing out in his forehead where he'd taken his hat off, and I could see he was older than he used to be and not so smooth. Because now he couldn't cover up how mad he was. But he stood still in his tracks, with his head and shoulder held careful and stiff, the way a tomcat stands that hasn't made up his mind how to jump, except he'd turn his eyes and look at the boys standing there with their mouths open, and then back at me, a hate-

18

ful, sliding sort of look. If he'd been a snake I couldn't have hated him worse.

"'Well, well, Sarah,' he says at last, changing his feet easy, 'I see you know how to take care of yourself all right. But it's a long ways back to Miami and I haven't seen my boys since they was little, and any father has a right to talk to his own children. You haven't got the heart to keep me from doing that just a minute, have you?'

"I had, though, and I would of if I could. But when he smiled at me like that I knew I couldn't do anything more with him than what I had, so I slammed the door and walked up and down the kitchen, trying not to listen to the sound of their men voices talking easy on the porch, and trying to hear what they said, and trying to make myself think I didn't care and that it would be all right anyhow as long as he couldn't get my property away from me. I remember I stood at the sink and kept wiping and wiping the same clean plate over and over again until I couldn't stand it any longer.

"But when I opened the door again McDevitt and the two boys were standing out in front with just their feet in the patch of light from the door, and he was talking to them and they were laughing. Pretty soon he went away and George carried his bag for him, and they must have stood awhile talking down by the gate, for the boys didn't come back for a while. It seemed like hours. When they did come they walked and acted real careless, joking and talking loud and cutting up with each other. But when they stood at the foot of the steps and looked up at me, standing stiff in the doorway, their eyes were shining and hard and they wouldn't quite look at me, the way men act when they think their womenfolks are standing in their way. If I'd been cold before, I went frozen all over then, for I see that McDevitt had turned their minds away from me a little so that there was something hard and cold come between them and me. They didn't want to talk to me much, and after they went to bed I heard them talking low and laughing to themselves at something.

"The next day they said they wanted to go to Miami, and I gave them some money and let them go. I couldn't have said anything to them against it, any more than I could have begged McDevitt to come back that time. It felt as if something inside of me was a hard lump that wouldn't let me feel anything. I wasn't going to have McDevitt say I'd kept them from seeing him. It was just as it used to be when he'd try to find out if I had a weak place he could get hold of, and I gritted my teeth to keep from showing it to the boys.

"They didn't come back for two days, and I didn't expect them to. I had a couple of nigras working for me then and I made them cut down all the orange trees I had and burn them. I couldn't stand the look of them. I had them drag the trees down to a cleared space at the edge of my land and the fire showed red through the pine trees. That night the boys came back as if nothing had happened, walking up the path, with the glare through the pines showing faint and McDevitt walking between them.

"I wouldn't let him set foot on the porch. 'I told you once and I tell you again, Peter McDevitt,' I says, 'that I won't have you on my place. The boys can do what they like. They're old enough to know better. But you, I don't have to have, and I won't have, and you can make up your mind to it.'

"George come up to me and put his arm around me and his black head, like my father's, was way taller than mine. 'Aw, ma,' he said to me, 'Grammer McDevitt used to say you were too hard. Dad never done as much harm to you as you thought. Joe and I think you'd ought to let him come and talk things over with you. He's had a hard time, too, and it would be nice to let bygones be bygones.'

"I didn't feel his arm around me no more than if it was a piece of iron, and I looked down at Joe standing there beside McDevitt, and he was as tall as McDevitt. For the first time I see that his hair that had been gold color when he was a baby had turned to be copper-colored like his father's, and his eyes were the same red-brown when he narrowed them. The two of them stood and looked at me, and George dropped his arm and looked at me, and McDevitt's eyes begun to shine and his nose came down over his mustache and his teeth under it were white and shining like gravestones, and he smiled as if at last he'd found the place where I was weak, and I knew it.

"That was when it seemed as if I didn't know what I was doing, except that I heard somebody telling them they could all three go away and never let me see them again as long as they'd rather have him than me. Then I saw them walking back down the road, all of them, as if they were hurrying, and I ran in and got my six-shooter and ran down the path after them, and I was shooting over their heads. When I'd shot all six shots I threw my gun away and went on stumbling in the dark after them, down through the pine woods where there was a reddish light from the bonfire still flickering.

"At the gate I saw McDevitt go on down to a car he had there, but Joe turned around and started to come back toward me, and George stopped and watched him, and then he began to walk toward me too. I stopped and watched them come, with their backs to McDevitt, and it seemed as if the hard thing in me was melting and softening and warming me all over. I come to myself all of a sudden and I could see Joe's face and George's, just as clear, without any kind of dark mist over them, and it seemed to me that it didn't really matter how weak anybody thought I was as long as I had my boys. I started to walk to them, too, almost crying, and I was just going to beg them to come back anyway, that I'd do anything they wanted me to. That was when Henry Marsh drove up and turned in my gate, passed the boys and leaned out and shouted at me that the pine woods in back of the place where the orange-tree fire was had caught and it was threatening the rest of my pines and on his side clear up to his grape-fruit grove. I didn't understand him at first, until he kept saying that the fire was creeping toward the pines. And I looked, and sure enough all that light wasn't just the bonfire but the palmetto flaring up and popping and flying and the flames climbing like ragged ribbons all the way up one dead tree that stood nearest. If I hadn't been so taken up with McDevitt I would have known the difference long ago.

"Well, there wasn't anything else to do but go and fight the fire. I guess George and Joe must have turned around and gone back with McDevitt, because I didn't see them any more that night. I rushed up to the house for some burlap bags, and then Henry Marsh and I drove as near the fire as we could get. I could see Marsh's men black against the flames thrashing at it. A fire in the pines down here isn't the same as a forest fire anywhere else. The fire clings to the woody soil and the oily palmettos and once in a while it gets up into a tree. If there's a dead branch or a rotten place the whole tree burns up then. The bark is made tough and heavy like scales, so that the fire can't hurt it if the tree is sound, and even young pines, if there isn't any-thing the matter with them, will burn only a little and not be killed. But where there's an old tree with its insides dead and rotted the fire leaps at it and the whole tree bursts into flame like it was tinder and the light of it brightens everything all around. Before you know it the tree crashes down and throws burning branches and ends of fire clear across a road or a fire path, and a new patch of palmetto will crackle up and blaze as if it was covered with kerosene.

"Through the smoke we could see the ground covered with blazing stumps and little edges of fire and an outer ring of flames where the fire was running toward my pine. Then a big tree that was burning fell like a fiery flag, falling straight toward the finest stand of them between there and the house, and I just went crazy. What I'd been with snakes or with McDevitt wasn't anything to that, I was so scared the pines would go. Henry Marsh said I snatched a wet burlap out of his hand and went at that burning tree single-handed, stamping and beating, with my skirts and my shoes in the flying embers, until he said it was a miracle I didn't catch fire myself. But all I remember was the heat on my face and a kind of wildness in me to get that fire out, no matter what happened or what it cost.

"And then suddenly that tree was out and there wasn't any more creeping ring of flame, but only black stumps and branches and the ground hot and smoking underfoot. The men had stopped the fire up on the other side next to Henry Marsh's grove and there was only some palmettos still burning in the middle and the smoldering earth where the fire had crept down into the peat and would smolder that way for days until it burned itself out. They got me back to my house and fixed up my burned hands and legs and feet, and I slept that night as if I was dead.

"The next day I sent word up to George and Joe that they could come back and see me when they wanted to, but I never said anything about McDevitt. And although they come back sometimes, it wasn't any use. I guess I knew it all along. Something had changed in them. McDevitt hung around Miami and I knew the boys saw him and were with him, although he never tried to come out here again himself. That night finished something for me. I knew I'd never dare to say his name to them again or ask them what they were doing. I never did. They got jobs in town, I guess, and when they come to see me I was glad to see them, but I never treated them like I'd used to, and they weren't the same with me.

"They brought me money sometimes, and I wouldn't take it and I wouldn't ask them how they got it, although they seemed to have plenty and dressed real nice. But I guessed things. They got to act more and more like McDevitt, smile like he did and not move their heads when they'd look at things, but only their eyes, and talk smooth and shifty. But sometimes they'd come back, or one of them alone, all tired out, and stay for a while, and all that would slip off them and they'd be just like my boys again, laughing and joking. I'd go in nights when they were asleep and look at them, great long heavy boys, the black one and the red one, sprawled over the bed."

The quick tropic twilight was driving the yellow light of the sun out of the clearing between the pine trees. The sky overhead was lifting and receding into a high thin dome of green quivering light into which the prickle of a star came suddenly.

Larry Gibbs did not dare to turn his head to look at her, stone-still in her chair. Her chair itself did not creak any more. But when she spoke again, except for the stiffness of her lips, her voice was deliberate and clear and dry.

"So I never let them or McDevitt see that I had a weak place, never once. I never said anything to them or pleaded with them. I never let them see me cry. I didn't cry. McDevitt went away finally, I guess. I guess maybe he got driven out of town. And the things that happened then—happened."

There was a long silence. Her voice said at last, in a breathless murmur, "And they can tell McDevitt—I haven't—cried—yet."

There was a man coming up the roadway to the house. Larry turned and watched him come. He was glad he would not have to say anything now. The man was thin and aimless-looking, and as he came up to the steps Larry saw he fumbled with his hat and had red rims to his blue eyes.

"Evenin', Mis' McDevitt," he said uncomfortably. "Mis' Marsh wanted I should step over and see if you needed anything, or if you wouldn't like to sleep to our house tonight."

Larry stood up slowly and turned to look at her. She was rocking again, but her profile was white parchment stretched tight over the boldness of her mouth and chin and her eyes were like smudges deep within their sockets.

"You're a right good neighbor, Henry Marsh," she said. "Tell Lizzie I don't want anything, thank you, and I wouldn't be comfortable anywheres else but here. I want to be up early in the morning. There's a man coming with some avocado seedlings. I thought I'd see how they'd do here. This young man is going back now. Maybe he'd give you a ride back as far as your house. I'm much obliged to you, I'm sure."

Her chair creaked slowly as the two men went toward Larry's car. Driving back along the dark road Larry spoke only occasionally to the thin man, who seemed much affected. He told himself it was ridiculous to be affected so much himself, and yet he could not forget her sitting there on that dark porch. He found he had dreaded, in leaving her, to see some evidence of the defeat and dissolution of what in her he had found splendid, that spirit which by repeated and hard-won victories had strengthened itself, had learned to do without all the ordinary happinesses. He saw now that he had had nothing to dread. She had maintained herself, like an old pine through many burnings, by the enduring soundness of its own wood. That, Larry saw, was his story, if he could put into English his feeling of so important and so abiding a thing.

2
A BIRD DOG IN THE HAND

$\mathbf{G}$EORGE HENRY HAYNES sat in the window of his room in the Hotel Corona-Biscayne, four stories above the crowded valley of Flagler Street, gazing upon the phenomenon of the city of Miami. From time to time he removed an intelligent and well-shaped forefinger from a calm forehead and made notes in a small brown note-book which smelled pleasantly like real leather. George Henry Haynes was jotting down stimulating phrases plucked like ripe cherries from the bent boughs of his contemplation.

All day he moved about in, but not of, this before-indicated phe-nomenon. He liked to sit here in the late afternoon, cleansed and su-perior, ripening the fruit of his observation. He gazed over tiled roofs, corrugated-iron awnings, traffic bells, blaze of billboards upon roofs, Spanish stucco façades; out to the sheer rectangular lift of occasional fourteen-story office buildings, gleaming blocks of white frosting or skeletons of black structural armor a-whirr with riveting; out to a tower in honey color and ivory, like the fine blossom of an unruly garden; out to the superimposed perfect bubble of the sky.

Into this the assembled architecture bit with jagged uneven bites, which in no way concerned the bubble itself or one white-heaped froth of gulf cloud, moving imperceptibly at an incredible height of airy blue remoteness. So remote also George Henry felt him-self, thinking long cool thoughts on the single tax, the chaos of new cities, the pernicious result of speculation in land values, the effect of sudden fortune upon civic character, the debasing result of the greed for land upon national culture. He thought of all these things in the manner of an intensive student of scientific sociology. When his mind dwelt with pure and lofty abstractions, where it was most at home, his eyes wandered above the sky line. When by that sarcastic necessity which requires the most perfect theory to take its base upon some rude fact, he had to cover his eyes, he gazed down, with the intent eye of a bacteriologist at a microscope, at an open niche of office just off the pavement below and opposite his window. He gazed down searchingly at the figure of Pomona Brown. It was quite characteristic of his feeling of remoteness that it never occurred to him that she might also occasionally gaze up searchingly at his.

Yet if a young man, tall, beautifully gotten up, with pale long hands, a pale beautiful forehead and rather a pale beautiful manner, sits every afternoon from four to six in a long window easily observable from the opposite pavement and never moves except to shift his gaze between the sky, a notebook and herself, how is any good girl to avoid observing it—especially when that girl is also the keenest bird dog of any real-estate office on Flagler Street? It cannot be done, that's all.

Pomona Brown, whether from her desk almost on the sidewalk or standing idly to survey the passing hordes of prospects with a fine calculating brown eye, was perfectly aware of him. And just as he made her a focal point for his practical researches in social phenomena, she daily gave him three large gold stars and the baby-blue ribbon as the most important on her list of to-become customers. Some day very, very soon, as soon as she got around to it, she took it for granted that the distinguished young man in the window would become the owner of a few excellent apartment-house sites in Vallombrosa Gardens, the Suburb Astounding.

If she had been told that the so-marked young man held passionate and intricate views on the immorality of the private ownership of real estate, she would have gazed at the speaker with the abstracted eye of one listening to the third act of an epic poem in early Hottentot. Pomona Brown was the best bird dog on Flagler Street just because her gaze was exactly as abstracted before all speech, all ideas, all human language, unless it was preliminary to or included such comprehensible utterances as, "Where can I buy a good business corner?" "Will you accept this certified check in cash payment for——" "Is this the dotted line?" Or those other good words, "How about a little dinner and a dance tonight?"

Within the slumbering depths of Pomona Brown's mind there were some unstirred germs of intelligence other than this. Anyone glancing across the pavement at her lucid brown eyes, her firm nose, her brilliant flexible mouth, her immaculate waves of shining corn-color bob, would not have denied her the possibility. Yet she never showed them, if they were in her possession. As a bird dog, none were necessary except those appertaining to results—real-estate results. A bird dog is known by the prospects she drags in. What it took to drag them, as Pomona was the first to state, she had.

The bird dog, to be completely explicit, is the latest thing in feminine types. Bachelor girls, salamanders, baby vamps, flappers and gold diggers have each taught something to the bird dog, yet she remains herself, more modern, more efficient, the most hard-boiled. Under a perfection of surface so hard and shiny you could not catch any of it in a door, all bird dogs are as cold as spring water and as direct as a locomotive. They live to sell real estate. They never believe anything they cannot cash at the bank. They are incapable of trusting anyone farther than they can throw the Isthmus of Panama. They make money easily, invest it shrewdly and have not to ask favors of any men whatsoever.

All that they keep in their sleek, beautifully waved heads are the prices of any lot in the city five years ago, last year, last month, yesterday, this morning and the next ten minutes. They know the difference between binders and options. They can figure commissions to a hundredth of one per cent. They know how to wear expensive clothes well, drive cars, dance and keep men in their place. For them, marriage is a future luxury to be justified by an excessive bank account on the part of the groom. Love is a foolish, expensive emotion felt for them by some men. They will take anything they can get and render back for it as little as possible. Their only passion is for their own safety and comfort.

Beneath a smooth and deliberately pleasing exterior, the bird dog is as tender and dependent and emotional as a solid-china door knob. There was an unmistakable accuracy in George Henry's choice of Pomona Brown as a characteristic civic figure. The Queen of Sheba who strolls up beside you at a counter of a department store and with flawlessly suave manner wonders if you would be interested in a lot in Valencia Villas this morning is a bird dog. The Madame Récamier who glides into a chair beside yours on a hotel porch and remarks that one would double one's money if one invested it before noon in a choice business lot in Mulgoba Manors is a bird dog. The sport-suited Cleopatra at the races who gives you a winning tip and suggests you put it to work on a remarkable residential site in Palmyra Plaza is a bird dog. They murmur at you on fishing trips. They entice you with bargains at polo games. Or, like Pomona Brown, they simply sit by the sidewalk and spin golden webs with fountain pens, while their eyes wander among the streams of prospects. They can recognize instantly the difference between a man with an unspent certified check burning his bill fold and one trying to conceal a second notice from his bank about that payment on Lot Nine in the northwest corner of the northwest section of Seminole Prairie, for which he may have to sacrifice his option on that hotel site on the bay front. It is the work of a second to cut the former from the crowd and turn him over, warmed and malleable, to J. Milligan Pritchett and his associated real-estate dealers waiting with plat maps.

"Listen, Jack," Pomona remarked to J. Milligan Pritchett, developer of Vallombrosa Gardens, the Suburb Astounding, "there's a bird over at the Corona-Biscayne goes by here in the morning loosing an eye at the map that sits up in that window every day that must have a sweet wad. Cora Bishop over at Tropical Townsites says she thinks he's got a tin ear or something the way nobody can sell him anything. They've all taken a whirl at him and he's come across with just exactly nine times nothing. The way I dope it, he's maybe looking for something big like an Everglades deal or a big subdivision layout. Bill James met him poking around forty miles out on the Tamiami Trail. Seems he can ask more questions than an income-tax blank, all about land. I think I'll drift over and see this bird. He simply hasn't been talked to right."

It really did not matter whether Pomona heard J. Milligan Pritchett say "All right, Miss Pom," or not. She was going anyway.

When her card was brought to George Henry he dropped his notebook because of a remarkable sensation that started in the center of his diaphragm and went tingling up to his ears. It seemed rather more intense than his usual devotion to social research, yet he could not consider it exactly unpleasant. The element of surprise lay only in the fact that she had been coming to see him, for he had been studying carefully her entire progress across the street. Flagler Street is narrow enough, and yet, with its continuous streams of automobiles, subdivision busses, brass bands and motorcycle cops, wider than all the waters of Jordan to cross. It had given him ample time to observe the shining corn-color curves of hair about her delicately rouged face, the splendid poise of her head and shoulders as she endured and ignored the contact of men's glances, the fresh color of her pale green crêpe de chine working dress, the immaculate staccato of her white kid sandals. He dashed into his bedroom to change his tie, wondering what in the world she wanted to see him about.

The curious sensations still curled about his diaphragm when she was seated in his best sitting-room armchair, her hands beautifully quiet in her lap, her feet uncrossed, her face unchanging under its mysterious rosy calm. When she turned her golden-brown gaze upon his face, George Henry felt an almost uncontrollable desire to do exactly what she might want him to do. He did not know that he was experiencing subtly the emotion which makes the bird dog famous. The fingers of his right hand were curving unconsciously as about the fat barrel of a real-estate agent's fountain pen.

Pomona Brown knew it, if he did not. To her the right hands of all obviously wealthy young men were created to curve in that practical manner.

"I just came over," she began in that creamy voice of hers, devoid of all grit or friction, "because I've been wondering if I couldn't help you. I know that you've been looking for something and I'm sure you haven't found it. I can tell you'd be very particular what you got. So I thought maybe you'd tell me about it and I'd get it for you."

The words, the tone, the manner, the power of the face were to George Henry something exciting and magical. It made him feel as he had once when he was a little boy at a circus and the remote marvelous fairy who rode the three white horses had suddenly thrown a rosebud at his own personal and familiar nose. There was something equally miraculous about this. Agitated under it, he stammered and patted his forehead with a perfect square of white linen from his coat pocket.

"Why, really, Miss—Miss Brown," he said, tingling under her gaze that continued to rest pleasantly upon his countenance, "I—ah—this is very kind of you—really extraordinarily kind. I hadn't been aware that—that is, I could hardly have hoped that you would——"

"I've seen you going by and looking at our maps, and I thought maybe you had some project that you thought was too large for us to handle. Now if you want——"

"I know what I want," George Henry exploded suddenly, with the desperate courage of a shy man; "I want tea. Don't you want tea, Miss Brown? We both want tea. Of course we want tea. We must have tea. And cinnamon toast and a chocolate éclair." George Henry advanced upon the telephone with the conquering stride of a theorist about to make his most passionate theory come true. "And then," he said, waiting at the mouthpiece, "I feel somehow—really, you know, it's extraordinary, your coming like this—I have so many things to discuss with you—room service, please."

Tranquilly, her fingers still crossed in her lap, Pomona watched him fussing with a small tea table and bringing over the bowl of roses and pulling at the window curtains, a tall, nice, blond-haired, gray-suited young man stirred by an excitement utterly incomprehensible to her. The brown and even shine of her eyes was unaffected by it. And yet deep within the previously slumbering mind of Pomona something pricked and stirred. The back of his head was adorably boyish. She thought that his hands were awfully nice. The stir within her was like some worm gnawing deep within the hard, polished, sound surface of an expensive apple. She did not believe in anything she could not cash at the bank, and yet the vague premonition of a feeling was creeping over her that she had found a bank book with her name on it in which the credit side was filled with figures in black ink. Its only manifestation was that she remembered a marvelous bargain in a hotel site that the Ocean Acres people were looking to buy. She'd like to see this nice boy make a nice quick profit.

A characteristic of the bird dog of hunting circles is that, having discovered where the birds are, the dog freezes into a point until the hunter is ready to shoot. The technical language may not be correct, but the idea is the same for either game or real estate. The bird dog does not close the sale. She only hypnotizes the prospect; and hypnosis is accomplished as much by remaining very quiet and listening as by a surfeit of distracting sounds. This nice young man, she was aware, contained vast quantities of unspilled conversation, undoubtedly carrying worthwhile tips like currants in a cake. She was the very one to help him spill it. Pouring his tea with the least possible clinkings and rattlings, she withdrew into a sympathetic soundlessness that for him was all one deep, understanding ear.

Before she had finished her first cup of tea, George Henry was well launched upon his deepest passion, the single tax and the public ownership of land, which led inevitably to a number of large, glittering ideas on the general lines of the complete renovation of all humanity. He exposed to her his earliest feeling that a serious-minded young man with money cannot be happy unless he is awfully agitated about the whole welfare of the human race. He gave her the tempo of college cloisters and the smell of libraries where he had discovered this, and been torn by the endless confusion and disagreement of political economists and sociologists on the question of what was the matter with the world and what was the best thing to be done about it. He had been eager at lectures and alert at private conferences with great scholars. And yet confusion had confused confusion. Until one day he had discovered accidentally by looking at it that, after all, earth was under the feet of him and of all men, and that he might do worse than take that as his beginning. From that the mists had cleared away. Everything became as clear as new ice. The public ownership of land—and all that that implied, which was a lot—had become his solution for all human ills under the sun.

"And so I came to this place of yours," he was saying at her second cup, "to study the social idiosyncrasies attendant upon the rapid buying and selling of real estate. My researches have taken me into every phase of the question and the result is that I am firm in my original premise that a decided stand must be taken by all of us who constitute the intellectual leadership of the world. I am convinced that the shortsightedness of the people in this regard is their unhappiness. They must be patiently and firmly led to think differently about everything they do. Their values are all wrong. 'Until there can be correct thought'—and here I quote, Miss Brown—'until there can be correct thought, there cannot be right action; and when there is correct thought, right action will follow.' These people, in their wild interest in making money, are not thinking at all. I assure you that extraordinary statement is not unjustified. These people do not think. How, therefore, can they act?"

George Henry remained for a moment lost in disturbed contemplation of his own ideas. Pomona reached over delicately and poured herself another cup of tea. Her serene gaze rested upon his head. His voice had been a pleasant murmur in her ears. It did not occur to her to wonder what he had been talking about. Men were like that sometimes. They liked to use lots of words. Her attention had been engrossed in something she had never felt before. It was a lovely, aching sort of pain just about the left middle rib. And yet it was not a pain so much as a conviction of this good-looking rich young man's utter helplessness. Never in her entire life had the possibility of a man's helplessness occurred to her. Her conviction had always been that the least you could do was to watch them like a cat and never trust them with a crooked penny around the corner. This knowledge was so new, so exciting, so devastating, that she hardly knew when he stopped or when he went on talking.

To George Henry she was the most wonderful listener he had ever known. His speech flowed and glittered because of it, took on dignity and proportion and scope. Suggestions previously vague came from his lips as well-rounded ideas, surprising even himself by their depth and reasonability. He grew taller as he talked, his dark blue eyes went black with the fire of his inspiration. He saw himself from this very tea table, under the gaze of this marvelous girl, striding out into the chaotic new city, recognized as thinker and leader, taking his place by the very force of his message as director of the whole stream of life that was pouring into this last new land. He could do anything—create a new tone in human relations, bring about a new way of human living, build a vast, contented, happy, orderly new civilization. Gazing into her eyes, he could see how simple and direct it all was. And when he saw within them a deep golden look begin to burn he knew she shared the vision with him, as he saw it, making it real. He felt even a little humbled before the soaring idealism of her woman's nature.

"You ought to get over to the beach and get a good coat of tan," she murmured in the rich pause he left. "Sitting up in this room all afternoon isn't good for you."

He sprang up and began pacing up and down.

"It is true that social reform is not to be secured by noise and shouting, but only by making people think. And that is why I have seen that it will be necessary to do something to make them think, to arrest them, if only for a moment, in their mad attitude toward land as merchandise rather than as the whole promise and potentiality of the future. I confess I have been at a loss how to impress this upon the minds of the real-estate agents I have met."

"You want to watch those birds," Pomona said softly. "Some of them would run you ragged. You leave it to me. I'll pick you up some gilt-edged stuff you can bet your shirt on." Her thoughtful glance was fixed upon his long, excitable hands. They would be strong hands if he ever got a good hold of anything, she mused, and felt herself secretly thrilling at the idea. She stood up with careful grace. "The tea was very nice," she said. "Thanks so much. I'll probably give you a ring tomorrow."

"But you're not going? You haven't had any tea—you've eaten nothing—I don't want you to go. You've no idea what it means to me to meet someone who sees my whole idea so splendidly. When will you—I must see you again—would it be too soon—won't you dine with me tomorrow?"

For the first time in her life, when she recrossed Flagler Street, Pomona was almost run down by a truck. Yet when she arrived at her sidewalk under the exclamations of a group of real-estate men who had seen her escape, she only smiled at them mistily. J. Milligan Pritchett was standing at her desk feeling expansive. The new subdivision was selling out nicely.

"Well, Miss Pom," he boomed, "find anything over there? Will he buy?"

Pomona sat down at her desk and powdered her nose slowly.

"Oh, I guess he will," she said vaguely, and sat staring across the street. If a certified check for fifty thousand dollars had been waved before her face she would not have seen it.

"That's fine, that's fine!" J. Milligan said heartily. "What's he want?"

"A guardian, I guess."

"Ah? Then suppose you take Jerry Lewis over and introduce him and have him close up something right away. I'd like to turn over that Shields tract, for instance."

"Jerry Lewis?" Pomona straightened up and stared at her employer. The brown of her eyes hardened into gold stone. "But that tract is south of cultivation line. It's under water half the time. It's nothing but saw grass and cypress hammocks. You can't—I mean, I don't want Jerry Lewis in on this yet. This bird is—I don't know—he's different. I mean, I haven't got his number yet. He hasn't told me yet what he wants. Let me have him a few days longer, please."

"Well, well—well, well! Little sister seems all excited up about something. Say, listen here, queenie, you're not fixing to double-cross us with this guy, are you? You're not holding out on us, are you? Because you know just exactly how far I'd let you get with that."

All the customers who had ever been led up to the dotted line by the finished smoothness of Pomona's work would have stared to see the eyes she raised to the clouded brow of Mr. Pritchett. There was softness in them, a hint of moisture. The assured voice trembled:

"No, of course not, Mr. Pritchett. You know I wouldn't. I don't work for any other firm but you. But please, please hold Jerry Lewis off for a while. I don't think—I mean this one isn't interested in acreage."

"All right," her employer said, equal parts of shock and suspicion in his tones; "but you'd better go home and go to bed, Miss Pom. You're losing your fighting edge."

"Don't you worry about me. I'm all right." The moisture was gone completely, and the eyes were hard. She reached out for her hat and slammed her desk drawer. "Only I tell you straight, if you send Lewis or anybody else over there until I say so, I'll quit you cold. Cold, what I mean. I hope that's sufficiently distinguishable."

She walked out and went home, her heels smart upon the pavement, seeing nothing at all. If she could find out who held that option on the hotel site before Tropical Townsites did, she could make a neat little profit for him. It was exactly as if parts of her brain which had previously lain dormant were now springing into activity. She spent an hour telephoning careless, casual questions to various friends of the bird-dog persuasion and learned exactly what she wanted to know. She was thrilled that she would have something to tell him in the morning.

But he was not in when she called him, morning or afternoon. He did not appear in his window. She grew tense and snappish with wondering where he was and what he was doing, and lost a perfectly good prospect who fairly walked in the door. Besides, he must know about the option immediately or someone else would snatch it.

34

Yet nothing of this was visible on her face when he called for her in the evening. The car he drove was shabby, but expensive. At the wheel his hands had force. His profile, as she gazed up at it, occasionally was stern and purposeful. They floated across the Causeway to Miami Beach, with the dark water around them, the dark sky overhead powdered with great sweeping trails of star dust, the city glittering behind them, the Beach glittering ahead. They were comfortably silent. Night and starlight and black water and speed were for the first time a rare and overwhelming mystery.

"Do you mind the wind in your face?" he said once, and she said, "Oh, no, I love it." And that seemed a subtly complete conversation.

They dined somewhere, on a balcony looking out at beach sand shining in the lights, and black palm fronds and a black ocean from which the reddest moon in the world slowly emerged with a great spatter and splash of light. They spoke platitudes about sand, ocean and moon, laughing a little as one does at the most brilliantly satisfying conversation. A delicious sense of adventure and fulfillment hung upon their eyelids. After that they drove across the Causeway again, and westward, until the Everglades stretched flat and vast and silvery about them and the wind was fresh and wet, fragrant with weed blossom and sun-dried grasses. Somewhere by a canal running full to the brim of moon silver they stopped the car. Deliberately, Pomona made him stop the car. All this wind and speed and moonlight was making her a little dizzy. She felt that the only thing for her to do was to cling firmly to the idea of options. The very sight of his hand on the wheel beside her was beginning to affect her strangely. Suppose he were to reach out and touch, ever so slightly, hers? What would she do? What would she do?

"I think I've got just the buy you're looking for, Mr. Haynes," she began briskly although the moonlight brought a lovely ripple to her voice. "An option on a hotel site that I know positively for a fact you can get for eight thousand dollars cash that will mean an easy profit of thirty-five thousand, six hundred dollars in a month. I know the people you can sell it to. I can fix the whole thing up for you, and I'll take a commission only on the resale. That's fair enough, isn't it? Can you get the money in forty-eight hours?"

The look that George Henry turned toward her, full in the moonlight, caught her eye, stopped her short, twisted something tight about her heart. It was as if she had hurt him horribly. He looked at her as at something foreign and a trifle loathsome. At least, so it seemed to her.

"I don't quite understand you," he said slowly, "after all I've told you about my feelings about the ownership of land. You mean—you didn't understand me yesterday? You weren't even listening? It seemed to me then that because you did I could do—why, I could make everything work out right, because you believed in me. And now you expect me to buy real estate."

They stared at each other with shocked faces, with eyes at last completely aware of each other as individuals, with mouths bitter with the sudden comprehension of the imperfection of all human understanding.

"I—oh—you mean—you don't want to buy anything? You don't want to make any money?" Pomona said. "I only wanted to help you. Why, I wouldn't even take a first commission. I——"

"You don't know—you don't see," he said, and his fingers on her wrist were painful. "To own land for myself, when there are others who can't own it, would be going against my deepest principles. Can't you see that all this buying and selling of land is wrong? Can't you see that it is what is ruining us as a nation, making people think of nothing but money? Can't you see that to force the price of land up and so huddle landless people in ugly cities is the reason for all the vice and crime and suffering of our day?"

Pomona blinked rapidly, with troubled eyes fixed on his face, trying to follow the sweep of his thought. His words fell on her unaccustomed intelligence like a great fog through which she struggled blindly. Never in her life had she tried to understand an abstraction. She was vaguely aware of protests she would have liked to make if she could have thought what they were.

She could only say feebly, "But—but then what would become of the real-estate men?"

In the full bitterness of his disillusionment, George Henry was reaching for his gear shift.

"Pah! Buzzards!" he said, and pressed his starter.

It was apparently his intention to start the car. The car was not started. The firm feminine hand that closed upon his arm held a bite in every finger, the anger of a woman whose tender emotion has been rudely challenged. He turned and looked at her in astonishment.

"Why, you—you poor flabby highbrow!" Pomona said. "You take that right back! Don't you dare to say that about real-estate men! I'm a real-estate woman. What do you know about anything anyway? You've read a bunch of stuff in books and you think you know it all. Why, there are dozens of honest, hard-working real-estate men in this town that could show you the big holes in every theory you believe in, just because they've done work and you haven't. You ought to be ashamed.

"Who started people owning land anyway? People always have owned land, and I guess maybe if it was as wicked and bad for people as you say it is, they'd have tried to stop it long ago, like murder and stealing. You make me sick. You never earned a dollar in your life and you don't know anything about the awful necessity of having to make it. You don't know anything about the needs that make people want it. You couldn't any more stop what's happening here than if you got out in front of the Pilgrim Fathers and told them to leave the Plymouth Rock alone. You wouldn't even be here in Florida if everybody else hadn't come here and advertised it and sold land; and yet I bet you wouldn't have stayed if you hadn't liked it, even if it did make you shudder. Don't you suppose developing and selling real estate takes brains and courage. Anybody can think up things people ought to do; it takes brains to make them do it. You'd never do it. You'd sit in a window and look at it and throw up your hands in holy horror at the idea of anybody making any money the way you don't want them to. First thing you know you'll wake up and find yourself dead without ever having lived at all. Before you get the right to be the world's best little fixer, you've got to get down on the street and take your share in it. You can't talk about what people ought to do until you've been people yourself. You can't—Oh, heavens, what's the use? You'd better take me home."

George Henry had taken the entire tirade in absolute silence, staring out across the shimmer of the canal to the utter silver rim of the horizon. When she had finished, he opened his mouth twice and closed it again. His head sat like granite upon his immovable shoulders and he did not turn toward her even when he must have heard the subdued catch in her breath behind her hastily applied handkerchief. If Pomona was indulging in so unusual a thing as tears, George was also white with a thought as new and shocking as a streak of lightning.

"You think I haven't lived?" he said finally.

"You cert'dny—don't dow—anything about itd," she said from the handkerchief.

"I hope you don't mean I ought to get out and sell real estate," he said, and his lips were tight.

The remark that issued from the handkerchief was to the effect that he probably could not sell a cubic inch of it if he tried until he was black in the face.

"You think I'm just generally no good?"

The small sound in reply might have meant anything.

"Then I suppose there is nothing else to do but take you home and thank you for a highly educational evening."

She implied that he was right, and he did.

Pomona did not go to work until noon the next day, but then she threw into it so much of her most compressed vigor that it was as if she were lost in a small cloud of her own making. She hardly glanced up when Jerry Lewis sauntered up.

"Well, well, little sister," he said in that lowered, slightly hissing tone which meant that he was particularly pleased with himself, "thanks for the sweet and lovely tip about your gentleman friend. He certainly came across handsome. The boss said to give you this check right now as your split on the commission. Many happy returns and all that sort of thing, don't you know."

Pomona looked up at him slowly, white to the lips.

"What do you mean?"

"Why, you know. The bird over at the Corona-Biscayne. The fluffy duck with the lovely wad and the large ideas—Haynes. The boss said as long as you weren't down I might as well go over and tickle him a little, and I sure tickled him some. Know what I sold him, kid? The Shield tract—all of it. Four hundred acres at five hundred an acre. Cash payment by certified check in the boss' upper left-hand pocket right now. And a sweet little split on the commission to a sweet little——Say, are you crazy?"

He stared down at Pomona's hands tearing the check into confetti. He stared down at her raised eyes, narrowed and hard and furious.

"No, I'm not crazy," she said, and her nostrils flared. "I'm

38

through. You can tell the boss so for me. He broke his word. He knows what I mean. And as for you, Jerry Lewis, selling a bunch of saw grass and water to a helpless boy who doesn't know marl from granite, I'll tell you what you are. You're a—you're a buzzard. And don't you forget I said it."

"Tell Mr. Haynes, Miss Brown must see him at once," she said to the telephone girl at the hotel five minutes later. She was not aware that she had crossed the street in front of a fire truck. She went up in the elevator without looking at herself in the mirror or fussing with her hair.

"What do you mean by going and buying land without asking me about it?" she stormed at George Henry as soon as she had entered his sitting room. "You swore you wouldn't ever own land. You swore it was all wrong. And then as soon as my back is turned you go and spend good cash money on the worst swamp in Florida. What do you mean by it?"

They faced each other, two thoroughly angry young things, quivering a little with complex emotions. George was the colder.

"Am I to suppose you have any interest in what I do?" he asked.

"No, you're not, and I haven't. I only want you to know that I didn't have anything to do with selling that land to you. I've torn up my share in the commission and I want you to get your first payment back if you can. You ought to be able to prove misrepresentation. And that ought to teach you never to buy land without looking at it. Never! That's a sucker's trick. You haven't any business being out without a guardian."

"I thought you said I needed to get out of my window and live like other people. If I'm a sucker, you're responsible. I hope you like your work."

Pomona felt her eyelids stinging with tears for the second time in two days, and the feeling made her perfectly furious. "Why didn't you stick to your principles better, if they were so fine? Why didn't you refuse to have anything to do with Jerry Lewis, if you think such things about real-estate people? Why, oh——"

She walked over to the window and blew her nose angrily. George Henry stood staring at her, miserable and bewildered. He started when she whirled on him again.

"You'd better get your car out tomorrow morning and take me

down there so we can look over that tract. You ought to see it, anyway, to know what you've done. Maybe I can think up some way of
getting you out of it. You come for me at nine o'clock. And for Pete's
sake don't buy any more real estate between now and tomorrow morning. Don't even look at a real-estate man."

George Henry could make only propitiatory noises in his throat
as she whirled from the room.

There is something about the sweet speed of a good car, held
steadily to an oiled road that leads straight and south to the place
where the horizon smokes into great white cloud, through a morning
whose sunlight is the newest, gayest, fizziest compound in the world,
across an earth marked with the glitter of grapefruit leaves and the
singing warmth of pine trees in the sun, which absolutely defies ill
temper. The top of the Florida morning was the very breath and aban-
don of adventure. Burdened with sternness as she was, Pomona had
not been able to repress a little hop and skip of delight as she jumped
into the car. George Henry, although bowed down with emotions in
conflict with the principles of a lifetime, grinned and settled himself
happily in his seat behind the wheel, echoing her own little shout of
delight when they had left the last subdivision.

She had a trick of crooning to herself like a happy little bug in
sunshine. Several times at a pert remark of hers George Henry
laughed. The pine smells and the smells of palmetto blossoms and the
reedy, watery fragrance of the open swales, where tall saw grass rippled
like a river of wheat between the pine land, blew across their faces,
were inhaled in great deep breaths that made the blood go singing in
their veins. Their eyes sparkled and their mouths were relaxed. And
by the time they stopped in Florida City for gas they ran across the
road for sodas at a drug store, talking blissfully and unconsciously all
the time. It was astonishing—only no one noticed it enough to be
astonished—how many things there are to talk about besides real estate and the single tax on a morning like this.

The low gray car turned sharp right at the Florida City filling
station and scuttled down the long straight road that suddenly took
on the air of having been completed just that morning for their espe-
cial benefit. The marching armies of the Caribbean pine, which had
seemed so much in retreat before the roads and the cleared lands, now
advanced straight to the road edge, a green-topped high wall of brown

40

trunks which seemed to wheel beside them as the car thrust its nose down the narrowing road. And when the last pine land vanished behind them and they flashed in sheer sunlight toward the sharp jungle walls of Paradise Key, with the shining fronds of the royal palms lifting like glittering banners into the blaze of blue, Pomona deliberately put a warm palm over George Henry's on the wheel and patted it.

"O-o-h!" she said. "Aren't they too marvelous?"

He turned and smiled at her, having adroitly caught her hand. So they ran more slowly through the green jungle of Paradise Key and emerged again like bold What's-'is-Name gazing with a wild surmise on a land never before dreamed of by them, or even yet believed.

For if the road by which they had come seemed new made and untouched, the earth upon which they now moved, in the rigid ruling of the highway, lay brilliant, never before invaded, touched here and there with glitter as if the first mists of creation had barely lifted from them. Under a piercingly blue sky the land lay, shut in only by the sky, a vast plain of high grasses, with here and there the somber green of hammocks of live oak or mangrove, like boats stranded in a tranquil sea. Beside the straightness of the road lay the straightness of a canal, filled with clear brackish water and with green things growing down the banks. All there was to look at was sky and flat earth, and yet they were so filled with the very essence of all light, with the very salt and vigor of all sea winds, that it had upon the two in the car the effect of a great heightening of experience. They did not speak at all, except for occasional rapt murmurs, and they seemed to see the same things instantly with the same zest, the same shock of delight. Overhead occasionally in the crystal air a buzzard soared and swept as if cleansing itself of the indignity of earth. And once, as they roared southward, an eagle lifted from a near-by tree and raced with them.

Then they came into a land where tiny stunted cypresses lifted their bleached whiteness above the wet green earth, a miniature forest of distorted ancient trees upon whose dead bones of branches the new green of leaves was scratched in a million tiny crosshatchings, misted and virginal. Behind them, here and there, taller hammocks of cypresses stood crowded together, whiteness showing through tangled green. Still the roadway was a blistering white line before them, and in the clear brown water of the canal birds dipped and flew up suddenly, scattering bright drops. Presently the country of the dwarfed white cypress lay behind them, and clear to the horizon the tawny saw grass stretched again, and the low mounds of the hammocks in the glittering distance were the darker green of live oak and button-wood. On a long gradual arc the road curved eastward and a stronger wind sprang at them, sturdy and brisk with sea salt.

"Look!" Pomona said suddenly, and pointed. "Look! This must be yours."

There was a faded signboard which read vaguely, "Shields. This Land for Sale." He stopped the car suddenly on that side of the road and they sat staring. A vast, breathing silence immediately spread about them, laid its hand upon them, as if it had been lying in wait for the death of the noisy engine. They lost themselves in it, tracing through it the infinitesimal creaking of an insect in the near-by grass, the faint sounds of the wind moving softly across thousands of silent acres. A bird flying far overhead cried thinly once, and from behind them another answered with a shower of silvery twitters. The car creaked and settled a little. George Henry drew in a deep breath.

"That—mine?" he murmured, in a voice that reached the girl's ears so strangely that she turned and stared at him. His hair blew away from his forehead. His eyes gazed straight to the horizon. Pomona found herself more interested in the strange expression on his face than in the land. "All that mine?" he said again. "Why, I—I never dreamed——"

As if waking from a mood in which her own familiar hard-shelled self had lain dormant, Pomona turned her head sharply to stare where he stared, swept carefully with a shrewd glance the neighboring surface of the grass and looked back at him. His expression had not changed.

She opened the door of the car, got out and stood in the road. Then she sauntered leisurely along it, peering at the soil which fell away sharply from the road in a ditch-like depression. She found a long dead branch and came back with it to the car.

"It's your land all right, Mr. Haynes," she said, in a cheerful business voice. "Come and look at it. I'll show you what I mean."

He clambered out of the car, still saying nothing, as if a new thing had wrapped him round with daze. He stood absently beside her as she poked vigorously in the ditch. He seemed not to be able to take

42

his eyes from the full expanse of the yellow-green earth or the dark-green shadow of the nearer hammocks.

"Look at that, will you?" she said. "You know how little rain there's been in weeks and weeks. You know how dry everything has been around Miami. Look at that. Right now that soil is sopping wet, and this is near the road. What'll it be like on beyond there, where it goes toward the sea? I tell you it's complete misrepresentation, unless they sold it as submerged land. In the rainy season this would all be under water. It's robbery. This stuff's no good to anyone."

He stared down at her stick, probing away among the stiff roots of the saw grass. It had disclosed soil as black as his boots, thick muck, oozing wetness. He walked off the road and down into it and the thick mud squelched around his ankles.

"Don't do that!" Pomona cried sharply. "Come back! You'll get stuck." But to her horror George Henry kept right on. "Here, listen!" she cried again. "Stop—George!"

He called back over his shoulder, "It's all right. There's a kind of path here. Firm enough. There's somebody over there on my land."

She looked where he pointed. Someone was evidently camping in the nearest hammock. A thread of smoke lifted. What looked like a piece of rag showed, hung on a bush. She would not have noticed it in the tangle of trees. George Henry was making his way toward it slowly, picking his way along through the saw grass. Pomona stared about her at the vast horizon. The whole world was suddenly empty but for the head and shoulders of George Henry, and he was moving away from her. The assurance of Flagler Street was slipping away from her. She was no longer shrewder and wiser and a better business man than he was. His vanishing figure was no longer helpless. She felt lost and lonely and deserted. With a little dismayed cry, she stepped gingerly down to the quaking earth and followed him. Her white-kid sandals sank in the thick mud. The murderous edges of the saw grass tore at her silk stockings and skirts. Once when she slipped off a hillock of dry earth and snatched at a handful of tough blades it tore her soft palm until the blood ran in bright drops. She wound her handkerchief around it and peered ahead for George Henry, called his name faintly. He was standing on the higher ground, looking back at her.

"Here," he said, "I didn't mean for you to come. Go back. You'll ruin your clothes."

"I won't," she said. "You oughtn't to come in here alone. It might be bootleggers."

"So you came to protect me, did you?" he said, and there was a queer light in his eyes. "You must think I'm pretty helpless. All right, come on." And he disappeared in the rude pathway that curved around tree trunks and over great interlaced roots, as if a furtive animal had burrowed through the solid jungle.

Then they were standing in an open space, facing a sort of hut, a plank platform with a roof over it. A pile of burlap bags lay on the platform. The camp was untidy with tins and bits of rags. A few pots and pans were hung on stakes driven in the ground. A kettle hung from a forked stick over a fire. As they stared, a man seemed to crawl out from behind a bush, straighten up and level a gun at them, full in George's face.

"What you doing?" his voice said shrilly.

Pomona dug her fingers into George's arm in sudden panic. And yet as she stood close to him, feeling the tension of hard biceps, somehow her fright left her. She could not see that George felt even a tremor of fright. She stole a glance up at him. He was smiling easily, straight into the man's eyes.

"Good morning," he said cheerfully. "You don't need to bother with that gun. Can't you see you're frightening the lady?"

Pomona saw the black circle that was the end of the gun begin to wabble a little. Presently it dropped. The man peered at them over it. He was a bent, bony figure, with a bald head and a nose like an old bird's, and his eyes were a blue so faded that it seemed almost as if he must be blind. He moved over to them, his thin mouth working a little. Pomona did not relax her grip on George's arm. Suppose he were to lift that gun again and shoot George suddenly.

"I'd put that gun away if I were you," George went on pleasantly; and he put his hand over hers and held it in a warm, strong, comforting grasp. "We're really quite harmless. My name is Haynes. I've just bought this property and I——"

"You—what?" The man's voice shrilled and broke. "You bought it?"

"Just bought it yesterday," George said. "What's the matter?"

The birdlike old man turned slowly and put his gun jarringly down on the planks of his hut, stood with his back turned to them for a moment. When he moved slowly back to them his face was twisted with emotion. "I—I'm Shields," he said. "I didn't think anybody would buy it. I've lived here right smart of a while. It—it kind of hits me all of a sudden."

Pomona expelled her breath in a long relieved sigh. She found that she had been trembling a little.

"Oh, you're the previous owner!" George said. "I'm glad to know you. I suppose they haven't got word to you yet. Well, now you can move away somewhere and live better."

The pale-blue eyes crept up to George's face and down again.

"Well now," he said, "I don't know's I'm so glad. I ain't exactly prepared for hit. I told them real-estate fellers they could try to sell, but I didn't s'pose anybody'd want to buy. This land's awful wet in the rainy season, and what with the mosquitoes in summer, I figgered they'd let me be."

"Gets pretty wet down here, does it?"

Shields looked up at him again, a note of eagerness in his voice.

"I sh'd say hit does. Why, some rainy seasons this yere hammock's the on'y thing out of water. Three-four feet of water all over the rest of hit. And soon's the water gits down a bit you'd ought to see the mosquitoes. Bite through burlap sacks, they do. Git up your nose. Drive you crazy. Sing at you outside a mosquito netting something terrible. You couldn't stand it."

"Well, you seem to stand it pretty well." George eyed him. "You look pretty healthy."

A proud smile cracked across the folded parchment of Shields' jaw.

"When I come to Floridy twenty year ago," he said, "I couldn't so much as walk. Now I walk once a week up to Homestead and back, and it ain't nothing. There ain't a weller man in the state. It's the sun done it. And the land is healthy."

"It looks good enough land, but if it isn't dry enough to do anybody any good——"

A look of brilliant cunning rippled up the birdlike old face.

"Don't you make no mistake about this land," he piped. "They ain't rich land like this nowhere. Old sea bottom, rotted rich way down. Why, you could spread this soil for fertilizer—spread on top of ordinary dirt."

"It is, is it? I thought so." A subtle sort of excitement seemed to be carrying from Shields to George Henry. The faded blue eyes were staring into his and they spoke directly and earnestly, as men who had arrived suddenly at a hidden understanding. "Then why did you sell?"

"I ain't sold all I got," the other said. "Land ain't enough. I figured I'd need a lot to do with it what's got to be done. With money, I could fix up my other piece, drain it and——"

Pomona broke in abruptly, out of an overwhelming feeling that she must stop at all costs something that was happening here, something that she did not understand, something that was exciting George Henry.

"You can't drain this land in a thousand years. It isn't enough above sea level. The water won't run off. And when Lake Okeechobee fills and overflows it's like opening a water faucet on it. You can't do a thing with it. It's crazy to think you can."

She might have had the unnoticed voice of an insect for all the two men noticed.

George Henry said, "You've heard of Holland, of course. I've been studying this proposition too. It'll take a system of canals and dikes. They've got to come to that yet—dikes."

The other blinked and nodded in swift delight.

"Plenty of wind," he said. "Windmills. Electric contraptions. I been figgering it. Dikes is right. You're a smart man. I thought nobody else but——"

"You'd be living," George went on, as if chanting a ritual; "not shut up. You could grow strange tropic things, rare crops. You could think things out. Sell only to people who'd promise not to sell—stay put—demonstrate how it could be done with a group."

"It'd take a powerful lot of money," the other said.

"Maybe," George Henry answered. "But if you've got it, why not? I suppose you wouldn't consider staying on to look after things. I've got to go to New York for an engineer I know. You could be building a shack."

"You get good engineers," the other said sharply. "No boys— men—men that can see it the way you see it. You come and live with them. Keep 'em up to the mark. Make them see it big. You're the right one to've bought it; do the right thing by the land. I didn't have the capital. You've got to have capital."

46

"And you've got to see it," George Henry said. "All right, we'll do it. I'll be down with this man next week. Come on, Pomona." And he turned and walked briskly back to the path.

Pomona followed him, her mind a dizzy fog. She had not understood half of what they had said. They had agreed to something which was vague but perfectly insane. It seemed to her that both men had completely lost their senses. The turmoil of anger, bewilderment, strangeness, uncertainty, fear, and a great pervading unhappiness boiled up in her suddenly as she stumbled blindly at his heels. She blundered into a sticky hollow into which she began to sink above her shining silken ankles.

"Oh!" she cried sharply. "Oh-h! I'm sinking in it! Oh, I can't bear it! This awful mud! Oh, oh——"

George Henry flashed around and with a sudden chuckle of laughter picked her out of it with one sweep of his arms and strode with her to the solid rock of the road. He was laughing happily in her ear as she cried limply, hot and miserable and disgusted, down his coat collar.

"So you're not a hard-boiled little business vamp," he laughed, setting her on her feet on the road, but still holding her tightly against him. "So you've come out of the street, have you, just the way you made me come out of the window? You didn't think you were going to jar me loose without getting jarred yourself, did you, Miss Smarty? Well, how do you like your future home?"

Pomona jerked her face from his shoulder and stared up at him with an indignant, quivering mouth. "What do you mean?" she stormed. "You're crazy! Do you think I'd live in the mud, like animals, eaten alive by mosquitoes? Have you had a sunstroke? Let me go!"

"Not on your life," George Henry said, gathering her in again. "You just didn't understand all that. I'm going to fix it for you. Drainage and dikes—that's the trick. It's going to take lots of money and lots of work. I suppose we could get a good house in Homestead. I want to be on the job with it. Hard, grilling work. But it'll be worth it. My Lord, you thought you knew real estate! You don't know anything about it. The real wealth isn't in selling land. It's in keeping land, developing it. I don't care how much it costs. This is my land—mine and Shields', not just because he homesteaded it and I bought it, but because the two of us are the only ones in the world that can see it and love it. Everybody else sneered at it but Shields and me. And if I put all the money I have in it, it will still be a good deal his, because he's loved it longer. Don't you see, it's not just the last frontier. It's the very end of the limit of speculation. We'll be the first really to love this land, that needs it so very much, that will be so wonderful. They all need to be shown how to take their land seriously. I've always taken land seriously, but in the wrong way. Keep still while I talk to you, you little vixen. It's all your fault. You got me into this. You made me see that I'd talked about the shame of owning land without a glimmer of an idea that owning land could be an emotion, an act of the creative imagination. It was land hunger I had all the time. The money my father and grandfather left me came from land. Land is my heritage. It's in my blood, the way the sea gets into a sailor's. Now I've found my place, the place where my roots can strike deep, the place where my—my children can grow up."

Pomona lifted eyes to his that were staring out over his land. She half opened her lips, but no sound came. Already his face seemed sterner, more bleak, controlled, as if the toil and hazards of his undertaking were already working upon him, sweating off the softness, replacing it with the clean hard look of a man who has found the work above all others which he wants to do. But if the softness had gone from his face, it had slipped into Pomona's. Her eyes were wide and brooding, her whole face that of a woman surrendering to an emotion which she recognizes gladly.

"You've got to marry me," George said harshly, bringing back his gaze suddenly from the horizon to her face. "You weren't living any more than I was. You're turning into a real woman. You've got to put this thing through with me. You've got to. I love you, you know. But the way I loved you before we found this wasn't worth anything. Now I'm going to love you the way a man can with his work and his life plain before him—a big work. And if you can see this the way I mean it, see us working together to build this right, the way you started me, why, you'll be worth loving like that as long as we both live. That's the way I mean it to be."

Before which Pomona Brown, the keenest bird dog on Flagler Street, raised to his face eyes blind with happiness and murmured, "I guess I've been kind of silly too. I guess I don't know—anything. But if you think you can teach me, so that I'll be some good to you—oh, George, please, I'll love you that way myself—all the rest of my life."

3

HE MAN

SMALL COLD SHIVERS of fright began rippling up and down Ronny's spine the moment his father stopped the car at the wharf on the bay front, and Gloria Cargill and Mrs. Kinney screamed with delight at the waiting parallel planes of the flying boat. In spite of the warm brilliance of the Florida morning at ten o'clock, in spite of the salt tang of the wind that snapped flags on mastheads and ruffled the blue water between the slips, in spite of the hilarious breakfast party they had all shared in celebration of Ronny's birthday trip to Bimini, his feet chilled and his hands went clammy and the bacon and broiled pompano sat uneasily within him. Yet the terror that from childhood had ridden him, the fear of high places, of falling horribly through thin air, and therefore, of all flying, was no greater in him at this moment than his fear of letting his father know that he was afraid.

He sat mute in the corner of the back seat, his slender hands gripping at his boyish bony knees. The lucky fact that no one ever noticed him much anyway gave him a chance to pull himself together. As his father dashed around to help out Gloria, and burly Colonel Kinney reached back a hand for his smart chubby wife, Ronny looked at himself deliberately in the little mirror over the wheel. His tan hid the pallor that he felt. His mild gray eyes steadied as he watched them, so that they would not betray him. That he did not show his panic more plainly gave him courage to get out of the car, carrying Gloria's green-leather vanity case and her flimsy green-silk coat.

None of the four looked at him as he came up, the tall awkward boy so acutely aware always that he could never be the figure of a man that his father was. Ronny looked at him now, shyly, with the spark of his adoration in his eye.

Andrew Burgess always dominated any group. His graying dark hair was bared, flying its shaggy crest of lock above the others. His bronzed handsome face was alert and eager, with only a few folds about the eyes to betray his years. Ronny thought again, as he had since a small boy, with that same little throb of almost hopeless devotion, that his father was the finest man he had ever seen in his life. To Ronny, who at school had followed breathlessly in the newspapers his father's polo exploits, his tennis triumphs, the purses and the ribbons that his racing stable won, Andrew Burgess was also the most brilliant sportsman in the world. His father never in his life refused a high dive or knew the weak sickness of great heights. Never in a thousand years would he have given up practice with the school polo team, as Ronny had, after being in hospital two months with a broken rib, because ever after that when he thought of playing polo the thunder of those following hoofs came sickeningly back to him, the trampling pain, the darkness, the oblivion. His father's ribs had been broken, and his collar bone and his leg, and he had played more dashing polo than ever, after that. But Ronny couldn't. He just couldn't, that was all, no matter how deep within him burned the bitter knowledge that he was a coward.

Sometimes Ronny thought that if his father ever discovered the depths of his son's weakness he would disown him. It was only that as a motherless sickly child Ronny had been given over to the care of the best of nurses, as a mild little boy to the most expensive of schools, that had saved him until now, he was certain, from being found out. This winter in Miami was the first time Ronny had ever been with his father for so many months. It was as if Andrew had suddenly discovered that he was about to be twenty and had decided to make a man of him. As a result Ronny had had desperately to try to live up to what was expected of him by a man who retained all his enthusiasm for sports, even if he were too old now for the more strenuous of them. Ronny had to give up entirely his rather studious, leisurely life. He had no time now for reading, or for the Spanish translations he had been so interested in doing with a young instructor at his college. And he gave up his beloved photography, which for years at school and summer camp and college had absorbed him. There was time for nothing now, and certainly no excess energy for anything but sports.

He struggled with them, with what valiance he could muster. He worked hard at a golf lesson every day, to improve his indifferent game, while his father and Colonel Kinney tramped their speedy eighteen holes every morning. He worked at tennis lessons for which he had no feeling whatsoever, because it had been one of the things his father had done best. And he spent hours every afternoon with his father and the Kinneys at polo games or at the races, where he bet and lost often, so that his father would not think him a piker, struggling wildly to conceal even from himself how supremely he was bored. It seemed to Ronny that nothing but luck and Gloria Cargill had kept his father from finding him out.

It had been all luck at first. His father happened never to have seen Ronny swinging rather wildly with a brassie, or practicing an overhand with his usual awkwardness. Ronny took care always to be swimming among the breakers when everyone else was diving from the tower by the pool. He rather liked swimming, anyway, if he could be let alone at it. He grew brown from work with a medicine ball every morning on the sand, put on a little weight and tried to remain inconspicuous. His father, incapable of imagining that any real man could be uninterested in the sports he loved, was only vaguely disappointed with him as yet.

If at times he looked a little puzzled at the quiet boy who took no prizes, broke no records at anything, would not play polo, was not handsome and dominant and magnetic, he had not thought about it long enough to be resentful. The boy was young yet. After all, he'd had too much schooling, too many women nurses as a small boy. It was a good thing he'd remembered to take him out of college. There would be still time for his polo.

"Stick with me, old boy!" he would shout to Ronny in one of his lavish moments, when a horse of his had won or he had taken a close game from Colonel Kinney. "I'll make a he man of you yet. Next year, when you're toughened up a bit, we'll look around for a couple of good polo ponies for you and you can get in on the practice games up at Aiken."

Those were the moments that Ronny, writhing inwardly,

hated most. It made the time when his father must find him out seem very near. It was to the putting off of that moment, which would have been the end of everything for Ronny, that Gloria Cargill had assisted.

Ronny did not really like Gloria Cargill. He did not really like big wheezy Colonel Kinney, whose talk was like his father's, all sports and poker and bootleggers, but somehow not the same, a thousand times more monotonous. He did not really like Mrs. Kinney, who was fat and flat faced, who wore the most expensive clothes in the most startling colors and played bridge like an inspired card sharp. He never knew what to say to any of them, and they had a way of screaming with laughter at some embarrassed speech of his and then staring at him curiously, with cold eyes, touched slightly with contempt. They always made him feel that they knew perfectly what a coward he was, if his father did not. But even they were easier to endure than Gloria, for all that she took his father's attention from him.

His father said that Gloria Cargill was the most marvelous woman in New York, and all his world of rich men and expensive women and racing and cards and sport and supper clubs seemed to agree with him. She was the youthful widow of a tire king and she spent her money like a spoiled empress. She was almost as tall as Andrew, with a lithe figure that was swaying and sleek either in a bathing suit or in one of her fabulous evening dresses. Her hair was wild red gold around the bold beauty of her face. Her brown-velvet eyes had little gold lights in them that burned when they looked at men, and the wet brightness of her mouth showed scarlet down the whole length of a hotel corridor or across a dance floor.

For Ronny the worst of it was that she had discovered that he was painfully shy of handsome women and therefore delighted in tormenting him. She could turn the whole force of her fascination on him, like a headlight, in which he squirmed and blinked miserably, to her laughing delight. She adored running a glittering hand suddenly down his coat sleeve, drowning him in her gusts of perfume, clinging with a burlesque of devotion to his arm and flashing her heady glance into his dazzled eyes. Once or twice Andrew had seen him blanch and jerk his hand back involuntarily and he had been furious, because an assured gallantry to women was to Andrew the fundamental of red-blooded masculinity. He lashed out savagely to the boy, if in a low voice, in one of those sudden rages which reddened his face uncontrollably. The whole thing fixed Ronny in his miserable sense of inferiority.

But if he secretly disliked Gloria, he was grateful to her for taking his father's attention. It seemed that everyone was watching to see if she would marry Andrew. Their world agreed it would be an excellent match, with plenty of money on both sides. Sometimes Ronny had moments of bitter jealousy of her, of this woman like a brass band and an express train, who thought she was good enough for his splendid father. But chiefly he was humbly glad to be effaced. And if she did marry him, perhaps his father would not mind so much finding out, as he must sometime, how much his son was unlike and unworthy of him.

Ronny thought all that over in a flash now, joining them in the full sun upon the wharf. He was trying to keep himself from staring at that flying thing. Gloria caught his somewhat rigid glance and smiled at him brilliantly. He had never seen her beauty so bright and polished and complete. She was all in a green so bright it made your eyes redden to look at it—green shoes and small green hat with a diamond and emerald pin pulled tight down over her blazing gold eyes. There was a flash of emerald light on her finger and a cuff of glittering bracelets on her wrist. And yet she dominated all that flash and glare with the sheer assault of her eyes, her lips, her poise, her conscious charm. Beside her, fattish Mrs. Kinney in her egg-yellow chiffon was almost inconspicuous. Not that Mrs. Kinney cared. Her voice was as loud as Gloria's, if not louder. Her laughter had edges. Ronny saw men around the wharves lingering and staring at the bright group, chauffeurs staring from parked cars and mechanics from the plane shed. The women especially seemed to be carelessly aware of the attention they were attracting. When Gloria glanced about her with quick casual glances, it was as if she trailed her laughter like an insolent plume across all the staring faces, fascinating them and knowing that she fascinated them, although they did not exist. That sort of thing always made Ronny's feet and hands seem enormous and uncomfortable. Now he tried to imitate his father's lordly buoyancy, knowing exactly how far he failed.

For one moment he caught the aloof calculation in the eye of the aviator fussing about the plane which was to take them up. Instantly Ronny's fear leaped and tore at him again. A line of perspiration was cold on his upper lip. He was afraid. He could not go up in that thing, to those terrible heights of thin air. He could not. He would not. He would tell his father that he wasn't well. He did feel slightly nauseated already, and dizzy, as if he were looking down from a high building. Little tremors crawled beneath his skin. Nothing in the world could make him go up in that thing, even his father's furious contempt.

Somebody gave him a soft leather helmet, and he buckled it under his chin with clammy fumbling fingers. Colonel Kinney was putting one on over his shiny bald spot. His father never wore anything on his head in Florida, and Gloria and Mrs. Kinney said their hats were quite tight enough. Then they were walking down the slippery plank and getting into the plane.

It was a three-seater. Mrs. Kinney and the colonel took the third seat and Gloria and his father the second. The women got in alertly, their high heels clicking on the deck, their sleek knees flashing among their skirts. His father motioned Ronny to sit next to the aviator, because it was his birthday treat. Ronny got in.

It was like sitting on a leather cushion in a high-sided tin bathtub, behind the smudged dimness of the short windshield. There were things—rods and handles—dangerous-looking things, between Ronny's feet, which he would not have touched for worlds, and behind, overhead, the loom and shadow of the great wings.

Gloria's jeweled hand patted his shoulder. "So nice of you, darling, to have this marvelous birthday!" she was crying, in that gay scream which made his very eardrums cringe. Suddenly the roar of the engine exploded in a thuttering numbness of sound that clamped mufflers on their hearing. Ronny felt his skin chill and crawl. They were off.

At the same time he had a flash of panicky decision that he must not clench his hands where this aviator could see them. There was something careless and matter-of-fact and young about him, which Ronny suddenly wished that he could emulate. So that, while the plane taxied out on the smooth bay water, rocking a little as it curved and thundered between the high black sides of oil tankers, past white bows of yachts, in an increasing blur of speed, he was equally concerned in watching his hands, fixed in a pose of relaxation on his knees. He was bracing himself for what he knew must come, the first sickening leap upward. It did not come. There was only a slight adjustment in the angle of the seat. The water at a distance looked lower than it had been. And he suddenly realized that they were up, although he could feel no sensation in himself but a quickening of his heartbeats.

All around the plane the sapphire level of the bay was deepening and lowering. The plane ground ceaselessly, climbing with a great, roaring steadiness the orderly staircase of the wind. There was reality in it, and stolidity. Ronny felt a strange sense of lifting upward into a freedom from earthly things, a consciousness of wide salt wind and tremendous reaches of sunny air. He had forgotten about relaxing his hands now, and his heart was pounding, but in him climbed, as the plane climbed, an amazement and a new delight. He was hardly afraid at all. It was astonishing. It was delicious.

As the plane wheeled, lifted its nose, climbed, wheeled and lifted in enormous roaring circles, the earth wheeled slowly beyond the side. The checkered green, the crowded glistening roof tops of Miami, stretching west to a mist of Everglades and sky, wheeled also. The blue bay floor wheeled, which was at this height bright turquoise, streaked with lime green, which whitened lightly on each side of the lean elbow of the causeway, where cars slid like beetles. Beyond Ronny's right bathtub rim circled the straight lines of trees and streets that were Miami Beach; the apron patches of green that were golf links; the small squares that were hotel roofs, house roofs, patches and rectangles of color flattened on the ground. Then, as they climbed higher and the plane lurched a little, heading into the vast sea wind, there before them, dim through the windshield, reaching out tremendously to right hand and to left, lay the ocean, a vast lavender miracle, wrinkling a little and reaching out, reaching out so enormously to the stretched horizon that it seemed to rise to meet it, to melt into it, and mingle, in the distance all one smoking, imperceptible blue.

High and far above it, yet somehow not remote, because there was nothing with which to measure the distance between, the plane snored straight eastward now upon the crystal level of its pathway, rocking a little upon its invisible cradling of air, strangely real, strangely prosaic, a thing of wood and metal, weighty, hard to the touch, solid to rest upon, commonplace in a world gone wonderful with high magic, all blue air and bluer unbelievable sea.

Beside Ronny the aviator's sunburned profile was calm. His hands moved only occasionally now on the controls. His manner was easy and assured. From time to time he glanced about him, out at the sea below his left shoulder; once across Ronny at the sky; and once, with a long narrowed glance, at something behind and overhead, at a wire or strut or something, which for some imperceptible reason had caught his attention. Ronny followed his glance with a little prickling thrill, but found himself nodding and grinning at Mrs. Kinney in the back seat, beyond his father's shoulder, and at Gloria's brilliant, enthusiastic face. His father and Colonel Kinney grinned at him briefly, eyes narrowed and faces still, with the manner of men enjoying themselves sedately. Ronny felt a sudden glow of friendship for all of them. Against the vastness of the background, underlaid still with the thought of his fear, they were familiar and dear and reassuring. He was overwhelmed with thankfulness that he had not shown them how much he had been afraid. The thuttering roar of the engines which shut about them so completely was not so noticeable. Ronny felt a sudden impulse to lean over and tell his father now all about how afraid of things he was. It seemed as if an ordinary tone could have carried and that in this moment of exultation his father would understand and forgive everything. As if Ronny did not know well enough, at the same moment, that the difference between his father and himself was more impenetrable than the roar.

The plane had been moving steadily upon its level above the vast wrinkled ultramarine of ocean for some thirty minutes now. Far behind, the mainland had melted into the mist that at the horizon blurred from sea color into sky color, like the bloom on a grape. Before them the islands were equally obscured. Occasionally the plane lifted or joggled slightly, as the wings bucked the booming trade wind, but on the whole it was stable, lulling into oblivion remembered fears. Ronny was growing happier and happier in knowing himself relaxed, even sleepy, under the numbing drone.

He could let his glance fall down over the side for a minute or two, with no feeling in the pit of his stomach. He grew bolder, making himself stick his head out almost into the wind to stare down. But suddenly then, like a dropped weight, he was hit by a dreadful image of himself leaping to his feet and pitching over there, head first and hurtling down the vast empty drop. The suddenness of it caught him in the stomach and the throat so that his spine crept. He withdrew his glance hurriedly to the comfortable commonplace within—dials and indicators, floor boards, the aviator's strong freckled hands, and his own feet. They helped to steady him physically, but horror still mounted within him, not so much at the outside world, perilous as it had become again for him, but at the suddenly revealed depths of strangeness in himself. Perhaps it was not only that he was utterly unlike his father but that he was different from all normal men. Perhaps within his very brain crawled the maggots of unbalance. At that moment he felt it was even possible for him to go mad and scream, and leap screaming over there. Ugh. Yet, of course, it was not so. It was only his imagination. But a he man would never have been troubled by fancies as sick as that.

It was at that moment that Ronny, fighting to calm the tumult in him by staring fixedly at the aviator's hands, saw the right one jerk as the whole plane lurched sideways. He saw the aviator throw a glance over his shoulder even while his hands and feet made curt gestures with the controls. The plane righted, but tossed violently before lurching again. Ronny, throwing a look back and up, saw a broken thing hanging and banging at one wing—a great blue hole and long rags of canvas. The vast circle of the sea below them was tipping up and circling like the surface of water in a tilted cup. The man beside him, working tensely, shot a look at him, a queer, tight-lipped grin, and the plane slid downward slowly, circling and nosing, with occasional moments of level. The engine roared as usual, and the air seemed calm.

The conviction that something was wrong, that something was awfully wrong, came to Ronny with a surprising slowness. The very worst things happened to him only in his imagination. When it was a matter of outward affairs which older men had always controlled so much better than he, it was hard to believe them capable of accident. The dark floor of the sea was rushing toward them in dizzy circles. And yet there was no horror in this for him, as there had been in the thought of plunging alone. Something had gone wrong, that was all, and the aviator had told him in that one glance that he was going to make a landing. Ronny had much more confidence in him than he would ever have in himself. They would probably land all right.

It was like sliding down an enormous shoot-the-chute, even to the water at the bottom. The ocean was there, rushing up to the pitch of the plane's nose, a ridged, blurry surface of deep blue. They were going to land all right. Ronny was certain. He was growing a little pleased with himself. There was even a breath of relief at the more familiar level after all that breathless height.

The engine subsided into a low growl. The wind screamed in the wires as if for the first time, and below grew the long rustling rumor of the waves. He could see whitecaps flashing now over brilliant sapphire hollows. Why, these waves were high, he thought confusedly, leaning back against the steepness. The faint scream of a woman behind him came only a second before the shock and bounce of landing, with the crash and drench of flying cold water. When their bouncing slide lost momentum they were immediately bucked about, tossed and dropped and flung on the strong new element as if in a light, topheavy dory. The hiss and surge of waves were around them, dark blue water hurling itself northwestward, blue black in the hollows and laced with snowy streaks of foam.

Ronny turned at once to look back and grin at his father, still exhilarated with himself and with his sudden sense of adventure. It was like looking at people whom he had not seen for years, who were changed, yet completely familiar. His father met his glance with a face like bronzed rock, in which the eyes were a little fixed. He and they all were engaged in the almost violent business of keeping their balance in the lurching dip and rise of the plane, topheavy as it was and beaten by the wind, upon the strong waves which rose before them, jagged and frowning, which heaved them up with an unremitting power and passed behind them for others hurrying and trampling on.

Gloria Cargill was clinging with one hand to his father's arm, and with the other was straightening her bright green hat. Mrs. Kinney's plucked eyebrows were lifted over the roundness of her eyes in an almost ridiculous expression of amazed protest, and Colonel Kinney, holding her tightly, was crimson to his heavy dewlaps, and swearing visibly. Ronny was happy that he had not yet revealed himself to these courageous people.

The aviator jerked off his helmet and became immediately individual and human. His blue eyes were anxious in a bony sun-reddened face. His bleached hair bristled on his head, and his eyelashes were bleached. Ronny remembered suddenly that his name was Bill. He looked more disturbed than any of them.

"Well, folks," he said, "I sure am sorry. That strut busted like a match stick. Somebody will get murdered for this, if I have to do it myself. Hope the ladies are all right. There's nothing to worry about, of course. Perhaps I can patch it." He crawled backward between them and onto the back of the fuselage.

"Want any help?" Andrew Burgess called, with his eyes warm and lively again. "Rotten luck. I've been ready for a bottle of beer for the last fifteen minutes. Hope this won't make us too late for lunch."

Ronny, looking up at Bill as he climbed over the seat and seeing the curious slant look he cast down at his father's nonchalance, knew as suddenly as if he had spoken that the matter was to be graver than that. He clung to the edge of his seat as the plane swung down in a smashing burst of spray that flew over them and stung their faces, considering the thing soberly. The violence of those Gulf Stream waves was still almost unbelievable. They had looked down so long upon the seeming flatness of this water. Ronny's clothes were getting wet and he shifted about on his seat to avoid the stinging spray that came inboard.

His father and Gloria Cargill were singing "Where do we go from here?" and "When do we eat?" with voices that seemed a little too boisterous. He knew that Gloria was showing what a good sport she could be, for his father's admiration, who watched her powder her nose and rouge, and do over her lips with the scarlet lipstick. Gloria was lovely, glancing sidewise into her tiny mirror, sidewise up at him. Mrs. Kinney was not singing. Her plump cheeks had gone a little sallow under the rouge, and her bright yellow hat and bright yellow dress looked startling on her. She sat hunched up very close to her husband, with her eyes fixed upon the lifting wave tops. Colonel Kinney patted her hand regularly and watched Bill.

As the plane lifted to a racing wave Ronny could look out over the sea to some distance to more racing blue wave tops with flashes of white boiling at their crests, under the dazzling beat of the sun. The horizon that had shrunk to this, from the vast sweep of the air, was jagged and uneasy with waves, and the sky beyond it was a remote unnoticed blue. It was the sea that had suddenly taken the menace that the air had had; the sea, looming and tossing around the incongruous smallness of the plane, an awkward alien, unfitted for this heavier element. It seemed to Ronny that they sat a little lower among these waves than they had at first.

The aviator, Bill, was slashing at a tangle of stiff canvas and wires and broken sticks under the lower wing. Ronny saw him slip and the tangle drop into the water, where it hung and splashed, held by a single wire. The plane veered suddenly at the crest of a wave and Ronny saw it plunge, stern down, on the wreckage. With a scream from Mrs. Kinney, a broken strut crashed through a thin floor board and in the jagged rip sea water bubbled smoothly, wetting their feet and ankles and legs.

"Hey, look here!" Ronny's father called suddenly. "We're getting wet! Here, Bill; come here and fix this! Put your feet up, Gloria. It's all right, Mrs. Kinney. We'll be all right presently."

Ronny had been certain his father would take charge of things. He was splendid. His voice was loud and confident and reassuring. Only Ronny could not make himself believe that nothing was the matter. Things looked bad to him. Bill's face told him the same thing, slipping and splashing back along the wet fuselage, like a whale back, low in the water.

The water was rapidly filling the cockpit. There wasn't any use being too cheerful, Ronny was thinking, climbing up to sit crouched uncomfortably on the back of the seat. His father and Gloria did it, laughing. But Mrs. Kinney had to be helped up and then held, perched precariously, her round dismayed eyes still fixed on the coming water. Colonel Kinney held her, with his ruddy face turning a curious congested purple. Ronny saw suddenly that the Kinneys were afraid, and he was sorry for them. It was dreadful to be afraid.

The plane had sunk with the weight of water in the cockpit, but now it seemed not to be sinking any more.

Bill scrambled wetly up beside Ronny and spoke to the others, "This isn't so good, folks, but it isn't so bad. The old bus is knocked out, but it can't sink any more and we're not so far from Bimini now. We may even drift quite near, the way the stream runs. Somebody's sure to pick us up almost any minute, because we're in the direct line of boats from Miami to Bimini and they'll report by and by that we haven't arrived. All we've got to do now is hang on."

His glance met Ronny's on the last words, and Ronny saw that in spite of his cheerful, matter-of-fact voice, his eyes were wide and unwinking. Ronny's own eyes were like that. As they stared at each other for a long moment, Ronny felt a sudden warmth of understanding and comradeship leap between them. After all, Bill was not so very much older than he was, for all the weathered maturity of his face. That glance linked them, by their youth, by their common ability to look at the situation, without too much fear or too much optimism. These others must be protected at all costs.

"Are you with me?" said Bill's glance to Ronny, and Ronny's answered instantly, "You betcha life." Bill withdrew his gaze abruptly to unlace his shoes and take them off. Ronny did the same, glad to feel his toes free in the water. He watched one shoe float a minute and then go over the side in a slap of water from a running wave. Bill was plucking up the wet cushions from the seats below the water.

"They'll float," he said briefly. "You hang onto this one, Mrs. Kinney. And listen here. The back of these seats are going to get awfully uncomfortable in about a minute. It would be easier if we all got down on the fuselage, even if it is partly in the water. Then the ladies can hang onto these cushions too. That's right, isn't it, sir?"

He appealed to Andrew Burgess, and Ronny saw his father brighten visibly, as if glad of something to do. "Perhaps you could show them, sir," Bill further suggested, and Andrew turned and slid back gingerly over the wet surface, lowering himself with one hand on a strut down on the incline, so that he rested with his legs in the water, but his body supported.

"It is better," he said promptly. "Come along, Gloria. Help Mrs. Kinney, colonel. Here, grab my hand. You won't get any wetter than you are now. It's not half bad."

Ronny and Bill and the colonel, splashing in the water, held Mrs. Kinney and lowered her, quite mute now, down to Andrew Burgess. Gloria went next, laughing. Her green silk dress clung wetly to her lithe figure, and she moved with much more assurance than the other woman, and seemed somehow more suited to the watery and difficult background. Her face was not so tense either, but somehow the bright spots of rouge on each cheek, the darkened eyelashes, the scarlet curve of mouth seemed to stand away from her face a little, as if the flesh were shrinking. After Colonel Kinney had followed them with ponderous caution and a very tight grip of Ronny's shoulder, the four hung there in a row, their eyes looking upward at Bill and Ronny clinging above them and at the jagged wave crests racing down upon them, with the same look. It was a mute look, guarded, expectant, a little humble. Their lifted eyes made something in Ronny ache with pity for them. They looked so helpless, hanging there, in the smashing dangerous water. They were looking at Bill and him as if the two had suddenly taken on an unguessed power and significance. Ronny tried to think of something else to do for them to still the tightness in his throat.

"Let's cut some of that wire, Bill," he said. "Maybe we can put it around them, so that they wouldn't have to hang on so tightly. Got a knife? I have."

They worked, balancing, slipping, plunging about on top of the fuselage, over which the highest waves sent a skim of water, twisting and cutting and clinging to the wing frames as they could. When four lengths of the wire had been hacked off, Bill slid down to the Kinneys, Ronny to his father and Gloria. There was enough to twist around the body of each, but it was hard to bend it around a strut so that it would stay fastened against the roll and jerk of the plane. Half the time Ronny was completely in the water, working with one hand, sprawling, while his father helped. When a higher wave reared above them, hissing, they had to stop working and hang on tightly, their heads and shoulders barely above the smother, their bodies banging against the wood.

Once Ronny lost the last piece of wire overboard and had to dive for it, clutching it luckily in the boiling depth below. But the swimming was actually a refreshment to him. To be able to move his cramped limbs freely and surely in this sea removed much of its menace. It was an element with which he was familiar. He came to the surface with a sputtering rush and an overhand that carried him easily back, with a grin for his father's anxious eyes. Ronny had even time to realize that he had never seen his father look at him like that. As Ronny put the wire about him Andrew's right hand lingered on his shoulder and he said, "Nice work, old chap."

Ronny was warm with gratitude for that. His father was being splendid. His color was good. His voice was assured. He joked occasionally with Gloria or Mrs. Kinney, putting out a hand to help when he could. That was what it meant to have been a good sport all his life, Ronny thought. He simply did not know what fear meant.

Gloria's hair looked funny, wet and plastered about her forehead like that. She had lost her hat somehow, but she was game all right. She was singing a lot of old songs, making them all sing things like On the Banks of the Wabash and Waiting for the Robert E. Lee. Even Mrs. Kinney smiled with stiff lips when there was anything to smile about.

There was not much to do after Bill and Ronny got the wires fixed. They all hung there, the four with the wires, Ronny and Bill wherever they could catch hold of something, half supported by the wallowing fuselage, bumping and hanging in the flounder of water, watching to duck a taller wave crest, and talking now and then, little bursts of talk that ran from one to another of the soaking figures. Their words lagged or renewed like a slow pendulum of vitality.

Presently Bill, who did a good deal of scrambling about, shinned up so that he could hang from the upper wing frame and peer, long and earnestly, out over the wave tops. Mutely everyone watched him. Ronny, standing on the fuselage above them, noticed that the whites of their eyes shone a little. Bill had been looking steadily at the same place for several seconds. He drew himself up higher, shading his eyes.

"You're looking at something!" Gloria called suddenly.

Bill did not answer. The faces were tense and a similar light seemed to be upon them all—a light of pallor and suspense. They knew that Bill was looking at something. Ronny leaped up beside him. At first he could see nothing but scalloped blue wave tops and the leap and flash of foam. Then, more to the right, he caught a steady flash that was a wave, but a wave breaking before a boat's bow. When he looked intently he could see, now and then, the gray pointed mass of the bow itself, appearing and disappearing. It was hard to tell how far away it was, or whether it was moving in their direction. Bill waited, motionless, and so did Ronny.

His father called suddenly below them, "For God's sake, boys, if you see something, tell us! And do something about it, can't you? Wave something! Shout!"

Mrs. Kinney shrieked suddenly, strained and off key, "Oh, make them hurry! Make them hurry! We can't stand this any longer!" And the other three all cried things, words and shouts mingled indistinguishably, a babel of sound at the water's edge, incapable of carrying, in that wind, more than a boat's length. Bill and Ronny waved their arms, waved Bill's coat, waved torn strips of canvas, and shouted as if a tension had given way.

Presently the breaking white from the boat's bow and the occasional glimpse of bow itself were gone. There were only the jagged lift of the wave tops and the foaming white of crests.

When Ronny really believed that the boat had gone, that he could not see it any more, that it had really failed to see them, or had ignored them, he stopped waving and let himself drop down to the fuselage. Bill dropped beside him and they stood looking down at the faces below them, the wet faces with the incredulous eyes raised to theirs. Ronny cleared his throat before he shook his head and said "It went."

"You mean it went?" His father's voice was suddenly harsh and there were reddish veins under the salt water on his forehead. "You didn't wave hard enough! You didn't try to shout! The hounds—to leave us—the dirty dogs! I'll have them arrested for it. I'll make them suffer for it, the dirty skunks, the lou——"

Gloria stopped him with a hand on his shoulder. Mrs. Kinney had gasped once or twice and her eyes had rolled in her plump white face, but Colonel Kinney had both arms around her.

"Hush, momma, hush," he said. "Never mind. That means we'll see others. The next one will come nearer."

There was then nothing to do but keep on waiting and keep on hanging on. There was no way of knowing what time it was, except that the blazing sun had moved slightly westward down from the zenith. The waves rolled as high, but it almost seemed as if the six had adjusted to their rolling, so that they did it automatically, knowing how high the highest would come. But the ferocity of the sun was an increasing agony. Ronny felt the sting of it under his wet shirt, along his tanned shoulders, and knew how much the others must feel it on the tenderer skin of their faces and shoulders. Colonel Kinney's bald spot glowed an angry crimson. He had lost his helmet long since.

And Ronny tore a big piece from his wet shirt and made Colonel Kinney tie it over his head like a hood.

All Gloria's make-up had washed off and her cheeks were red with sunburn and her nose already blistered, Mrs. Kinney's pale face was bright rose color, and both women's lips were swollen and blistered from the salt water and the sun. Ronny tore other pieces from his shirt to tie over their faces, and the sun was instantly angry on the bared places on his neck and back.

It was a relief to dive into the water after a dropped cushion or to swim around a bit, after their various positions on the fuselage, and yet Bill was right when he warned him, in a low voice, not to tire himself. Ronny contented himself by hanging over the cockpit edge with one hand and letting his body float on the lift and drop of the waves. The sense of high adventure was burning steadily in him; the sense that here at last he was encountering an experience which he could remember all his life.

The waves that came racing at them from the southeast, with their curious impersonal violence, surprised him with their endlessness. It was amazing that there could be so many of them, hurrying and shoving forward, in their leaping up and down. As the blazing sun crept slowly down the long afternoon slope, so that it shone redly in their smarting eyelids, the light changed upon the waves, whitening their leaping tops, intensifying the dark sapphire of their hollows, shadowed in the trough with glossy black. It might have been a gloriously exhilarating sea to sail a boat over. But sunk almost to the chin as they were here, there was little gayety in it. Deep blue could be bleak, Ronny was learning slowly, and flashes of white sinister, just as the plane that had been so powerful and assured, taking off from water only that morning, floated here so incongruously; alien wreckage that just was able to support itself and their clutched and uncomfortable lives.

The silences were longer between the choppy snatches of talk. Gloria did no more singing. Ronny remembered, as if she had been some other woman, how she had looked that morning, waiting on the pier. That gay brilliant figure had practically no point of resemblance to this sodden one with the drenched, salt-matted hair, the pale swollen lips, the brilliant green silk only dank clinging fabric on the arms and shoulders, the nose and eyelids reddened. Her consciousness of charm, too, had gone—that powerful vibration.

Ronny looked at her now only with pity and concern for the pale woman, silent, with closed eyes and miserably clutching hands where the great emerald still flashed incongruously in the wet. Mrs. Kinney managed somehow to look more like herself, with her plump short figure in the soaked yellow silk clutched by her husband's arm, with a piece of Ronny's shirt tied over her head and forehead. There was in all the faces, it seemed to him, a growing look of withdrawal, of remoteness, as if each one were drifting away from their relations with others to the silent place where ultimately human life exists alone. When one spoke, it was with a forced utterance. A smile took more strength than it had and was more automatic. All their attention was centering, more and more, on the sheer act of endurance.

The sun, just above the western horizon, burned and flared upon their faces, under their blinking eyelids, and the blue waves changed slowly to a cold green against a vast rose-colored afterglow that held no loveliness for them. In half an hour it would be night, and there was no boat.

Ronny was thinking lingeringly of juicy beefsteak and baked potatoes and a steaming cup of coffee, or fried onions, or even just an orange. Anything to relieve this withering abominable taste of salt in the mouth. It seemed to him he must have swallowed quarts of salt water already, and his tongue and the lining of his mouth were blistered with it. The feeling of too much salt water swallowed was cold and uneasy also in his stomach.

Bill came floundering beside him. "Look here, buddy, le's you and me try to turn this bus around, so the plane'll be away from the wind. Maybe she'll ride better that way for the night."

Suddenly Ronny saw the night—the night. "Sure," he said to Bill, grateful for activity. But something about his heart was cold.

It was harder to swim than it had been. There was no longer refreshment in the swash of water over his body. The wind skimmed stinging hatfuls of spray over a wave top into their faces. When they reached the rudder they clung to it and breathed a trifle hard, planning their concerted effort. Presently they let go and began pushing, thrashing tremendously with their legs, breathing or gasping when they could. The huge thing was unwieldy and hard to start and, once started, the wind often caught and forced it back on top of them. Ronny's legs began to feel the strain of it and there was a pain in his laboring lungs. Floundering and struggling side by side there, Ronny found that he and Bill were staring grimly into each other's eyes, as if the very abstract intentness of the look, in such moments as their faces were clear of water, was some sort of permanence. And at the moment when they got the thing half about and the wind took it from the new angle, whirling it as they wanted it to go, Ronny caught a twisted grin on Bill's face, a grin and gasp of triumph that reached to him as a glorious thing. It was tremendous. It was unconquerable, he felt, grinning back as best he could as they both hung and panted on the turned plane. He felt warm all over, as if with a great achievement.

By the time they were ranged beside the others again, along the fuselage, the anxious pale faces turned to them, the bodies floundering and awash, the color had gone from the watery world. There was only a brief green streak of twilight where the sun had gone. To the east the waves were black against the tremendous looming purple of the night. Stars were quivering in the enormous rondure of the sky that overhead took on a strange metallic blue and cast upon them a faint luminance that was less than light and only a little less than dark. By it they could see their own dark shapes, the black parallels of the wings. On the black water the white crests flashed and lengthened and disappeared, ghostly in the dark. The waves snarled now as they leaped toward them. The hissing spray stung like thrown pebbles as it struck their blistered, puffy faces. There was a little relief in the darkness, for the sun no longer burned into their eyeballs, but in its place the phantoms of the black lonely water started about them and the blood went thin.

"I suppose now"—Mrs. Kinney's voice came suddenly and a little shrill, from the shadow she had become—"now that it's dark, nobody can see to pick us up, even if a boat did come?"

No one spoke. It was what everyone had been thinking, Ronny was sure. But it had not been spoken before in so many words.

Then Bill said simply, "It's not likely, Mrs. Kinney. But in the morning it will be different. They'll have heard from Bimini, and the boats will be out sure. We've been drifting a bit or they would have found us sooner."

No one spoke again. They set themselves, somehow, to endure the night. Through the noise of the wind humming and shrieking in the wires and of the waves hissing and slapping against the wood, Ronny could hear few sounds which would indicate that human life was here, clinging perilously to what was almost wreckage. His arm ached dully and continuously as he held it tight over the edge of the cockpit, and his bumped and floating body smarted in places where the skin had been rubbed off. Yet he was growing queerly drowsy. His eyelids dropped and a hazy swimming took the place of thought within his head. He must even have dozed once or twice, for a sharp pain in his elbow roused him or a slap of choking water in the face, and he recognized miserably again, what, for a second of blur, he had forgotten—the lost floundering in the dark, the misery in him and in the figures about him.

Once or twice he heard Colonel Kinney speaking gently to his wife and her sharp whimper, as if she, too, had wakened abruptly from a wretched doze, perhaps one in which she had dreamed of warmth and safety and being dry, to the reality of the roaring and sinister dark. Once he heard Gloria swearing to herself, as if unable to stand it any longer, and then stopping abruptly, knowing that it did no good.

The stars were gold and silver overhead in the vast dark vault, and it seemed to Ronny that their tangled and glittering patterns were dragged slowly across up there, like a remote panorama for how many human eyes below them, raised in agony and mute endurance. Only decoration, after all. He must have dozed again, hanging by the other elbow, cheek almost in the water, for presently he started out of oblivion with a hand on his shoulder.

It was Bill, his voice low and humble.

"Look here, buddy," he said slowly and with difficulty, "we'll have to look out. They've begun to slip off. Mrs. Cargill's wire keeps coming unfastened and your father went down once. Coming up with him I hit my head a bit. Would you stick around and watch them while I catch my breath?"

"Hurt bad, Bill?" Ronny whispered anxiously. "Here, hang on to this edge. Hook your elbow over. Take your time, old man. I'll be on the job."

He swam slowly down the side, catching here and there at a foot. "Don't mind. It's me," he said hastily. He counted the dark heads and shoulders out of the ghostly foam. One, Colonel Kinney; two, Mrs. Kinney; three, Gloria; four, his fa— that head disappeared even as he looked. Instantly he dived, groping downward in the strangling, rushing depths. There was only water in his frantic reaching fingers. Then he felt hair, a shoulder, caught at a thrashing arm. They came to the surface together, staring into each other's shadowy faces, gasping.

"Dad," Ronny whispered in agony, "did the wire come off? You must have let go. For heaven's sake, be careful. You can't tell when——"

For a moment longer the bulk of Andrew Burgess hung and shook a little in the dimness. "Thanks—old boy," he said then. "Guess I wasn't holding on tight enough. Yet hanging on—hanging on's—not much worth while."

"Hush, dad. Don't," Ronny whispered. "They'll hear you. Think how we'll talk about this when we get back. Just think of the experience of it."

His father said nothing. Ronny hung and watched the stars and tried not to think of those boiling black depths he had encountered, or of the queer tone in his father's voice, or of hot, yellow scrambled eggs. The wind played three distinct wailing notes among the wires, high when the plane was tossed higher on a crest, low and humming in the hollows. The jerk and ache along his arms helped to keep him alert now. He hoped that Bill would be all right. Then Mrs. Kinney cried out, either in a doze or waking from it, and Ronny ached with pity for her, because she sounded like a frightened child trying hard to be good. Ronny could hear the patient fatherly drone of Colonel Kinney's voice, trying to console her. His own father changed his position restlessly, and then Gloria, in one of those restless moments which passed among them all like a long shudder. The night crawled on.

There was no way of knowing what time it was and yet it might not be more than ten o'clock, Ronny thought. People ashore were just leaving hotels to go out for the evening, or dressing gayly for a dance. How strange it was—they here; those other people over there, hundreds of them, thousands of them, laughing and well fed and happy, walking around on pavements under bright lights. He could see them vividly, hear the murmur of their voices, the scuffling of their feet on sidewalks; and yet they could not think of the six here, even imagine them, or their helpless plight in the black devouring ocean, unless there were headlines in a morning paper. How queer things were.

And the stars far overhead moved slightly and slowly on their steady courses and the black water lifted and lashed and fell, lifted and fell, lifted and fell, and the wind hummed its three notes interminably. Ronny's head swam a little with a creeping weariness. His body was clammy inside and out and it was extraordinary how his arms could ache.

Then Gloria's wire went loose and she slipped down with a choked gasp and her head went under, and Ronny dived for her—dived with desperation, so that he crashed full into her, down there in the strong surge, and came up with her weight caught in his arms. She coughed and tried to swim a little and spluttered and tried to conceal from him that she was crying in sheer wet misery. Then he could not find her piece of wire. It must have gone down too. He put one arm around her and held her tightly while she recovered herself. Their wet bodies close together warmed each other feebly and he was grateful for it. Her shivering stopped slowly and she put out a hand to a strut and held on, so that he was relieved of her weight. He took off what was left of his shirt and tied it around her and around the strut, but warned her hoarsely not to trust it too much, torn and sodden as it was.

Then he dozed a little, locking his grip and jerking it tight again before it quite relaxed. It seemed to him that a second of real sleep, half a second of sleep, would be an oblivion so delicious that it would make up for everything. It was always just ahead—just ahead—and then salt water smacked in his face and he was wide-awake again and his father's head had disappeared, and he had to dive twice before he brought him safely back again and held him while he recovered from the longer immersion.

A fear that was not like any fear he had known, yet clutched coldly at his heart. Was it really a possibility—could it be possible?—that he might lose someone down there? Was death really so near to any one of them in this casual adventure?

The stars slid a little; the waters hissed; the wind screamed. Time was an interminable agony, welding impossible moment to impossible moment that crawled, crawled, crawled. Gloria slipped in again, and

70

then his father, and then Colonel Kinney, losing his wire, and Ronny dived again and again. He had lost track of the number of times. He was not even sure which one it was he hauled heavily to the surface, clinging to him and coughing weakly. Now his right leg was getting cramped. The pain shot up the stiffened muscle, needlelike and searing. Suppose it caught him down there next, when he most needed all the strength he had? He was ashamed to rouse Bill, but he had to, and he heard his own voice, husky and humble, as Bill's had been.

Bill roused instantly and took charge. Ronny hooked his arm over the cockpit edge, and the doze that moved upon him was delightful. Yet it seemed only a moment when Bill was calling him again, exhausted, and the stars were altered and it was hours later.

As Ronny moved out to be among the others, and Bill hung, gasping, he counted them carefully, to make sure they were all there. His hands lingered on a shoulder, and he saw that it was his father. After a moment his father's voice came to him wearily. "Still—hanging—on," he said. "Don't go doing—too much now. We—depend on—you and Bill—a lot."

The night went like that, passing so slowly, with such a minute succession of incidents, of wretchedness, that it seemed impossible that it could ever end or change above a half-drowned world.

So that when Ronny, floundering on a wave top, with one arm holding up Gloria, happened to see in the east a streak of pale color he stared at it for a long time with puzzled, bloodshot eyes, wondering dully what it could be. The glow widened, the sky and sea around it turned pale gray. A streak of burning gold swelled into that. And Ronny cried out suddenly, in his surprise, "Look; it's morning!"

The tender light fell on faces sodden and strained almost beyond recognition. But even as the light grew white and radiant over the crested wave tops and the strange emerald of the waters, animation came into the faces and they were once more his father and Gloria and Mrs. Kinney and the colonel and Bill.

As if light were the supreme necessity, the supreme miracle, they sought it. It was hope; it was food; it was safety; it was life. A faint burst of animation, exclamation, broken words, feeble, husky laughter passed among them like a renewed pledge. They were once more capable of watching the sea to the west, where any moment now a boat might come. Yet no boat came. The flash of spray was only the edge of a higher wave. The drone was only the wind in the wires. Bill, lifting himself up with greater difficulty now, peered out above them over an empty sea.

Presently the reassuring warmth of the sun had changed to the agonizing glare of yesterday. Their faces were a raw crimson against which the wave edges were knife cuts. Their salt-crusted lips were swollen and cracked. Their eyes were bloodshot and inflamed. Ronny and Bill managed to find rags enough about them to make masks to tie over the faces of the four. Ronny and Bill dared not mask themselves. They had to be on the alert now, both of them. For now that the flash of hope was over and the sun glared nearer and nearer to noon, the others slipped down more easily into the blue depths. It was easier to find them there now, that was all.

It must have been afternoon when Colonel Kinney, slipping down almost without a splash, eluded Ronny's grasp. Beneath the surface the big body was only a whirling shadow which Ronny caught lightly once and lost. When Ronny's lungs seemed bursting he shot to the surface empty-handed, with despairing eyes for Bill's anxious look. One full breath and he was down again, fighting down amidst the strong heave and swirl of the waters, and Bill was with him. Twice they clutched each other fiercely. There was no other shape.

Gasping dreadfully the two hung together on the fuselage, staring into each other's eyes. There was nothing to be said. Ronny was thankful for the mask over Mrs. Kinney's eyes. She need not know yet. She was like a dead thing, hanging there, half held by the wire about her, with one hand locked about a strut. She clung as if by no volition of her own, but only the gripping tenacity of the life within her, straining to go on. The sun beat down upon them. The wind screamed steadily in the wires. The eternal water roared and hissed. No one had said anything for hours and hours.

It was late afternoon. "Ron," whispered his father feebly through his mask, "where's the colonel?"

"Gone," said Ronny after a moment. "I—lost him."

His father tore off his mask suddenly. Beneath it the contorted swollen features were almost unrecognizable. "He's lucky," his father rasped. "Why not? Why not?"

"Hush, dad," Ronny said patiently, "they'll hear you. There'll be a boat before long. There must be."

Andrew Burgess said nothing more. Ronny stared at the haggard,

72

bitter face where the stiff gray hairs bristled about the chin. It smote through his numbed brain suddenly that his father—his splendid father—was an old, old man.

The sunset flared hideously down upon them. Another night came slowly from the west. And Gloria, tearing off her mask, leaned back abruptly in the rag that held her, and tore free. Her lips strained back from her gaunt face in a queer tense smile and she threw both hands over her head and went down suddenly, before Ronny could guess what she had intended. And below there was only the swirl and the silvery bubbles of his own and Bill's frantic search.

When they came back again it was almost night, and Ronny was shaken by a paroxysm of grief which he had not even strength enough to express in sobs. He remembered vaguely how beautiful she had been on that morning, ages ago, when he was a boy, before the flight began.

In that night his father disappeared. It was a night such as Ronny had never dreamed possible. He and Bill were left alone in all the lost world, hanging mute and feeble on each side of the faintly warm figure of Mrs. Kinney. Her wire still held. With the mask off, under the stars, her face was not so ravaged as the others. From time to time she moaned a little and they took turns in chafing gently her clammy hands and feet. She was something infinitely precious that they had left to care for, in the whirling chaos in their minds, in the roaring black about them and the high black over them, punctuated with the glittering smear of stars.

When the sun at last broke up the permanence of that night they blinked their salt-incrusted eyes at each other unbelievably, to see the sun, to see that they were still there—three nameless, shapeless beings, under the incredible light.

Ronny turned his head presently to see a boat come surging toward them with a great fan of spray at the bow—a boat with men in it, with young, dry, smooth faces looking anxiously at them, and waving. Ronny watched it come with no emotion whatsoever. He had always known that it would come. But now that hardly mattered.

When hands clutched and hauled him up, he fought them until he saw they had clutched also Bill and Mrs. Kinney. He felt himself in a dry boat, with something to drink burning his throat. But he felt nothing. There was nothing to feel. Until they told him, gently, that Mrs. Kinney had been dead for very many hours. Then he cried with terrible retching sobs, vaguely ashamed that Bill should see him so.

4
TWENTY MINUTES LATE
FOR DINNER

*I*T WAS EXTRAORDINARY to Hobey, even in the surge of
his emotion, how suddenly the thing finally happened—the decision
which it had never occurred to him that he would make. It started
abruptly out of the hidden channels of his mind, complete, to change
the whole nature and direction of his life.

One moment he was as he had been for the last three years—
secure, in spite of the lift of delight in him because of Evelyn, a slow
wave that poured over him, warm and strong as the Florida sun, briefly
appearing between the low white cloud layer. He sat on the barracks
step, wallowing in both, thinking of nothing very much except
Evelyn—vaguely happy. He was aware equally of his own brown paws,
loosely clasped, sticking from worn dungaree cuffs; of his Navy shoes
planted in rough white coral; of the gray governmental buildings of
the Coast Guard about him; of men's voices, familiar and droning,
from open windows and from the boat slips on the bay side. He heard
the thrash overhead of palm fronds in the stiffening sea wind and,
from the southward, the gradual approaching snore of an airplane,
which was the commander coming back from a patrol out at sea.

It was all exactly as the years of his enlistment had been—
simple, understandable, uncomplicated, male. With the moment of
change almost upon him, he savored it below his abstraction, waiting
to ask the commander for an extra hour of liberty, so that he could
get down to his mother's place in Miami an hour or so before dinner.
Because of Evelyn. The very name in his mind was a sting of delight
in the haze of his content.

74

The next moment it was changing; it had all changed. Like the sudden rearrangement, to an utterly new pattern, of the same bits of glass in a kaleidoscope, everything was different.

There was no longer any hope of simplicity and directness for him. He had only made himself think there was, because his mind had desired it so. Nothing very much happened, and yet everything happened, leaping up in him like slow explosive, three years laid. Charlie Brown came by with the mail and gave him a letter.

It was smooth pale orchid, addressed in Evelyn's handwriting like a cobwebby, uneven picket fence. His blood stung in his chest as he held the letter in his hand and looked at it; thumped in his ears, just as it did when he looked at her, at the soft curve of her upper lip and the clear mysterious blue of her eyes. He turned it over and over in his hand, trying not to grin too self-consciously, waiting until Charlie Brown and Saunders, one of the motor machinists' mates, talking above his head, should have gone on. The thick paper was creamy to his fingers. The sun ceased to glare upon it, being shut off by the low, whity-gray clouds. The sea wind ran chill and damp across his eyelids, wet salt across his lips, and they were saying that it was a tough life.

"I'll say it's a tough life," said Charlie Brown, lighting a cigarette.

Saunders borrowed his match. "It's a tough life, awright. M' girl ga' me the gate last night."

"That red-headed girl you was with the other night in Miama? What she give you the gate for?"

"Yeh. Swell girl, awright. But she ga' me the gate. First she was letting me take her places and buying her dinners, and then she ga' me the gate."

"Maybe she saw you with that blonde in Lauderdale one time and got sore?"

"Nah, she never—I never went with any other girl since her. She knows 'at, awright. She knows 'at. I was simple about her was how it was."

"Well, what's her idea? Must of been some idea, swell girl like 'at."

"Yeh. Well, it's a same old line. You know. Didn't your wife hand it to you? She made out like she couldn't stand going out with the Coast Guard on account of not liking probition and us chasing the rummies. All like that. Says we're on'y cheap probitioners, snoopin' around with a hand out for what we can get, and double-crossing the rummies when we get it. Gee, I was sore. And then this Coast Guard trial comes up down there, see, and she knows a girl was cousin to the rummy that got killed, and they said the Coast Guard on'y got him because he hadn't paid up, and like that. I told her we wasn't out for probition specially. I tried to tell her about being under orders about preventin' smuggling pearls and dope and Chinks or anything. But she ga' me the gate just the same. Gee, I was sore."

"Yeh. It's tough awright. But you can't tell a woman anything. They all ack the same down here. They think these rummies are swell, like movie actors. It doesn't get you anything arguing with 'em. You can't tell 'em anything."

"That's the third girl ga' me the gate on account of probition. What do I care about probition? It's like I said to her, I said, you got to do what you're told or you get court-martialed. We got to. It's like there wasn't anybody else to do the dirty jobs but the Coast Guard. We didn't ask for probition. We got it wished on us, same as any kind of contraband. But I couldn't tell her nothin'. She's going with a boot-legger now, I guess. I was sore."

"Yeh, I been sore myself. But you can't tell 'em nothin'. They like things romantic."

"Yeh. That's right. I sure was sore."

Hobey sat still, listening to the voices moving over toward the office, where he could not hear the words any more. He was turning and turning Evelyn's letter in his hand. Then he ripped it open.

That was the moment when the thing happened. His world—his secure masculine world—crashed about his ears and he was Hobart Allen, 3d, again, back in that fussy world his mother and his Aunt Agatha and the Allen money and the Allen social position had wrapped about him mufflingly since he was born. Womanish and sub-tle and indirect and confusing, he was in it again, up to his ears. Be-cause Evelyn wrote the thing he had not let himself imagine. She would not marry him if he re-enlisted next Wednesday when his time was up. She said she was wild about him and he thrilled her to death and she adored his exquisite mother and his Aunt Agatha and it would be too marvelous to be Mrs. Hobart Allen, 3d, and live in the West-chester house, but she simply could not marry anybody who had so little ambition and so little regard for his mother's wishes as to be satisfied with being a kind of prohibition agent all his life. She would marry him next month, if he came to his senses and refused to go back to that weird life of wearing a uniform and stopping people's yachts and being ordered about by men whose incomes wouldn't pay his mother's butler. He didn't love her enough if he couldn't be glad to give that up. And he must come early tonight, because she couldn't wait to see him, and she trailed the word "Darling" all across the last page over her signature, that poised there, delicate as a butterfly.

It was exactly like that trick she had of fluttering her eyelashes against his cheek impishly, when she would not let him kiss her—a butterfly flutter of a caress that shook him down to the heels of his boots.

He folded the letter and put it in his blouse pocket. He was licked. He knew it. There wasn't any use fighting any more. He might have known he hadn't had a Chinaman's chance from the first. He saw that perfectly clearly. The decision was made in him, like a tremendous overturning. And, once made, he had left no other emotion than a slight dizziness. It was Evelyn. She was the most adorable, the most marvelous, the most——

She would marry him. Perhaps she was right about his laziness and his lack of ambition. And yet, he remembered, as if from a remote distance, he really had wanted to keep on going up in the service. Next to Evelyn, the thing he had wanted most in the world was to pass his officer's exams and be an ensign. Certainly he had worked harder, actually worked longer and steadier and with more concentrated enthusiasm, than he had ever worked in his life before, or been allowed to. His two pampered years at college, with his mother taking a house off campus to be near him and making him give up after that because she worried about his eyes, had been nothing like this.

He looked down at his brown, thickened hands. They had been pulpy that summer his mother and Aunt Agatha had left him alone in the Cape Cod house when they went to San Sebastian. It seemed to him that had been the first time in his life he had been left alone. He knew perfectly what he was like then—a slight, mild youth, studious and awkward. His mother had always been so distressed because he would drop the tea cakes. Once he had spilled scalding tea on the bishop. Yet that was only three years ago. He had to grin, looking down at his brown right fist. It had held other things than teacups since then. It had known blisters and bruises and grease and frostbite. It had pulled at ropes and on oars. It had gripped boat hooks and pistols and heavy paintbrushes and chipping hammers. It had scraped decks and cleaned brass and tended engines and scrubbed his own clothes and peeled potatoes. It knew the kick of a wheel in bucking seas and the satisfying smack of a right hook to the jaw. There was that time he had knocked out Lefty Flynn, cold. Next Wednesday he had been going to re-enlist. He had been careful not to mention that to his mother and his Aunt Agatha. He remembered, as if for the last time, fleetingly, how it had begun. He remembered himself pounding blindly down the beach to the Coast Guard station with Aunt Agatha's telegram crumpled in his hand. They were coming back. It had been the first summer that he had sailed a boat all he wanted to, with no one watching him with binoculars from the upper balcony to see if he were in danger. He had capsized three times in winds too strong for the other boats and taken two swimming prizes and got his feet wet constantly and spent hours hanging around the Coast Guard station. So that, when that cable came, something leaped in him and he enlisted.

He had been in uniform when he met them in Boston, and he was browner than they had ever seen him, and heavier, and his hands were already calloused and his mind was rooted and grounded on content. For the first time in his life he had been able to meet with a little detachment the nervous crisis of their dismay. He could even endure his mother's hysterics. It showed him, more clearly than anything had ever done, that, in spite of their gentleness, their rapt devotion, their tea-rose complexions and their small, vague hands, there was something in their love for him that was smothering—oh, very loving, very gentle, but like having your breath slowly shut off with rose-silk pillows faint with attar and edged with ancestral lace. Blue serge and hip boots and sou'westers and wet feet as a matter of routine, and gray seas smashing up into a narrow gray bow, were lungfuls of rousing sea air, after that. They had had to accept it.

Until he had seen Evelyn he had intended to remain in the service always.

He had to hand it to them—the suave, shrewd little ladies. They had got what they wanted with the inevitability of admirals and diplomats. After the first, they had not cried or protested. His mother, whose nerves had always held him in secret terror, had not once been hysterical after the first few months. Aunt Agatha's jaw line, well concealed with ivory lace and a pearl choker, had not once asserted itself. When he had been transferred to Florida they had taken a house in Miami only the second winter. And when the base was transferred to Fort Lauderdale, they had not been plaintive about it. They had worked carefully and discreetly and slowly. He had been perfectly aware of that. He had laughed a little to himself, watching them accent the masculine bareness and rigor of his life with their own cars and servants and delicate luxury. It had not worried his content, in the slightest.

But then they had sent for Evelyn. They had made no mistakes about her. They had not praised her too much. They had spoken of her only casually, as poor Cousin Sarah Garnett's youngest girl, who would be so grateful for a winter in Florida. They had not insisted that he get away from his work to see her often. They were, as he knew so well they could be, soft and innocent and watchful and utterly determined. They put him on his guard with all their softness and subtlety.

But nothing had made any difference from the first moment when he had seen Evelyn. The warmth in him grew now to a great, dazed glow. She had walked straight out of a door into the full, blistering dazzle of white light on a white beach, with the sapphire and white thunder of ocean beyond her, all shapely gold, laughing, and the dazzle had leaped to his veins and his throat and his head, and stayed there. She took the life out of everything else and crammed it into her own gesture. Behind her everything paled. The content that had been in him was nothing; his ambition, nothing. When she clung to him with the soft palms of her hands the poignance of it ran him through the heart—as it did now.

That he had planned to re-enlist next week fell from him like an unimportant memory. A fever to see her, not just think about her, swept him to his feet. It was incredible that he had never seized her roughly and kissed her, and kissed her, as he meant to now.

The commander's plane swashed across the bay to the runway, a huge khaki-colored bird, clumsy now that it was out of its own element. Hobey walked slowly down toward it. He'd speak to the commander right now. He could shave and dress at his mother's, to save time getting there. He hurried, lost in the color of his own thoughts. What a rotten whity-gray day it had turned into, to be sure. The sea wind was altogether too searching for his idea of a Florida December. He noticed, for the first time, how, without the sun, the whity-gray light lay drearily on the gray board buildings and the rough white earth. The palm trees struggled in the wind like bedraggled birds. Gosh, imagine spending another three years here, being told to do things and having people, his own people, furious with him for doing as he was told.

He forgot even the slight formality the Coast Guard likes, even in its less official moments, and spoke to the man loping up toward him from the beach.

"Look here, commander," he said abruptly, "I've got to——"

"There you are, Allen," the commander said to him softly, like a man bringing good news. "You remember that black boat? It was about twenty-five miles off Hillsborough when I saw it, heading southwest. Looks as though they were making for Baker's Haulover, coming from West End. The way they were going, if you get right out on a southeasterly course you ought to pick them up off Hollywood. You better take out the chaser and go look. Take Saunders and Charlie Brown and Perkins and Willis and Anderson."

The words were clear, but they did not quite penetrate the warm mist that was in Hobey's head, now that everything was changed for him.

He went right on saying, "I've got to leave early for Miami because——"

"What'd you say?" the commander said. "You remember that black boat—the one that got away from us last week? Yes, I know it's your liberty night, chief. That boat looked as if it weren't making all its usual speed. Better snap into it."

There was a black boat wallowing out in that gray sea somewhere, out in the stream, and this tall person with the slow, keen gaze seemed to expect him to do something about it. Hobey half opened his mouth to ask him what. And then he didn't. The word "Evelyn" had drawn veils across his thinking. But somehow the Navy shoes on his feet were carrying him, running, back up to the house for his cap and his jacket and the Navy automatic in its holster on the belt that went around his waist. He heard his own pipe skirling shrilly, heard his voice shouting the names. The thumping of the weapon against his hip as he ran was not so real as the thumping of the resentment in his heart, but his body hurled itself back across the strip of sand, along the dock and curving down onto the chaser's immaculate deck with the blue legs of his crew swarming into action behind him.

The boat's get-away from the dock, with a bursting roar of engines, down the bay to the ship channel, already running swift with greeny-gray water before the push of the gray wind, the long rolling swing out into the slate and livid leaping white of open sea, and southward, was a thing which, half an hour ago, the blood sang in his veins to feel. Now he felt nothing.

One of the seamen had the wheel. It was the boy named Willis, he recognized vaguely—one of the new boys who got rattled when some local newspaper charged the Coast Guard with graft and murder after some battle with the rummies. He didn't look rattled now. He was grinning and the two others on the deck behind him were grinning into the teeth of the wet wind whipping across their faces. It used to get him like that, too, Hobey thought absently. There was something about this action that got you. Or it did once. Now, there was no response in him any longer to the surge of a deck under his feet and the ensign snapping out and the sea running white astern. It was all blank for him now, except for his impatience at being kept from Evelyn.

What the deuce did he care about this smash of water and roar and tension of excitement and black boats, if it meant the capture of every infernal rummy from Canaveral to Key West? He was out of it now—out of it, out of it. It didn't concern him. He was through. For the first time in three years he rebelled hotly against the idea that anyone at all could make him do something, when he, Hobart Allen, 3d, wanted to do something else. When Evelyn had said they could be married next month.

The worst of this sort of wet, rolling, chill, stern chase, he thought vindictively, clutching the weather rail and staring resentfully but still watchfully out over the tumble of gray sea under the whity-gray scud of cloud, was that it was quite likely to amount to just a half less than nothing at all. If the black boat were a real rummy they wouldn't be bringing her in openly at this time of the afternoon with any evidence on board. Or if it were the same boat they had seen, her engines were so much more powerful than their own that she would walk away from them. And if it were not a rummy, it would mean only hours precious to him wasted on some disgruntled fisherman tourist who would go back and complain about being rudely overhauled by the rude Coast Guard that had nothing better to do than go poking about sticking their noses into a private and respectable citizen's private and respectable business. Even if the same citizen had voted for a tariff.

And yet the chaser was a great craft. He had to admit that. She was taking the short, choppy, 'longshore sea like a gray, leaping cat. The stinging white foam flew from the impact of her forefoot on the ridges and the bleak racing wind lashed at her, rising to it splendidly. But she ran lightly, staggering and shuddering only a little to some heavier shock of water, answering her helm valiantly. They were heading, roughly, southeast by east; taking the plunge and chop of the deepening waves that ran northward, slaty green now, marbled with glaring foam, as the Gulf Stream deepened about them. The flying wet clung to their faces and blurred their eyelids. Hobey clung to anything he could reach in the bucking plunges, peering ahead for whatever he might discover, feeling sure that whatever they found would be worse than useless anyway. The thuttering roar of the engines was one with the smash and shock of tons of sea water, leaping and smashing and breaking along her sides. The troughs of the running seas were glossy, greenish black.

The boat was discovering a nasty little pitch and toss in the cross seas that turned the boy named Willis whitish-yellow about the jowls, and Hobey motioned for steady old Saunders to relieve him at the wheel. Because of that sea, Hobey's resentment burned deeper. It was the miserable kind of pitching any man might be sickened of, if he had to stand too much. There wasn't any romance in it, nor any sense of adventure. It was just a wet, rotten job that anybody would be crazy to say he liked.

He really had not been expecting to see anything. Surely the black boat must have changed her course and got away out of that by this time. They had been a good half hour now. There was no land to westward, only a dirty smudge with a white splinter sticking out of it that was the high tower of a building. The clouds were rolling heavier overhead, like long wads of dirty cotton batting. Pretty soon it would rain, to add to the joy of life in dirty weather on the Gulf Stream, and after that it would be colder. Any rummy who ventured out on a day like this was crazy.

The sea before him was empty of everything but thrashing gray-green and blackish water, lit with boiling white. He looked back and saw that the white sliver had disappeared, and the land. He looked forward and a black dot was there—black and a snowy flash of white—that broke and flashed, broke and flashed, with the black rolling, but moving steadily between.

The men had seen it as soon as he had. Sooner. And a little smothered tightening of excitement ran among them. The boy named Willis turned from a yellowish white to a sudden pink. Saunders at the wheel, for all his fifteen years of service, narrowed his eyes and chewed slightly in his grizzled cheek. Saunders always did that, Hobey thought absently. But where interest should at least have quickened in himself, there was only that blank place. He watched the alternating flash of black and white ahead, and signaled for all the speed they had, but it hardly seemed to him to matter whether they caught the thing or not.

They were gaining on it slightly. Something must be wrong with the black boat's engines, or else they had not seen their pursuer yet. Hobey waited, brushing a hatful of spray from his eyes. The black wedge was growing larger. Yet at this rate the chase might lengthen out indefinitely, with the black boat disappearing eventually in a burst of additional speed. And the chaser roared forward, doing her best. The distance grew only very slightly less. And then it seemed to Hobey that the black boat's speed suddenly increased.

It was useless to hail in this wind. But they should hear shots. From habit he looked to make sure his Coast Guard ensign and pennant were showing. Then he nodded to Anderson, who stood ready, rifle in hand. The three warning shots cracked out, high up, over the black boat's smothered bow.

As far as Hobey could see, nothing happened. The black boat

was not stopping, and they, with all the speed they had, were just holding the distance between them. It was impossible that the boat had not noticed the shots. Hobey had the gun fired once more.

"Better use the Lewis gun, chief!" Saunders shouted. "If he knows we've got one he'll likely quit!"

Hobey clicked back the charging handle. The quick staccato barks rose sharply above the engine roar and the crash of the spray. As if traced by a finger, a line of torn water crept up past the black boat's bow well off to one side. This was as it should be. The orders were strict about firing at or too near boats unless absolutely necessary. And who wanted to hit a man for a load of liquor, even if the orders were specific?

The width of the gray troughs between them slowly grew narrower. They were running up on the black boat now, which had not stopped, but was proceeding more slowly, as if limping away. But still there was no sense of excitement in it for Hobey. It was all according to regulation, the usual formula for stopping boats at sea. Then they curved about to draw alongside and Hobey heard the black boat's engines thumping haltingly.

"Darn nerve he's got!" the boy named Willis yelled at Hobey's right ear. He was bright red with excitement now, and Hobey's eye lingered on him with a little amazement. A day or two ago he had not been unlike that too. Now, what in the world was there to get excited about?

They were alongside the black boat, and Hobey waved and yelled to them to pull up. It was a long boat, decked over except for an open cockpit where the helmsman stood, sheltered by a weather hood. He looked down into it and full into the eyes of a man with a narrow, sallow face, who stared at him fixedly with little gleaming eyes under lowered lids. The black boat's halting engine stopped abruptly and Saunders dropped over into it with a line to make fast. Now that the roar of the engines was blotted out, both boats lay and wallowed deeply in the deep sliding troughs, and the sounds of wind and smashing water were suddenly louder over them, in a kind of silence.

The body of a man lay aft in the black boat, on a layer of bags in the cockpit, giving and rolling stiffly with the rolling of the boat. It was a dead body. Anybody could see that. Hobey's glance leaped back to the eyes of the man watching him. That one had made no motion since the boat had stopped, but hunched there, one elbow over the wheel, his narrow face lifted boldly.

"Why didn't you stop when I ordered you to?" Hobey yelled down at him from the side. Something of all his resentment crackled in his voice. "Don't you know a signal when you hear it? Get aboard there, boys, and open up that forward hatch!" The sallow-faced man said nothing, his small black eyes fixed on Hobey's under yellowish lids. Charlie Brown and the boy named Willis watched their chance as the gunwales tossed and lifted, bumping against their fenders, and dropped over the black boat's side to join Saunders. Perkins and Anderson remained on their own boat. Hobey jumped over into the boat after the others. As the boys worked at the hatch cover he clambered aft to bend over the body.

A sudden harsh cry came from the man at the wheel: "Don't touch him!" he said, and his voice hung on the wind for a moment.

Hobey straightened up and looked back into those narrow eyes. "Why not?"

"Because you killed him!" the sallow face said.

Hobey's scalp stirred. He looked back at the body. It was so terribly dead. Low down in the back a ragged hole was blurred in the coat. Hobey looked at that a long moment. Then he caught his breath, bent down and turned the man over by the shoulder. The face was pasty white under a smear of grime, and the shirt front had been sopped with blackened blood. Hobey put him down again gently. He felt a little shaken. This had never happened to him before. Or had it happened? He glanced forward again and met the eyes of the man there, gleaming and ratlike and watchful.

Old Saunders left the hatch cover and came toward him. "He say you shot him?" he asked under his breath, looking down at the queerly shrunken thing at their feet.

"He says so," Hobey said.

Saunders leaned and put a hand down slowly. Then he stood up and grinned, murmuring into Hobey's ear, "He's stone cold. Hours ago. Watch out," and went back to the hatch.

Hobey's caught breath went out in a great gust and he jumped up on the deck forward without another glance at the man at the wheel. They got the cover off. Hobey looked in. Burlap bags made a solid floor under the gray light, reaching into the shadows. It was evidence, all right—a big haul. The breath of the Willis boy was exultant at his shoulder.

"Anything the matter with your engines?" Hobey said abruptly to the sallow man. "They sounded queer."

The man said nothing, dropping his lids slightly over his fixed gaze.

Hobey considered. "We'll get some of this stuff aboard and lighten her," he said. "She's too heavy forward to tow well. Hey, Perkins! Stand by to stow some of these bags!" He braced himself by the mast on the deck to the sullen plunging of the boat. His brief glance passed once over the man at the wheel and the body aft. "Snap into it, Willis," he said. "The sooner we get this aboard, the sooner we get back."

The bags were passed up over the hatch coaming, from Saunders below deck, to Willis and Charlie Brown and so across to Anderson and Perkins on the chaser. Hobey watched them, holding to the mast so that he could keep an eye on the man still loafing by the wheel. He saw himself being watchful. Yet now that the action was over, the whole area of his brain was given up to impatience at the delay. At this rate it would be an hour before they could get back to the base, another hour before he could be in Miami. The slow, monotonous bucking and plunging of the two boats—the black one and the gray one—the gray roll and toss of the breaking seas under the hissing gray wind, worked in him a gnawing protest that was anger. Down in the black boat the engine-room door was slatting.

The man in the hatch sang out that the forward compartment was empty. Hobey had counted sixty bags.

Saunders looked up at him and said, "Shall we take any from the engine room?"

Hobey realized that he had not looked into the engine room. Often they stowed cases there, each side the engine. The open door slatted and banged. Without bothering to get down into the cockpit, he bent over the break of the house, holding the door with one hand and peering down into the shadows. There were bags——.

It was only the sudden roll of the boat that prevented the blow that caught him over the ear from stunning him completely. He felt himself knocked down into the cockpit, but even as he rolled over, with his hand to his holster, he felt his automatic jerked away. As he staggered to his feet a crash of sound and flame brought him up, standing, and in a kind of whirling redness he saw Perkins crumple slowly over the chaser's gunwale and hang there, his arms swaying idly, with a fan of blood from his chest leaking brilliantly down the wet gray side. The bottle that Perkins had snatched to throw from a torn sack had splashed into the water.

He saw the face of the man in the hatch staring, with a sort of gleam in the whites of his eyes, and his arms go up slowly, and the arms of the two others on the housed deck went up also, and their eyes stared, hard and a little glassy, at the sallow man turning Hobey's automatic upon them and grinning a little.

"Now you can get your hands up too, mister," said the sallow-faced man. "Get up out of that hatch, you, there! Keep those hands up and claw air with 'em. . . . You too," he said again to Hobey. "You put your back up against the house where I can see you. And, you three, start bringing them sacks back here, where you got 'em."

Hobey's mind jerked like a caught fish in an agony of anger and helplessness. "Fool," he said to himself bitterly. "Fool;" and watched the tuft of Anderson's yellow hair creeping along the gunwale of their boat toward the gun forward. He tore his telltale gaze away and jerked his arms to draw the sallow man's gaze. But that was all the good it did.

"Keep those arms up there!" the sallow man yelled at him, and waited until Anderson had made a plunge from the cockpit to the ex-posed deck forward. Then he fired and the shot smacked out dully over the wash of water. A splinter leaped from the deck and Anderson fell backward, sprawling limply, out of sight. Both boats tossed and rocked and plunged to the swing of the seas, and Hobey stared, without blinking, at the dead arms of Perkins, swinging also.

"Anderson," he called out, and his voice croaked, "did he get you? Did he get you, Anderson?"

Over the chaser's bow, yawing slightly under the wind, a flung sheet of spray leaped and fell like small shot on the deck. The sallow man said to him conversationally, "There's daylight through him, all right. Just like the man you killed. They don't say much after that." Then he raised his voice, meeting Hobey's eyes with a long, sneering glance. "Hey, Bill!" he called. "Hurry up! Come out of it!"

From the shadows of the engine room, where, in the first place, he had neglected to look, Hobey, with his hands tingling in the air, saw a brown negro emerge—a grinning brown negro with thin, long arms and legs. He was over the side and into the chaser's cockpit in one ungainly scramble.

"Now, you there"—the sallow man pointed with Hobey's automatic—"you can stow those cases back. Get 'em over, Bill. . . . Keep your hands up, you," he said to Hobey.

Hobey's back was against the deck house and his arms in the wind, and in him was one black seethe of rage and humiliation. It burned his throat so that he swallowed twice, tightly clenching and unclenching those useless fists of his, with the wet wind streaming through his fingers. What a useless fool he had been. Two good men cold in less than two minutes, and his fault—his fault. Where he gritted his jaws was a dull unnoticed ache. Not one of these men had been armed, in spite of the pistols on their bulkhead. There was only this automatic of his anywhere near—in those sallow fingers. As the rummy's coat blew back he saw another pistol snug in its holster.

Saunders and Charlie Brown and Willis were dropping the sacks back into the hatch with the deliberation of a slow-motion picture. Old Saunders was great. Nothing had disturbed him. Every gesture he made carried insult. The eyes of all three of them, as well as Hobey's, with his useless hands in the air, turned from whatever angle to stare with rigid lids at the man who held the weapon on them. Their nostrils were stiff. The Willis boy's face was yellow-white again, and he was frightened, Hobey saw, but he was controlling it. He'd be a good man yet, with another year in the service, Hobey thought with a detached corner of his brain, watching the sallow man, watching the long arms of the negro passing sacks to Saunders, watching, out of the tail of his eye, the grim mouths of his men and their backs, bending over the hatch. But the rest of his mind was fixed on the dead arms of Perkins, swinging and swinging.

The negro held the last of the sacks on the rail, waiting for Saunders to take it. Good old Saunders—he was taking his time. There was defiance in every line of his elbows. He clutched one end of the sack carelessly, heaved it across. It slipped through his fingers, and with the smash of glass, came clear brown liquid running over the deck.

The sallow-faced man swore a thin stream of vitriol. "Line up there, you three!" he yelled at them, and Hobey saw that Saunders had managed to flick him on raw nerve. There was a livid look on the sallow face.

"Line up for'ard there!" he said. "Turn your faces for'ard and get those hands up. Way up." The automatic was in his left hand, his right clutched the butt in his own holster. He stared at Hobey for a moment and Hobey saw his broken teeth. "All right, Bill," the rummy said to the negro on the chaser. "Got your matches? Get in there and start a fire in that engine room."

The negro looked at him and then down at something in the cockpit and so back again, with an odd sort of hesitance. "Dis mahn here—'e isn't dead!" he said shrilly. "'E moved now, fo' true!"

"What difference does that make?" the sallow man shouted at him. "Do as I tell you! Get that fire started and get back here to cast off that boat, or I'll leave you burn up with it. Hurry up there! Faster!"

The negro swallowed, looked down, fumbled in his pocket and started toward the engine-room door.

"Anderson!" Hobey yelled, and a prickling quiver ran down his spine. "Anderson, can you move? He's going to burn the boat. Can you move?"

Anderson's voice came indistinctly through the sounds of wind and water. "Can't. . . move my legs. Can't . . . move them. I'm shot in the back. Don't let them burn it—don't——"

"You Bill!" the sallow man shouted. "Get started there!"

Anderson cried out again, and the Willis boy shrieked suddenly.

Hobey's voice leaped out and jerked the negro's head around as if he had struck with it. "Put that man aboard here," he said—"put that man aboard here, you, before I——"

But it was the sallow man who spoke last for only an instant, swinging his automatic around straight at the negro's right eye.

"I'll give you three minutes to get that fire started, Bill," he bawled, "before I put a hole in you! You hear me?"

The negro's head disappeared. Anderson was moaning "Don't—don't." The boats heaved and bucked. The seas broke and banged and smashed, and the wet wind hissed in the snowy foam. Hobey caught the tail of Saunders' eye with the tail of his. Defiantly, they had all turned around. The Willis boy's lip was bitten through. But all four of them—Hobey and Charlie Brown and Saunders and even the Willis boy—stood leaning a little forward, with their hands clutching and clutching the empty wind, their eyes glaring at the man with the automatic.

He stood, with a kind of lounging alertness, by the rail. He eyed them through dark slits, listening. The sea made too much swash and hurly-burly to let them hear the sound of matches striking. Hobey's eyes were scalded with staring. A thread of smoke blew out suddenly from the chaser's engine room and disappeared.

The Willis boy went suddenly very sick. He clutched his stomach and retched, plunging blindly for the boat's side. The sallow man, having looked at him with brief disgust, turned and deliberately spat over the rail into the sea.

In that half second Hobey plunged. He had the sallow man's throat squeezed like a sponge in his hands that craved murder, murder, and he was not aware that the automatic had bumped on the deck. He was past worrying about firearms. They were down in the cockpit, twisting and mingled somehow, but he was aware only of that throat and his own thumbs, rigid steel, pressing in. The black eyes bulged within a few inches of his own crazy glare. He did not know whether he was cursing or not, or when they rolled and banged against the deck house. He did not know anything but the savage, indomitable satisfaction of his own fury.

The body under him went limp and he hauled it up and flung it down again, snatched the pistol from the holster, his own from the deck, flung them somehow into someone's hands by his shoulder and crouched over the long inert frame. His hands were opening and shutting still because they were still hungry.

The eyelids in the pasty face twitched over congested eyeballs and the man gasped and lifted his head up gingerly and drew himself back in a defensive huddle against the seat. Hobey wiped his face with his cuff, and reached out for his automatic and put it into his holster and stood up.

Saunders and Charlie Brown were over on the deck of the other boat with the negro between them, and there was no drift of smoke anywhere. The Willis boy was over there, too, lifting Perkins' body from the gunwale.

Hobey straightened up, watching the man at his feet. His head was quite clear now, and his thoughts were orderly. They'd have to get this bird tied up.

"Tie Bill up," he said to Saunders, "and then come over here and tie this one and yank him aboard. We won't take any more chances."

Saunders stood and looked over at him. His grizzled face was like iron.

"You'd be wise to shoot him," he said harshly, "same way you'd smash a snake. Shoot him where he lies. It'll save trouble in the end. There's that stiff aboard there. He said you killed him. We know you didn't. But you can depend on it, he and his friends will raise a howl and try to fasten it on you. Shoot him now and keep out of trouble, chief. God knows it's too good for him, after what he's done."

Hobey looked down at the cornered man on the deck. He was a rat—a livid, murdering rat. Murder was nothing to him, because he was outside the law anyway. He had killed Perkins and shot Anderson, and he'd been perfectly ready to burn Anderson alive. Shooting was too good for him. If he had been shot by accident, it would have been all right. But if he didn't do it now, it was perfectly possible that he, Hobart Allen, 3d, would be arrested on a charge of murder.

And if he were arrested for murder, would Evelyn——He stirred uneasily, watching the sallow man breathing more naturally, staring at him with his hard small eyes. Evelyn—it seemed as if it had been days since he had thought of her. The thought of her now held no flush of delight. What place had it here, on this wet deck where there had been blood? But Evelyn—would she——

The boats thudded against the fenders. The spray flew over like blown snow. Anderson was moaning again and they were attending to him. Only old Saunders stood and looked at him with his grim cold eyes.

"Shoot him and have it over," he said again—"for your own sake, sir."

Hobey looked over at him curiously. You didn't get called "sir" like that until you wore stripes. The word did something to him, warmed a slow spot in him, in the chilled clarity of his mind.

He looked back at the man on the deck and slid his automatic definitely into his holster.

"Nope," he said, "it can't be done. Whatever happens, I guess

I can stand it. I know you'll see me through. Come over with a rope and tie him."

Hobey was exactly twenty minutes late for dinner. The shaking racket of his old car died before the wide veranda of his mother's Miami house, and he got out and walked up the steps out of the salt and windy dark in a kind of mental breathlessness. It had seemed, vaguely, much later than that. Yet, as he stalked through the door the second man held open for him, the breathlessness gave way to a grim, slow calm. He remembered, as of time long past, that his Aunt Agatha was very difficult about people who were even five minutes late for dinner. It really did not matter, he decided. In the long hall mirror he saw himself against a softly lighted silver wall, as a dark, unkempt figure, unshaven, with his blue uniform wrinkled and whitened with dried sea salt. That did not matter, either. If his mother cared to delay dinner, he would change.

It was curious how he had managed to keep his mind away from Evelyn these last hours.

He came down the dim, great living room quietly, among the tiny pointed flames of candles, his wet shoes soggy on the rugs. Against the pale tinted walls there were great masses of some tropic flower that gave off a clinging, poignant sweetness. He saw the dark shadow of his figure passing the dim pools of the wall mirrors, toward the three women in silver by the white fireplace where the flames streamed upward.

He wondered a little, moving more slowly, why they had all chosen to wear silver tonight. It made them seem so much alike. His mother's was gentle silver, under a gray-and-silver shawl, and his Aunt Agatha's was stiff silver, with her long chin line over her pearl choker. At any distance he recognized her anger. He had to look at those two closely, so that he would not see Evelyn too soon.

She was there, at the piano in the corner, and the fine gilt of her hair and the frosty silver about her worked the old miracle in him.

He stood at the edge of shadow looking at her, and the emotion she set loose in him ran like a faintness along his tired body. He found that he had been weakly hoping that she would have ceased to be so lovely to him. But she was lovelier, more exquisite, like a tiny silver statue seen from a long way off. He dreaded the moment when she would turn her eyes upon him.

So that he spoke hurriedly, knowing his voice harsh. "I'm sorry to be late, mother," he said. "I was detained."

They turned, startled, to look at him. His Aunt Agatha's anger was haughty, and his mother wore that nervous stiffness about the mouth which showed that she felt he had slighted her purposely. But Evelyn just looked. Yet how alike they were—the fragile, silver, feminine figures—how alike, and how remote.

"It does seem to me, Hobart," his aunt was beginning, when the second man, moving down the room, said, "Telephone, Mr. Allen, please."

"It does seem to me," his aunt went on icily, with her formal head-of-the-family manner, "that you should show some respect to your mother and our guest, however little you may feel it. No, don't answer that telephone now. You have kept us waiting twenty minutes and you arrive in this extraordinary condition, which I——"

"Sorry, Aunt Agatha," Hobey said calmly. "I think I'll have to take this call."

When he spoke into the transmitter the commander's voice was immediate and crisp to his ear. "Chief? Thought I'd warn you. The minute we got your man in jail he called up his lawyer and they are going to get out a warrant for your arrest. Murder. It's just about as you told me when you brought him in. There is a lot of bootleg money behind him and they mean to push it, perhaps as part of his own defense. They may overhaul you in Miami, or wait until you get back here. I'm starting out right now to wire the commandant and see about bail for you. Of course, you understand that the Government makes no provision for bail in a case like this. It's up to you, from now on, as a private citizen. But I'll get it somehow. It might be well to get back up here fairly soon."

"Yes, sir," Hobey said distinctly—"yes, sir. All right."

"And while I think of it, Allen, I want to say I've been talking to Saunders and the others. Saunders told me he advised you to shoot. I get Saunders' idea, of course. It would have simplified things. But you were absolutely right. It wouldn't have done. Not for the service. And perhaps it will be a good thing for the service in the end. But I want you to know I think it took guts to do what you did, knowing the mess it would probably get you into—guts. And I'm behind you every ounce. Get that?"

The grimness had grown in Hobey, listening, but with it a strong and surging warmth that ran in him through every muscle and nerve end. But all he said was: "Thank you, sir. That's great of you. Thank you. I—it didn't seem there was anything else I could do. But I've been wondering—will this make any difference about re-enlisting next Wednesday?"

"Absolutely not." The rough warmth of the man's voice made Hobey's throat tighten in spite of himself. "I should say not. And if you get cleared at the trial—which we'll have to see that you are—I'll see that you get some mighty strong recommendations to the board, if you can pass your officer's exams. You can depend on it."

The trial! Hobey went slowly back into the fragrance and gleam of the long room. Tonight he would be arrested for murder. He would be tried for murder, when he had deliberately not murdered. He saw clearly that stiff body, rolling under the gray light in the bottom of the black boat. Was there any possibility that he had killed him? He saw the three waiting women, delicacies in silver, beyond that. He would be arrested for murder. It was kind of queer, when you stopped to think of it.

But, of course, it simplified everything too. His course was so utterly clear. They must not be alarmed. They ought never to know anything about dead men in dirty boats. It would be best to let them know after—well, afterward.

"I'm afraid I won't be able to stop for dinner after all, mother," he said steadily. "I'm awfully sorry to have kept you waiting, and then to have to run off like this. I hope you will forgive me. That was the commander asking me to get back to Fort Lauderdale directly on a—a matter that has just come up." Against the raised emotion of Aunt Agatha's voice, he went on, saying deliberately, "I want to tell you that next Wednesday I'm re-enlisting for another three years."

He had to look at Evelyn then. He had to. In their assaulted silence he looked at her, and he saw what he had dreaded. She stood up slowly and looked at him, and her beauty moved in him like pain. It shook him, even as he saw the loveliness of line and contour in her face fixed in a coldness that was absolutely clear to him. It was not just that she would never marry him now. It was that she had not loved him, ever, so much as her own will. It was only he who had loved. He saw that equally clearly. And yet the hard simplicity of the thing he was doing steadied him in spite of the pain; made, for the moment, the pain seem only part of the course he was now following unhesitatingly.

He looked from her, turned completely away from him, back at the other two—the older, more fragile women. It was curious that for the first time in his life the childish threads of fear of their anger, their nerves, their insistence, fell away from about his heart and he knew in its place a strong surge of tenderness for them—an active, pervading tenderness that went out to their vague soft hands, their small, withering, proud faces. All this thing he would have to go through would be much more horrible for them.

He had not thought of that before. Now it tore at him savagely. It would be dreadful for them. Strangely, in that moment he knew for them that same ache of protection they must have felt for him, when he was little, against all the fervid dangers of their own imaginings. He could not protect them from the consequences of living, any more than they had been able to protect him.

It was a gripping, almost an agonizing emotion. It swept him clean of all thought of Evelyn. It made him suddenly years older than these two little silvery women. Was this what it was like to be grown old, to have helpless things to protect, whom you could not protect? He felt himself gathering all the strength he had, to help them bear it. They were so fragile. They had so little resource against the thing that would happen to him any minute now. There was a pain in his heart like nothing he had ever felt before, and it was for them entirely.

He heard his Aunt Agatha saying, with that graciousness in which her anger was lost at the challenge of an emergency: "But, Hobart, surely, you don't need to decide that so abruptly, without consulting us. Your mother and I will think it over. Here is Bemis with a fresh shaker. We will wait ten minutes while you change. But you may drink your cocktail now."

He looked down helplessly at the tray of gleaming little glasses. What a mess everything was—what a mess! He wanted a cocktail badly.

"I'm afraid I can't stay," he said slowly. "I will telephone you in the morning and I may be able to see you. I think I won't have a cocktail. Thanks. No, don't worry, Aunt Agatha. You know we aren't prohibition agents. It's just that——" Why should he be thinking at the same time of his mother's delicate profile and of Perkins' dead arms over the rail, swinging and swinging? A horrible mess. But at least, he saw suddenly, his own course was direct and clear. It had the straight simplicity he had always wanted. Well, he had it now, all right.

And, in a way, in spite of his concern for these two, it was good to have it. He threw his head back and grinned, if a little soberly. "It's just that—Well, maybe I've lost my taste for them." He went over abruptly and kissed his mother's hand. The poor, little, gentle thing. "Good night, honey," he said, and went out.

5
PLUMES

*T*WO-GUN GEORGE JOHNSON gave it out around the Cape Sable and Shark River country that he was watching the egret rookery at Cocos Lake. That meant that everyone else, in the code of that country, would courteously lay off.

There was some little surprise that the long white had gone back to Cocos in numbers enough to make it worth one's while to shoot. Its great rookeries that had once whitened the blistering blue Florida sky with their tens of thousands had been shot out and forgotten long ago. Besides, with the American law on, there was no market at all, except in Europe, by way of Havana, and no prices to speak of even for Grade A live plumes, in comparison to the great days of the plume industry.

But Two-Gun was keen for any extra money he could pick up in addition to that which he earned by mackerel seining and occasional sponging; so the word went out. Only one man in all that last end of Florida, where the low green land goes back to the green-running sea that made it, received the word with something other than casual acquiescence. He was the one man of all of them to whom it was dangerous to feel anything else.

He called himself John Pinder. Once, years ago, he had come down the East Coast on a house-boat trip, now only a half-forgotten, glamorous memory, and it was then that he had picked up, carelessly, the idea that to be taken for granted down the keys one should be named Bethel or Pinder or Sands or Roberts or Curry. He sat in his dinghy and stared with narrowed eyes at the wake of the passing fish boat from which the word about Cocos had come, and felt in himself a ripping shock of anger that was so different from every emotion to which he had schooled himself in the past three, the past ten years, that he could only cling to his battered gunwale and grind his teeth together and shake. He was an escaped convict. He was a man in whom the shadows of bars lay burned across his heart. He might not have, he could not possibly allow himself to have, any sort of emotion beyond the extremes of constant watchfulness, of constant caution, beyond a silent, aloof, moment-by-moment hoarding of the immense fact of freedom. He crouched here in his boat on the free and glistening water, raging, and told himself savagely he was a fool.

But there it was—that unaccustomed anger—boiling in him still. It was a tide that surged in him so violently that its violence frightened him, as if it were an aberration strong enough to lead him back all the way, prison shoes on his feet, prison clothes on his body, prison air in his lungs, prison thoughts in his head. What business had he with it, an effete emotion from an existence lost to him by his own guilt? They weren't anything but birds. He forced his hands to rebait his hook. It was only weakness and sentimentality in him to flare up so at the idea of killing birds. What were they but nit-witted handfuls of feathers? It was the custom of these people of the coast to live off the country, and it was upon the good will of them—their tolerance, their silent acceptance of him—that all his continuing safety depended. He choked back the last of his anger with the thick, remembered smell of prison. It was gone, he told himself.

What he should really have felt, he was perfectly aware, was gratitude that he had become one of those to whom the word from Two-Gun was passed so casually. Nobody would hear it who was not considered right to hear it, moving up and down the intricate, monotonous, lazy, glittering coast. It was being passed laconically, along with other news, from fish boat to fish boat, from fish boat to palmetto shack, among all that labyrinth of watercourses threading the interminable mangrove, brown canals rippling among saw grass, level sea meadows misted with the sun. It was passed back again along that milky-green southern sea that is half Atlantic and half Gulf, under the diamond-burning sky, as vast as Eternity and as remote as Judgment. It was being murmured among the crews of the occasional white-and-gilt cruising house boats, behind the backs of tourists intent on tarpon or sailfish, who could not be expected to be interested in birds. A plume buyer in Havana might hear it, and presently a discreet shop or two in Paris or Berlin. It was being spoken freely where brown-faced fishermen sat on their heels and narrowed their sea-colored eyes against the sun, on fish wharves at Key West or Fort Myers, or among the corrugated-iron shacks of the Ten Thousand Islands. There was, in a way, no particular secret made of it, and yet somehow no one heard it who might have been expected to pass it along a little too freely nearer Miami, where the solitary game warden of three vast Everglades counties might have pricked up his ears. The more he thought of it, the more John Pinder was profoundly thankful that he had been included among the hearers. It was a complete reaffirmation of his security.

It made him almost believe that he was one of them. There was little difference from them in his appearance, he knew, rowing back to his small gray fish boat, in dirty khaki pants and sneakers and faded shirt and wide palmetto hat. His face was hardly less sun-burned, sun-cracked, sun-blistered than theirs, his calloused hands only a shadow less clever at line and fish grains and scaling knife and landing net. If his face were heavier, his eyebrows heavier and blacker than most of the concise, straight-eyed faces about him a little later, selling his catch at the mackerel boat from the Key West market, they did not indicate any great sense of difference. He never spoke very much, knowing that by his accent he was plainly not of these waters. But he always listened.

There was much easy talk on the mackerel boat, where the solitary fishermen congregated for supplies and conversation after unloading a catch. A great feller for picking up any extra dollar he could see, was Two-Gun. It was a sight the way he'd work for it, month in, month out, as if a few hundred dollars wasn't enough for anybody to sit in the sun with. One of the Bethel boys—the squint-eyed one— was telling it, paying it out in slow, easy sentences:

"How Two-Gun come to see these yere long whites was, he was huntin' for otter up beyond Snake Bight, and not findin' much. Along toward sundown he see nigh about a thousand long whites risin' and fallin' to no'th'ard, and he sez to his son Fred, 'Fred,' he sez, 'them long whites is fixin' to nest up at Cocos, by damn if they ain't.'

They was a few plumes a'ready glistenin' in the sun. They was settlin' to roost right smart near there, but Two-Gun knew, anyway, they wasn't sleepin' yet where they was goin' to nest. So he's left Fred up there and he's give out the word that he's watchin' them. The rookery won't be ripe for a couple or three weeks yet."

"They hasn't been so many long whites seen together in a good few years," old man Luke Thompson said, spitting over the rail. He could remember when you could make all the money you wanted for a whole year, just off two-three rookeries.

The man John Pinder, filling his water bottles, listened and said nothing. He had heard enough drawling talk of the good old days to know that a rookery was not considered ripe to shoot until the nestlings were out of the eggs, and the birds, with the beautiful nuptial plumes that caused all the trouble, had sacrificed their natural shyness and tendency to scatter at the first shot to the care for their young. You could shoot right among them then and they'd only rise a little and come right back anxiously to their own nests. The Bethel boy with the squint said he might go up to Cocos with Two-Gun if Two-Gun would let him. There was more gossip then—some small talk about young Bill Robertson's getting drunk and beating up his father with a hammer, an argument about the price of sponges and a little mild speculation about the house boat that had just gone up Shark River. There were some big bugs on it from Washington—senators or somebody. Old Luke Thompson complained the country was getting ruined with all these outsiders. John Pinder stowed away an extra tin of smoking tobacco and shook his head easily at a man he had never seen before, who asked him if he was any kin to the Pinders up at Islamorada. Two or three men nodded as he nodded, shoving off. Nobody paid any attention to him, more than that, as his boat chuffed away, his mackerel money jingling in his pocket as he steered with a knee at his tiller.

They were, in a way, all his people now. They had taken him in. They would even stand by him with their silence if it were necessary. The Bethel boy's mother cooked grits for him sometimes at their shack on Northwest Cape. Charlie Sands, who owned the mackerel boat, had been buying his fish for two years now. He'd often bring him some special canned goods from Key West, or the New York newspapers. He was happy, he assured himself; he would be richly fortunate to live here and die here, in this strange sea country, under the free great winds. His throat thickened a little, knowing what it meant to him. That was exactly how senseless his rage had been. The way of these people must be his way. He could not afford, he should not be able even to experience, any emotion foreign to them. After all, he had been here only three years. If pursuit ever caught up with him and these people chose to give him up, there were ten years of prison still ahead of him. What was a handful of birds, alive or dead, against that grim fact?

Yet now, in the middle of the afternoon, when the mackerel were still running well, he was heading for Shark River and for birds. His emotion had disturbed him to such an extent that he allowed himself now suddenly the trip that he always took—a sort of pilgrimage—at this time of the year. Now that the nesting season was so near, the Shark River rookeries might be filling up with all sorts of birds—the little heron and the great blue heron and the white heron and the Louisiana heron, the ibis and the water turkey and any number of others. It had been, since the first time he had happened on them, a sort of secret festival of his own, just to go and fill his eyes with the sight of wings; his eyes that had never quite lost the memory of white-washed masonry walls and bars before distant dirty glass. Perhaps he'd even see some egrets, but he turned his mind from the thought of those, frowning. He must not think especially of egrets, or of that rare thousand Two-Gun George had seen, their nuptial plumes glistening in the sun, rising and falling in the silent country near Cocos. Not for anything in the world would he acknowledge to himself even that in his first rage at the idea that these last of the long whites were to be exterminated it had flashed over him that it was up to him to go up to Miami and pass the word to the game warden. It would have been an absolute betrayal of confidence. He would be here still, wouldn't he, and the sea and the sun and the quiet-spoken people whom he liked, who asked no questions, if every last egret in the world were obliterated from the memory of man? Well, then.

Up the Shark River he chugged absently by the house boat lying at Tarpon Bend, showing only a slow arm in acknowledgment of a raised hand from a lower deck. Big bugs from Washington were nothing to him unless they filled the upper reaches of the river with a clamor of outboard motors and exclamations. His small gray boat churned at the clear water stained brownish with mangrove roots between the narrowing and widening walls of mangrove, its surface all a-leap with fish.

Kingfishers clucked and darted across river before his absent eyes. A few redwinged blackbirds ker-lonk-a-lee'd from the low bushes. A phoebe or two caught his eye casually, and the little myrtle warblers, scurrying along the lower branches. But these were not the birds he had come to see. He hardly turned his head toward the coot and teal, in increasing numbers up every little wandering tributary, that, as the sound of his boat passed, scuttered up from the water like an alleyful of tricycles. His mind lingered a little on the house boat he had passed, for all his real unconcern. Once, a lifetime ago, he had been a guest on a house boat like that. What an extraordinary way of life that had been, he thought, looking down at his scarred and dirty hands.

He remembered, as if he had read about them, his emotions of that time. It had not seemed like the high tide of his ambition then. It had felt only like the first wave of his success. He was to have gone on from there, making money, marrying a beautiful wife, owning house boats like that, railroads, cars, becoming a figure in a world not then quite attained, now as distant as a dream. He had been young. That was a strange, unreal thing too. How had it happened that he had made that one unbelievable, irremediable gesture? How could it possibly have happened that one easy mistake could have changed everything? Was he really a criminal through and through, predestined to theft, or had it been only one of those curious and wandering impulses which must come to all men, but which surely are not always followed so promptly with an avalanche of disaster? He felt only a sort of chronic nausea that he could have been so stupid.

He could see his own mind then, as objective as if it had been the mind of someone else, his thoughts as strange to him now as the motions of his hand, transferring hundred-dollar bills from the cash drawer to his hand bag. What an extraordinary thing to have done! He had thought he would pay it back to the bank within the month. To think of letting oneself be tricked by that ancient illusion. There were hundreds of men still in prison who had been as blind, as weak, as stupid.

Still, in prison—He took a sharp breath and stared about him suddenly at the low mangrove tops, dull green against the piercingly lovely blue, at the clear quiet water, the brown water, that was his roadway now. All that other life, his own curious acts, were dimmed for him by the sour reality of prison. But how was it possible that he was not there now? That was the unescapable reality. And yet he had escaped. He was not poring over a ragged atlas in the prison library, where a few hours a week he pasted torn pages and gave out love stories to trusties. He was not staring and staring at faint marks on a page that indicated vaguely this remote and unknown coast. He was here, breathing the perfect softness of the air, burned with its sun, as if by some blinding trick of chance he had been let off with a blessing. If he had planned his life with half, with the smallest fraction of the intensity with which he had thought of escape, with the wit and courage and passion with which he had seized the merest hint of chance for a get-away, he would be now—he would be now——.

He could imagine nothing that he would be now, except himself—this self that had taken the name John Pinder. The way he had come was so plain behind him that he had given up long since thinking what he might have been. He was humbly grateful for this. The fears in the night, the watchfulness, the isolation were not much of a price to pay for what he had here. He wondered sometimes if he would not have to pay more, to pay adequately, for this beatitude.

Ah! There, high up, far over the distant tree tops, where the river receded straightly before him, there were the first small white-flashing specks that were birds. The sun lay westering behind him, so that his shadow reached forward on his gray deckhouse and he stared with the curious catch of breath that the first view of those rising birds always brought him. His face, raised to them, his reaching look, was drained of everything but a kind of clear happiness. There were the birds.

As if the sight of those first white flecks had been the signal, from the right came suddenly, high overhead, a great, widening fan of white birds and of blue birds, a great pouring sheet of herons, the rustling of whose wings high over his upturned face was the rustling of a great sheet of silk. They had risen, they had lifted, they had passed overhead, bright and unbelievable in the sun, and it was as if his heart had been squeezed suddenly with delight. He breathed again deeply as they disappeared, settling far to the left. After them, as his boat proceeded forward at low speed, guided by his unconscious knee at the tiller, streamed the brilliant squadrons of the air.

They lifted, far away, from unseen tree tops, with the restlessness of before sundown; they sprang upward from close at hand, bright explosions of thousands upon thousands of wings. They crossed and recrossed above the pathway of the river, soaring drifts of birds, bursts and festoons and mile-long fluttering ribbons of birds; birds in blowing streamers, in ordered ranks, in far-spaced floods. Their whiteness as they turned and flashed against the blue, against the sunlight, was the whiteness of white petals, of new snow, of white foam bursting from a riven sapphire sea. The blue of the herons' long bodies was the blue of steel and of the horizon. The blue flashed and became white. The white turned, in one wheeling turn of thousands of identical wings, and became blue, became dark, became shadow feathered against the sky. And in the sky still the only clouds were distant wings. Far off and continually there were wings, the swift and airy deliberation of uncounted wings, in a fine world of air, inviolate and unstained.

There were a few egrets among them. The watcher from the boat noted them with a twinge of uneasiness over the clear delight of his heart. They flew singly and level and immaculately white, a little aloof from the others, the great beak straight, the feet tucked together straightly behind, only the dazzling white wing spread oaring into the air.

He tried to forget them, naming over the names of the others with the recurrent pleasure of recognition—names he had learned painfully, here and there, from men who had known. He told over the list of herons—the little blue herons, and the white herons in their thousands, the green heron, and Ward's heron, and the black-crowned night heron, and the graceful thing they called the lady of the waters. He greeted the stately, fine craft of the ibises—the white ibis and the black-and-white wood ibis, trailing their long legs, and the water turkey, and with each recognition his delight was a rare thing in him.

Presently, beyond the amazement of the wings, the sky was stained violet and an enormous pale moon whose shadows brimmed with soft violet rose and hung in it, and the last of the white birds sprayed against it, moving overhead.

The birds were almost all settled now, so he turned his boat back

104

reluctantly. He could see the nearer flocks against the darkness of the trees, a close-set whiteness. To the west the sky burned its immense crucible of raw bronze and vermilion. The very air was stained a fine rose gilt. The boat moved downstream and the night flowed a softer and darker river behind it, and the moon moved higher, reddening in the dark. When the silent man had gone for half an hour, with no thought in his head but a lightened and happy musing, he turned and saw the river ebony behind him and the long, polished grooves of his wake brimming with the silver of the moon. The stars were there suddenly, swarming where the birds had been.

The brightly lighted house boat was garish and uncomfortable to him in the breathing, airy dark. He looked at it slowly, with eyes that gathered their memories back. He was going farther down the river to tie up to a bank he knew, build a fire, eat and sleep. This house boat, and the people on it, were nothing to him.

Two figures of men at the upper rail, dark in the darkness, moved as if they looked at him, and within the cabin a woman's voice sang crooningly a song he had known. His hand, even as he stared gravely, jerked at the tiller. With no conscious thought except that this was the one thing in the world he must not do, he was running alongside, flinging a rope to be caught on the lower deck. He was over the rail, running on desperate, silent feet up the stairs to the deck above. His glance, as he stood there, met instantly those of the two men watching him. They were smoking cigars and made no motion, except that alert turning of their eyes.

"Look," he was saying to them, in a harsh, forced murmur-- "look. Doesn't anybody on board here care anything about birds?"

The shorter of the two men squared about his square shoulders. "I do," he said, with something of the other's abruptness. "What's wrong?"

John Pinder hesitated then. He must not do this. He could still keep his teeth locked. He could go back now, quickly, and not say anything at all.

"Egrets," he said, and stood peering at them, panting a little, as if he had run a long way. "There's a thousand egrets coming in up at Cocos. They're being watched. They're going to be shot out."

"How do you know?" There was a sting in the shorter man's voice. He moved slightly forward, and in the light from a stateroom window the man Pinder saw a flare of black eyes in a shut and silent face.

"I know." John Pinder was not panting now. The thing was done. One way or another, his face was set irrevocably on this course. "I was talking to the men who are going up there—to Cocos. The rookery won't be ripe for another three or four weeks. There won't be any long whites left in Florida, more than a few handfuls. And nobody cares."

John Pinder stopped and stared suddenly at the shorter man, because in his face he saw a black flood moving. The tight mouth shut tighter and the nostrils bent. It was rage in that face opposite him—curious, unexpected rage, as his own had been. The short man shook the rail with a heavy fist, turning to the other, who had not spoken.

"For twenty-eight years I've struggled to save those birds," he burst out with difficulty. "For twenty-eight years I've raged up and down this country trying to make the people save for themselves one of the rarest things they've got. I've fought to put the legislation through that put a stop to wearing egret feathers. I've kept wardens on this coast and in the Everglades. I've raised money and I've spent money to keep these birds from being butchered. And after twenty-eight years it's still going on. I tell you, the people don't care. They don't want anything left that is as beautiful as these egrets. All they want is shooting and killing and a handful of money that'll be spent on foolishness the day after tomorrow. I tell you, it makes my blood boil so—It's enough to make me want to quit everything right now; it's enough to make me sick and sore with regret that I ever lifted a finger."

He was silent abruptly, and John Pinder and the other man, watching him, were silent. The black current alongside whitened with the moon. One of the Negroes in the crew below laughed richly. The stocky man turned and walked down the deck. When he came back his face was still dark with anger, but his voice was quiet.

"Look here," he said. "How'd you know I was here?"

John Pinder spoke slowly. "I didn't. I don't know who you are yet. But I was so angry that I hoped there'd be somebody here who could do something. I don't know what."

"What's your name?"

"John Pinder."

"You're not from around here. You talk different."

"I—no, sir."

"What are these egrets to you?"

"Nothing. What should they be? Only it seems to me a shame to let them be killed. Even if there wasn't any law, I'd hate to hear they were killed."

In the lighted cabin the woman's voice began singing again, to a piano. It was a rich, low, lovely voice. John Pinder kept his eyes on the stocky man's face. Such men as these had once been his friends. Their clipped Northern accents were grateful to him. A light sigh shook him, waiting. What was the use of thinking about that now?

The stocky man looked up at him. "I don't know who you are," he said slowly. "I guess I can find out. But it doesn't matter. Do you think, if I gave you the authority, as I can do—made you an accredited Audubon Society warden—that you could keep those long whites at Cocos from being shot out? There'd be salary and equipment. You'd need somebody to help you. You know what you'd be up against. Will you do it?"

The song went on softly, it seemed to John Pinder, a long time. He could not seem to speak.

"We're leaving here in the morning," the man went on, "or I'd go up there with you. But I'll try to be back in a month. I want those birds protected. They've got to be."

John Pinder said slowly, "I'll do what I can."

There were two things he had to do first, he told himself, eating grits and fish next morning, by his little fire. The first was to go and talk to Two-Gun Johnson. It was the only square thing to do. Then he had to see about getting someone to run supplies for him up to Cocos—perhaps old Luke Thompson. There was no one else that he could think of whom he could depend on. His heavy, unshaven jaw set itself grimly, turning over his engine and shaping his course down the river. There was no use at all now in worrying. His hand was set to this act.

He passed, on his way to the Gulf, the house boat from Tarpon Bend. Men, the stocky man among them, were leaning over the after rail, and they waved at him as he came up and by. He looked at them slowly and at length, lifting a deliberate arm. He had joined himself with them definitely, as if in some hidden way he had never quite left them, criminal and outcast though he knew himself to be. He passed them and did not turn his head. There was never any use in turning back one's glance.

After an hour or two he picked up sight of Two-Gun George Johnson's boat in the morning shine of the broad gulf. The mackerel were running well this morning. Two-Gun looked over at him calmly under the frayed edge of his wide palmetto hat. Two-Gun's grin was always slow and steady. John Pinder stopped his engine a little to windward and let his boat drift nearer.

"Hey, Two-Gun!" he hailed. "Want to talk to you!"

Two-Gun stood up in his cockpit and waved him nearer. He was a big man, burned yellow brown, calm, with calm eyes and huge hairy fists resting on hips narrow under the pillowlike diaphragm that swelled over his belt.

"What say?" said Two-Gun.

John Pinder waited while the boat drifted nearer. Two-Gun's youngest boy glanced up at him incuriously, bent over a net. The boats joggled on the dance of the water, and the radiance of the immense sky, dusted over with a thin white haze, seemed to hold them suspended in a flood of absolutely pure light.

"I thought I'd tell you," John Pinder said. "I'm going up to Cocos to take care of that rookery of long whites. I got the regular job to do that from the head guy of the Audubon Society."

Two-Gun's glance was calm upon him. "Mighty obliged for the information," he remarked slowly. "I was watchin' that rookery up there myself. My boy Fred's up there now."

John Pinder's glance was fixed in his. "I heard that," he said. "It's too bad too. But it seems they want to keep that rookery from being shot out. And wood ibises. I understand they don't want any more of that wood ibis up there to be killed and salted for the Key West market. I just thought I'd get you to pass the word along."

"I'll pass it along," Two-Gun said after a pause. "Well, I take it right kindly of you. Funny how news gets around. Somebody must of gone up and told somebody on that house boat some things."

"Yeah," John Pinder said steadily. "Well, I'll be getting up to Cocos in a day or two. Thought I'd just tell you."

"I take it right kindly of you," Two-Gun said again. "You might tell my boy Fred he could come back out."

John Pinder nodded and bent to his engine, but Two-Gun spoke again, very leisurely, seating himself on the gunwale and spitting into the water. "Thought I'd just ask," he said. John Pinder glanced up into Two-Gun's eyes, gone curiously small and heavy, like bullets. "You any kin to Ben Pinder at Islamorada?"

John Pinder shook his head, waiting, breathing very slowly.

"Or any of Bill Pinder's folks, down to Key West?"

He shook his head.

"Just thought I'd ask. I don't know's I been seein' you down the keys or around more'n two-three years."

"I been down three years this time," John Pinder said.

"They was two-three talkin' a while back how there was a man to Key West said he'd seen you some place in the States before."

"I reckon," John Pinder said. "I been all over."

"This feller said he seen your pitcher some place."

John Pinder shook his head. "That wasn't me, then. I never had my picture taken."

"Somebody else, likely. This feller was positive. I'll have to ask him again when I'm in Key West. You goin' up to Cocos, then?"

Two-Gun's youngest boy was listening. John Pinder looked at him and at Two-Gun's placid bulk, and grinned, a little stiffly.

"Yeah," he said. "I promised the man. I'll be up there."

He did not look back at Two-Gun as his boat picked up its steady, thudding progress. His heart expanded a little with excitement. He was glad. It was open battle between him and Two-Gun, he saw clearly enough. Two-Gun had warned him. Well, action was good, after three dreaming years.

He had a little trouble, as he knew he would, convincing old Luke Thompson to help him. He sat on the front steps of his frame and corrugated-iron shack on Northwest Cape and talked him into it. Even then old Luke would not have agreed if it had not been for his daughter, a lanky, straw-colored widow who welcomed the money. Old Luke was uneasy. He said over and over he didn't like to do anything George Johnson would take as unfriendly. A chance like those egrets didn't come any too often nowadays. But the money finally convinced him. It wasn't as if he would do anything actively himself, John

Pinder explained. It was just hiring him to run supplies. Old Luke champed his almost-toothless mouth under the pale frazzle of his mustache and flickered his pale eyes.

"He'll get your stuff for you from the railroad," Eva May finally said for him. "He's awful tim'rous, pappy is, befo' anythin' happens. And then it most usually doesn't."

John Pinder strode down the beach, crunching thousands of delicate white shells under each heel, not too satisfied, but lashed now by a vast impatience to be off. Nothing would be right for him, he was certain, but to be settled at Cocos, with Two-Gun's boy warned off, definitely doing his work.

He whistled a little, running along the palm-fringed coast, looking forward along the sea, flashing and brightening its strange green before him. He had never been to Cocos Lake before, but he knew exactly how it lay—at the end of a watercourse that was half narrow tidewater river and half abandoned canal. The entrance to the canal, after three hours of steady going, was marked by crumbling white spoil banks. And within, as he turned his boat's nose up it, away definitely from the gulf, the canal lay straight as a ruler before him, the canal banks narrow on each side. There was just water enough for his shallow-draft boat.

For an hour he ran as straight as an arrow, staring about him with real pleasure at a strange white country; white mud, from which curious whitened dead mangroves emerged, and dull white water, thickened with the calcareous silt. Presently the white country opened out to wide dry sea meadows, with distant islands of palmetto hammocks swimming in the mirage of the white sun.

But beyond that, as the canal turned and straightened again, the delight that the sight of wings always brought him stirred in him suddenly, for on each side of him were vast flats covered with a skin of water so clear that the clouds stood motionless in it, darkened only in great patches of small, feeding water birds. As the throbbing of the boat neared them they skittered and lifted into the air, heeling about in a thousand tiny flashes of white, never quite leaving the teeming fishing grounds, but crying plaintively at the interruption—the thin, reedy crying of thousands of sandpipers and their kind.

Beyond them, in another hour, the canal became only a wandering river among low bush mangroves, which at times seemed to shut him in completely, like a land-locked pond, but always somehow opened out a little to his prodding bow. And in other places there was the canal again, with tall saw grass like wheat on either side, rippling in the steady wind.

It was well after the middle of the afternoon, and he began to be a little concerned about getting to Cocos before dark. As it was, Two-Gun's boy Fred could not leave until next morning, even if he went willingly. And then there was a flash of white to his right. He snatched his gaze from the shallows to stare. They were the egrets.

The nearer ones, disturbed by his boat's noise, had risen nervously, and behind the first a magnificent flock burst whitely into the air from some hidden feeding ground. Their white lifting, their dazzling white suddenness against that sky sent through the watching man that old inexpressible shiver of delight. But this was deeper even than anything he had known. They were his egrets, his own and lonely responsibility. He watched them as long as he could, so glistening white, so remotely lovely, so strange against the sun. There was undoubtedly the glisten of nuptial plumes among them. They would nest very soon.

And there at last was Cocos, beyond a low last swamp of mangrove and wandering channel, a still, bright surface of broad water. He pushed out into it cautiously, after a slow passage of the entrance shallows. He stared about, not denying the thumping of his heart. There was the wide encircling rampart of mangroves; half-dead, white-bleached trees, shattered in some blow; their few leaves faintly green in all that sunny blue and white. Fish jumped and flopped before his slow bow. The lake's expanse was utterly silent except for the sudden, harsh voice of a fish crow overhead. Along one side of the lake he saw the dead trees covered with a rookery of motionless great white-and-black wood ibis, who did not stir from their stick nests and fuzzy-headed young for all his noisy passing.

On a point of land beyond, where the mangroves had been cut back for a footing, was a palmetto shelter and a boat. Two-Gun's boy, Fred, was sitting in the stern, watching him as motionlessly as the ibis. A rifle rested by his hand. John Pinder steered that way, grounding his boat's nose against the muddy bank after cutting off his engine and leisurely tying up to a projecting root. Then he looked over at young Fred Johnson and nodded gravely. Young Fred nodded, with still eyelids, hardly looking up from his work of plucking a freshly killed ibis.

John Pinder spoke first, looking over at the bulk, the sun-blistered face of Two-Gun's boy, through his newly lighted pipe smoke. All the Johnsons had this imperturbable calm.

"I'm John Pinder," he said. "I was just talking to your dad this morning. I was telling him I'm the new warden of this rookery, to look after the egrets. And he said to tell you to come on back."

Young Fred Johnson's thick hands went on among the ibis feathers, but it seemed to the other there was a quite perceptible jerk of the elbow toward the rifle beside it. A decided touch of red went working up the young cheek bones.

Then Fred said, "You're kinda wrong on that, Pinder. I'm the Audubon Society warden up here. I been watching this place more'n a week."

"I know," John Pinder said. "I've known a lot of men to give it out they were wardens, but that's only so's they can have the rookery to themselves. That's not the kind I am. The head man of the society put me on this just the other day. I got papers to prove it. He's paying me a salary. It's straight about your father. He said to tell you to come back."

John Pinder's rifle was where it had been—in his cabin. He looked over quite simply at young Fred, his hands empty on his knees. Reluctantly young Fred's eyes came up to him, wavered and fell back. There was the slightest possible twitch of uncertainty on his young mouth. John Pinder knew he had won out. The boy was not sure enough. He didn't dare risk picking up his rifle and ordering John Pinder off.

He left the next morning. They had eaten the roast ibis together and young Fred had slept on his platform under the palmetto shelter, solidly, all night long, leaving his rifle in his boat. John Pinder sat by the fire and watched. The mosquitoes were bad, but anyway, he could not sleep yet. There was too much to think about. He thought and young Fred snored. John Pinder turned his eyes toward him at intervals. He found himself liking the boy's solemn, burned, plump face. He liked, with a definite warmth of affection, all these silent people of the coast. He liked their hardiness and their independence. He admired their neat-handed sea manners, their amazing shut-mouthed capacity for endurance and for survival. He found it strange that out of that flash of civilized and almost forbidden anger he had come to set himself against them. The night was soft, domed with the myriad dust of stars. Across the lake came occasionally the stir and squawk of uneasy fledglings. He dozed, waiting for the thin dawn.

Young Fred left at first sunlight, not quite meeting John Pinder's eye. There was no overt act of hostility about the boy, except that infrequent sidewise glint, but after he had left, John Pinder stood and watched his progress across the lake with a curious sinking into depression. His mouth set in old and bitter lines, as if for the first time he was tasting what it was to be set apart among men. Young Fred Johnson never once looked back.

It was the very morning after that that the egrets came in. He had been sitting motionless in his dinghy, fishing in the middle of the lake, and suddenly saw the white lines of them dropping to the trees from their low flight. They came in by dozens and fifties at first, and there was a great restlessness and uneasiness among them, a shifting of slim white bodies and long wings, a clamor all along the southern side of the lake. By night there were hundreds of them already beginning to bring in sticks for their flat nests. The next morning more egrets were arriving, many in full nuptial plumage at its freshest and most dazzling. By nightfall of that day the whole lakeside was populated and the hasty twig nests being placed everywhere that the matted, half-dead branches would hold them, five feet from the calm water or higher among the leafless tops. It looked as if all those gaunt, bleached trees had suddenly burst into a strange heavy blossoming of white-feathered bodies, whiter in the sun than any whiteness the watcher could imagine.

He remained for hours in his boat, motionless, given over utterly to his absorption in them, in his renewed delight. He could think of nothing else. He ate casually and awoke often in the starlit nights to listen to the sleepy stir and scuffle of hundreds upon hundreds of nesting birds.

It was a week before the rookery was settled to the regular business of egg laying; several weeks, at least, before the first fuzzy-headed fledglings were cracking at their pale blue shells. In that time everything had dropped away from the man John Pinder but the strange, unhuman life of this still lake, soundless except for wind noises and water noises and the constant activity of the birds. As if the egrets had sensed its coming with the beginning of nesting, the last of the occasional cool winds ceased. The days were still and brilliant with warmth from the almost cloudless blue; days that moved slowly in a rich and enchanted stillness; halcyon days in which the little boat of the watcher hung or slipped slowly over the motionless bright water; in which the very heart in his breast was soothed and brooding, like the white beauty of the birds.

He had almost forgotten old Luke Thompson until that one's boat pushed its nose out of the tangle of bushes at the entrance and throbbed across the lake. Old Luke brought all the supplies John Pinder needed—a tent and plenty of water—but he was obviously reluctant to stay, glanced only nervously over at the phalanxes of the feeding birds. After he had been fed, he sat smoking, his eyes paler and more indefinite than ever.

Eventually he said, "Two-Gun George hain't exac'ly give up the idea of comin' up here, I been hearin'."

John Pinder only nodded. "I'm not surprised," he said.

Old Luke went on nervously, "Well—um-m—he was down to Key West a while back, and when he come back he give it out he'd found out things about you. He said there was a feller in Key West right glad to know whereabouts you was."

John Pinder nodded again, his face without expression. "I take it kindly of you," he said. "I'll be here. You'd better be getting back now, hadn't you? You won't more than make it by sundown."

Old Luke was infinitely glad to go. John Pinder paid him and watched him disappear. Any day now, he told himself, he could expect——

He busied himself with his camp, with fishing, with shooting the many water moccasins that began hunting among the bushes for unguarded birds' eggs and younglings fallen from the nest. The life of the rookery was noisier, more vital, more preoccupied than ever. Father and mother birds joined in hunting food for the fledglings that now bobbed and squawked from every nest. The raucous fish crows were active, gobbling up stray minnows and little birds. There was a sense of life renewing itself, perpetuating itself, with purpose and with passion. And behind the slow beat of wings, the going and coming of the birds, the days were serene.

The event which had so slowly been gathering its menace for

the watcher shattered suddenly the hushed and golden time. He heard at last, late one morning, the slow, purposeful beat of a boat coming along the watercourses toward the lake, and with a gathering of excitement he rowed the dinghy over to a sort of outpost he had made among the farther mangrove bushes, from which he could command the last quarter of a mile of the approach. He had his water bottle with him, his rifle, extra ammunition and some food. Whatever was to happen, he meant never to be quite cut off from his supplies.

He crouched among the mangrove, behind a shelter of dead branches he had piled, watching. Presently the gray of a boat's nose emerged slowly into sight down that narrow alley of brown water. The figure of a man bulked large in it, and as the course curved he could see two heads in the dinghy towed behind. That was because Two-Gun's boat was a little deep draft for these shallows. John Pinder stood up as they came, leaning on his rifle, watching them. They could see him easily from that distance. His heart thickened a little.

When the boat stopped full in the channel, he could see Two-Gun's calm face plainly. It was at a distance that spoke curiously of hostility, near enough for talking or for shooting, not anywhere close enough for casual friendliness. Two-Gun stood, looking at him. He waited.

A figure rose beside Two-Gun, behind the bulk of the deck house. It was a man, red bearded, whom John Pinder had never seen before. He stood and stared at the warden's figure. From the dinghy there was the grate of a gun butt against a gunwale on the still air.

The red-bearded man, thinner than Two-Gun, a little stoop-shouldered, spoke with a harsh directness. "James D. Evans, he said— and the name rang queerly over the flat clear water— "I have a warrant for your arrest. You escaped on March 15, 1927, from Boundbrook Penitentiary, Pennsylvania. You might as well give up peaceable. We've got you covered."

No look of triumph changed the calm gaze of Two-Gun, who had come for his egrets. The man who had called himself John Pinder, whose name had once been James D. Evans, saw no change in him, breathing as slowly as he could himself, stiffening his face against the shock of his surprise. Always, deep in his mind, this was the thing that he had been expecting. It had been inevitable. And yet, as he steadied himself there, he felt as if actual tissue was being torn in him, so painful was the destruction of his living hope, of his persistent illusion of safety.

"Well," the red-bearded man said, "no funny business now, Evans. Just throw that rifle of yours in the water and we'll come up and get you."

There were tones in that harsh, contemptuous voice to which his feet had moved obediently, left, right; left, right, in clumsy prison shoes; tones before which his eyes had dropped. Old habits of obedience ran curiously now along his tensed muscles. But that was when he had been only a number. His name was John Pinder, he told himself desperately. He was the warden of this rookery. The two rifles in the dinghy, resting on the shoulders of the Johnson boys, contradicted that grimly, firmly, under the sun.

"My name's John Pinder," he cried out loudly, against them. "I'm warden of this rookery here, and you can keep out—you and your warrants. I shan't let the Johnsons shoot up my birds."

He dropped suddenly, as he spoke, below the barricade of branches, and only a fraction less suddenly a rifle cracked from the dinghy and a bullet zinged where his hat had been. Through a chink in the bushes he saw that Two-Gun and the red beard—who was evidently an old chum of his, endowed with the brief authority of a deputy sheriff—had dropped below the line of the deck house, as if anticipating an immediate return of fire.

He was thinking hard and desperately. He could not shoot to kill, or even to wound seriously. Things were bad enough for him as it was. All he could hope for was to discourage them, keep them off for a while longer, frighten them away if possible. Frantically he clung to that hope. It was all the hope he had.

His first shot carefully nicked the gunwale of the dinghy, where a shoulder showed, and a bit of rifle. He heard a confusion there and knew that the boys were scrambling into the motorboat. He fired again, just over an incautiously protruding hat, and then flashed into movement, crawling back carefully along a little pathway in the brush toward his own boat. There he huddled and waited, a half second only, until—blam-m-m—three rifles clapped like one and the bullets hissed and thumped in the cover he had just left. It was, as he had feared, no sort of shelter.

Now he leaped up, shooting twice into the wood of the boat,

up and down again and on all fours back to his first place. An angry voice shouted and bullets scored the boughs where he had been. If he could keep them guessing for a while——

The position held for an hour or two, through noon and the first imperceptible arching downward of the sun. It grew hot, and in the windless air behind the bushes the mosquitoes sang and nipped. The water in his water bottle turned lukewarm. On the boat the noon quiet lay heavy, with occasionally someone whistling, and now and then a shot as the changed sun sought out the shadows in the bushes. For the most part, the man who had called himself John Pinder sat hunched up, his rifle over his knees, the perspiration wetting all his face, his back and shoulders. He racked his brains with a dogged and weary tenacity. How would anything hold these men except the direct fire of his own rifle, aimed to kill? And he could not do that.

He moved once, incautiously, where the bushes were thin, and a rifle slammed instantly. The bullet flicked through the twigs and gouged his leg lightly. He tied up the wound, with a sober face. It was quite evident that they were placing their shots to exact intent. The fact of his resisting arrest made everything quite simple for them.

But suppose even now he ceased to resist arrest? His mind shivered away from that, from the whole implication of that idea. There must be something else that he could do, even now, to fulfill his trust here. He moved slowly from time to time, in the breathless shadow of the bushes, seeking another peek hole and occasionally shooting harmless shots that glanced from gunwale or from deck house, simply to tell them that he was still watchful. His wounded leg throbbed a little dully, although the bleeding had stopped.

Presently, as if the noon siestas were over and action definitely on foot, there were sounds from that fish boat, now almost grounded in the shoals. He listened intently. There were grating sounds, dragging sounds, occasional thumps, which at first he could not understand. After those stopped, a hand turned the motor once or twice and it was clear to him. They had transferred ballast and dunnage to the dinghy, to make up for the weight of the boys. The keel must have swung clear of mud, for immediately the roar of the engine startled all the sunny quiet and three pelicans sailing low overhead. He peered among the bushes. The boat was crawling deliberately forward, at low speed, but irresistibly gaining ground among the saw grass, the twists of darker water among the sun-warmed shallows. He shot twice, hurriedly. Instantly a fusillade of shooting hailed him from rifles along the gunwale. They raked the bushes time and time again, so that he crouched and dodged and started. He could hear the swishing of the bushes along the boat's side. Then it had passed, it had emerged, with the rifles still keeping his head down, into the full depth and bosom of the lake.

He heard the speed pick up with a kind of horror of despair. They were in it now. He had been useless to keep them out. If he could only have shot to kill. Yet by this time they must have known that he dared not. The very sound of the engine was bold and invading.

It was not until dark that he ventured to crawl into his boat. There he ate food hastily, staring out across the water to the camp he had left. Two-Gun's boat was tied up there and a little cooking fire pricked the soft dark ruddily from among the ashes of his own breakfast. He could even hear voices raised jovially from time to time. The men must have been drinking.

But they were none the less alert. His oars had dipped ever so cautiously in the deep shadow beyond the firelight, but a rifle had cracked toward him and a bullet splashed. He shot then himself, defiantly, and nicked one of the men on the shoulder. He heard the voices as the man shouted angrily. He was glad that he had drawn blood. Perhaps, if he had not been so careful at first, it would have gone better. A hot surge of anger rose in him; he had a desire to row nearer and kill them all deliberately, one after the other, as they moved incautiously in the firelight. It was what any sensible man would have done, he told himself. But he sat motionless, nevertheless, staring over his folded arms, listening vaguely to the sounds of men and, from the distance, the sleepy sounds of the as yet undisturbed egrets. The starlight grew so bright he could see the sleeping and waking white bodies clearly among the darker masses of the trees. A sort of spasm twisted all his face, for the thought had squarely come to him, "Suppose I do give myself up? Suppose I strike a bargain with you and give myself up?"

His oars dipped from time to time, moving like an uneasy spirit among the remoter darknesses of the lake. The fire dwindled to a spark in the distance. He moved or stopped, rowing or brooding for long moments of time, staring over at it. The trouble was, he saw clearly, he had been wrong from the beginning. It was like that old Hindu idea of an act loosed into the world, spreading like the ripples of a stone in a pond. No matter what he did, he could not escape that. And he was beginning to see, like a great spread of weariness, that his second mistake had been to try to evade. He had got off too easy. He had not seen the thing through. That was the fact that dragged at him now, with this curious lethargy. There was one thing he could still do, and he could not bring himself to it. His boat drifted idly and he dozed in the cool breath of dawn.

It was the sustained crackle of gunfire which jerked him abruptly awake in the broad dazzle of the first sunlight. He started and stared, his eyes unbelieving. Four guns were being shot off unhurried. No bullets came in his direction. It was then the fact burst in upon his thinking with the deadliness of a bullet. They were doing exactly what they had come for. They were shooting up the egrets.

Digging his oars into the water with that first bite of realization, his boat shot out across the water direct for them. Only, once or twice he turned to stare. Even at that distance he could see clearly the confusion at the rookery. White bodies of birds were falling every moment, catching in the lower branches or floating in white flecks on the water. Those as yet unharmed were rising a little way from their guard by their nestlings, screaming stupidly, distracted, but dropping again as if they had been tied by the leg—tied by the inevitability of parenthood to the end which was upon them. Long-legged lovely adults, with the shine of their perilous plumage behind them, were rising and screaming and falling. The deadly gunfire carefully poured across them, as searching as the sun. Already large areas of the brush were empty of grown birds. The fuzzy-headed young in the occasional untouched nests squawked hungrily.

The man who called himself John Pinder forgot everything but rage. He stood up in his boat and shoved it savagely forward with one oar, and as he drew nearer he shouted as he went, hoarsely, as a man does who cannot bring himself to believe that what is happening is actually permitted by life, by whatever justice there is, to go on. No heads were turned to him. He saw plainly the men who were shooting from the gray boat, anchored opposite the rookery. One man sat in the stern with his shoulder tied up. The red-headed deputy sheriff shot occasionally, looking around him, talking and smoking a pipe.

John Pinder stopped shouting, stooped and picked up his rifle. As he stood there, he could easily kill all of them; but his gun cracked only once—a shot that went whistling over their heads.

Two heads turned, three. The fire ceased. And in that hush, while they stared at him levelly and without any emotion, he let his rifle drop and cried loudly, "Don't shoot any more and I promise to give myself up! Don't kill any more birds! I am Evans! I will give up!"

The faces stared at him. He breathed hard, his hands twitching on his rifle. He cried again, "Will you promise to stop shooting?" and half lifted his gun.

The shot that smoked from the rifle of the deputy sheriff in the boat was a smacking blow in his side. He spun on his heel with the vicious force of it and only saved himself from going overboard by a twist of his whole body that in the same moment revealed to him a fiery agony of pain. He sat, and his boat righted itself and drifted a little, before the bright wind, nearer to the bushes.

In the gray boat there were low voices and a laugh. And then, one by one, the orderly guns picked up again their raking destruction of the rookery. Two-Gun George Johnson, who had given it out that the Cocos Lake egrets were his, was leisurely resuming business.

The man John Pinder opened his eyes on the coolness of over-hanging branches. His ears were filled with the quiet swish of leaves alongside. The boat was motionless. In the distance the guns were a remote trouble in his mind. It was surprising to him how much blood could be in the bottom of his boat. His hands, where he tried vaguely to stuff his shirt into the place in his side, came away brilliant with it. He ought to do something about it. It was bad to lose as much blood as that.

He found himself, however, staring vaguely at an egret that had been shot and had fallen here, half in the water, half clutching a branch. The bird had somehow righted itself and stood motionless, with a long red stain on the pure white features of its breast. It stood and gazed incuriously with its black, shiny glance at the man in the boat. It was as if all its unguessable bird thoughts were turned inward with a passionate direction upon an event shaping itself in its most hidden fibers, an event portentous and unshared, beyond any memory now of flock or fledglings or of its kind. There was no fear in the bright bird eyes, only a mute undeviating attention to the slackening and precious ebb of its heart.

The man John Pinder stared at the bird and something cried out with a frenzy of protest within him; the unnumbered cells of his own body cried out that this was death. He did not want to fail, with those methodical guns still in his ears. He would not die, he told himself fiercely. But his eyes lost their glare. He let the guns slip from his thoughts. His face quieted with that same passionate and mute intensity, that inward absorption, that the bird's eyes held, still clinging to its branch.

When the worst had happened, when mistake and failure and pain had fulfilled themselves to their uttermost, against the last desperate protest of the mind, what was this left, this something delicious, this respite, approaching cobwebbily along the avenues of himself? Was it this that had said to the outcase, "Struggle"? Was it this that had murmured to the defeated, "Victory"? He did not know. He rested, smiling a little, his eyes upon the dead bird in the water. How much were they paying for plumes? That, too, was unimportant. He had seen them for a little while, glistening in the sun.

6
BY VIOLENCE

*I*N ALL THAT WIDTH of lonely water there was no other
boat. Young Martin Gomez stared with black eyes somber in his
smooth, amber-tanned face. He had not expected there would really
be another boat. And yet, with a heart blistered with his first encoun-
ter with grief he had as good as stolen this boat that had been his
father's and come seeking—come seeking—he did not know what.
Something incredible to solve the churning uncertainty of the problem he faced. Yet there was nothing more here for him than there
had ever been—empty, bright water, enormous blue-lighted sky: to
the west the blank sickle of the horizon cutting the Gulf of Mexico;
eastward, toward all Florida, only the low barrier of the silent and unending mangroves. Yet somberly as he stared, he was expectant.

The stinging spray from the too-narrow bow had plastered his
cotton shirt to his bony, small ribs, over the raw sore of his heart.
The roar of the most powerful engines in the Ten Thousand Islands,
that had been his father's pride, was almost silent in his ears. His soggy
sneakers were braced where his father's feet had braced themselves.
His bony, small hands clutched knowingly the long rope rudder lines,
just as they had a good three hours back in Chokoloskee, taking the
boat out like an arrow under the very noses of his Uncle Harvey and
his Uncle LeRoy. They had bellowed and shaken their big fists at him
from the upper gallery of Smallwood's store. But Martin had not
cared.

For the first time in the last dreadful two weeks which had
changed his universe for him, he had escaped. There must be some-

thing he could find to do, some money he could make somehow, that would show them they had to listen to him, that would keep them from sending the children away to the mainland. His father would want him to keep the children together and safe on Chokoloskee Island, where they belonged.

And yet, with all the numb helplessness of childhood that was hardly past for him, he was hopeless of doing anything against his uncles and his loud-voiced Aunt Lulu Belle Hannaford, from Fort Pierce, and his keen-tongued little Grandmother Gomez. They had dinned in his ears ever since his father's funeral, "Martin, you mustn't act like a little boy any longer. You must try to realize——" But they wouldn't let him speak for his father or for the children, or take the boat out, or do anything. Their talk poured over his head, a deafening flood. They were tall people and big people, and they talked loud and acted violently always. Once he had been charmed by that in them, thinking his Uncle Harvey and his Uncle LeRoy great men. He had admired them, assaulting the silences of his slighter father. That was the way real men should act, the way he would act, he had assured himself often. Now they loomed incredibly formidable. He did not know what he could do against them, if this sudden tearing flight away from all that did not produce some miracle to reenforce him.

Because the children must not be parceled out among distant kin on the mainland. His father distrusted the mainland. The little girls were too young. The baby was lame in one foot. Through the uncertainty in him, and the burning grief, Martin knew that one thing. The children must be kept home. He must keep them. And he could. If only something—something incredible——

It happened so unbelievably that for all his quick-silver sharpness of glance he did not at once credit it. It was too marvelous. He had been running closer to the monotonous line of mangroves, in his vague way south. Yet with a glance trained to see everything, in that gulf-coast world where a landmark may be only a darker shadow of water, a subtle alteration in a curve of shore, a mangrove branch reaching up taller than the rest, he knew where he was and where all the sand bars were. The mouth of Lostman's River should open widely here. The leafy shore shifted its look a little. The mangrove barrier opened to the one view where the eye can plunge straight eastward up the center reach of one of those west-coast rivers which is no more than a haphazard valley of water in a continent of mangrove, a river which moves and brims and breathes at one with the milky immemorial sea. In that one moment before the branches below the river mouth obliterated the straight glance, Martin looked and saw.

The welter of half-adult emotions in him gave way before a yelp of pure joy. He whirled the bow eastward up the stream, for there was a boat up there, in trouble. It had been only a spot and a flash, but he had seen that—a boat in trouble—and his the only other one for lonely, watery miles north or south. There was a job ahead. They might be rich people. He yelped again, happily, and jiggled with boyish delight in his squashing wet sneakers.

His face was intent for the channel and the gliding walls of green, from which the din of his engines came back to him pleasantly enlarged. The muscles around his mouth stretched into an uncontrollable grin.

He figured that the boat he had glimpsed might be two miles up the river. Somebody had been waving something, small in the glittering distance. They must have been watching for the one-minute glimpse of him, crossing the open patch at the river's mouth. He began expecting it around every curve. Several times he saw it clearly, before the curves of the channel screened it with leaves. And then, with almost startling unexpectedness, he came upon the boat, just when he was deciding that he was following the wrong channel entirely. It lay long and shiny and superb, with its shining mahogany bow thrust, as if at full speed, straight into the mangroves and the mud. Its stern was hopelessly under water. It was like no regular west-coast boat that he had ever seen; more like one of those glossy, elaborate, speed toys millionaire yachts sometimes carried. It made his father's boat, that was so much admired in Chokoloskee, look stubby and commonplace in comparison. He could only stare at it in awe, having switched off his engines. From a captain of his own destiny he reverted suddenly to being an embarrassed small boy.

Two men were staring at him from the boat's forward cockpit. His glance, encountering the curious fixity of theirs, could not get away. Their faces, turned abruptly to his, were set and still. There was actually a kind of hostility in them, as if they were holding him off, warning him not to come any nearer, by the coldness of their double glare. Immediately, however, Martin felt he must be wrong. Their faces changed, wrinkling around the eyes with the same grin. Of course they were glad to see him. They had waved for help, and they certainly needed it. Assurance lifted again warmly in him, and he pulled his boat, with its following dinghy, nearer by the overhanging branches.

The men said in the same breath,. "Hi, there," and "Well, well." Martin grinned back at them shyly.

He had touched the other boat's gunwale before he saw with a start that a third man was sitting stiffly on a tilted seat of the half-submerged after cockpit. At first Martin thought he was hurt, he looked so queer. The other two wore caps, but his head was bare and his dark hair was blown every way over his pasty yellow face. His eyes, under thick lids, hardly seemed to look at anything. He sat there just about as he must have been sitting before the boat struck. He sat as people sit waiting for something, as Martin's Grandmother Gomez often sat on the porch of her house, looking out over the sea and thinking how old she was and how many things she'd seen. That was a silly idea, of course, because this man wasn't so old as that. But his eyes looked old.

The tall man who had straightened up first—the one with the long face and the long lead-blue eyes—was saying, "Well, well, well, we're in luck, after all. Imagine finding a boat so quick in this God-forsaken wilderness. You'll take us to the nearest town, won't you, kid?"

Martin nodded, inarticulate with pride and pleasure. They'd pay the full guide rates without question, he assured himself shrewdly, warping his boat alongside. The second man—the heavier one—pulled off his cap and lit a thick chocolate-colored cigar with a mother-of-pearl lighter. He was shorter than the other, but he had the same sort of figure—narrow-hipped. His eyes were some kind of yellow-brown, set a little oddly in his face, as if the bony cavity of one had been pulled down a little, making his whole face askew. His mouth was full of gold teeth as he bit at his cigar. He did not look like the taller man, and yet he did. They were alike in the way both men had looked at him at first— cold and fixed—and the close way their lips were set, and something in the way they turned their eyes without turning their heads. Neither of them would stand it to have a boy get fresh, or anybody, he guessed. He gave a last shove, fended with a pole, and held the boats together.

"Good work, kid," the tall man said. "You're the buddy for us, all right, all right. Well, Julius, all we got to do now is move."

It was the shorter one who was Mr. Julius. Probably his first name. Martin stood holding the boats together, looking up at them. Mr. Julius was rolling his cigar around in his mouth. There was something he was mad at. The tall one began passing bags to Martin. There were two light suitcases, bright tan with gleaming locks. There were binoculars and a vacuum bottle and a lunch basket. There were two coats. Mr. Julius put on his over a flannel shirt, which seemed unnecessary. That was all. There were no fishing rods. They didn't seem to have any of the things that people would have on a trip on the west coast.

Mr. Julius said abruptly, "I don't like it, Sam." The tall man's name was Sam, then. "I don't like it this way at all. I told you you were a fool not to pay more attention to the chart of this coast."

"Aw, tie it," Mr. Sam said. "The chart didn't show the river was so narrow up here, that's all. The boat's not hurt bad. Anyway, you can't pull anything now. The kid's here."

Mr. Julius said, "It ain't neat, that's why. It ain't accordin' to the way things oughta be done. I never did a job like this and I don't like it. Whadda we goin' to do? You got idears. You tell me."

"Why, we're just goin' for a nice little boat ride with this smart young fellah and pretty soon everything'll be all nice and tidy. He'll take care of us, won't you, kid? Di'n't I tell you we'd get a break?"

He winked elaborately down into Martin's wide eyes. His voice was loud and a little raucous, and to Martin he did not seem to need to be as cheery as he was. He stepped into the boat, steadying himself on Martin's bony young shoulder. Martin endured the almost painful wiriness of his fingers. As the boy looked up again he saw the end of a funny sort of gesture Mr. Julius made, with his hand in his coat pocket. As soon as Martin's eyes were full on him the gesture ceased abruptly.

Martin found himself looking almost at a level into the eyes of that third man he had only half noticed, sitting with blank face, stiffly, as if he had been waiting a long time. Martin stared into his eyes and the man's eyes faintly came alive and stared into Martin's. A constriction moved the boy's stomach muscles. The man was fix-edly, horribly afraid.

It was fear such as Martin's fourteen years had never seen in a human face. And he had seen several kinds of fear, too, as any boy would in that world island of his, surrounded and penetrated by the untouched, raw wilderness and the naked, uncontrollable sea. He had seen people's faces in hurricanes when the raving water almost closed over the island. He had seen the face of a man just bitten by a water moccasin. He had seen his father's face the time his baby sister had had convulsions. But this was different. There was no suddenness in it, as if it had lasted so long now it had driven out the human look from the man's face. It was like the fear of animals. There was paralysis in it, like the time the rattler had got into his rabbit pen. He hated it, violently, with an increasing sick wrench at his stomach. Nobody, especially a grown man, had any right to be as scared as that. It did queer things to Martin's idea of the grown-up world. He held on to the boat and hated the pasty-faced man as he felt hatred for a barra-cuda in the fish box that he had hit and hit again, that would not die.

"You, Williams, come on. Get a move on, can't you? Get into the boat," the man named Sam spoke harshly from behind Martin. There was a heavy emphasis on the word "Williams." Martin, looking up at Mr. Julius' face, was pretty certain that a wink had gone with it. It was the way you spoke when you signaled something to Packy Davis. It made Martin think the man's name might not be Williams. That's the way it sounded.

Mr. Williams got up then and climbed across Martin's shoulder into the boat. The boat rocked under his stumble and Martin had to steady it before Mr. Julius could get in. He trimmed the boat neatly enough. The three sat in the swiveled fishing chairs aft and on the gunwale and Martin had to move around them, stepping lively and neatly between his engines, the rudder lines and the side of the boat. He was absorbed instantly in the job of getting the stern clear and the boat off down the channel. He was self-conscious about it, too, because it had dawned on him suddenly that for the first time in his life he was responsible for a boatload of people. He was in power and he was alone. It stiffened his spine and aged his look a little, glancing warily over the side and handling his steering lines cleverly.

The infinite, impenetrable mangrove ranks slid backward slowly on each side. The morning sky overhead was turning to the hot platinum of nearly noon, and here among the tree walls the air was a hot stream against the skin. But the water deepened later, so that he could give his engines more gas. When the cloaking roar rose thickly in the ears, he was certain that Mr. Julius and Mr. Sam spoke in quick undertones, hardly moving their lips. But he would not have tried to listen, in any case. Speak when you are spoken to and never hear anything that is not meant for you is fundamental good manners among fish guides and their children, all up and down that keen-eyed, shut-mouthed coast.

But he could not keep his heart from pounding with excitement. How they would stare at him along the wharf at Everglades, bringing up a lot of tourists in his father's boat. He glanced back pridefully at his tourists. And instantly that dreadful other sensation was there, waiting for him. It was that man Williams' thin hunched shoulders. It made Martin remember the look in his face. It wasn't any way for a man to sit, or for a man to make a boy feel. He turned his head hastily back to his steering. He hated any man that would let himself look as—as helpless as that. But the deeper, the agonizing thing about it was that Martin saw suddenly in them a likeness to his own father's bent shoulders, sitting on the porch steps in the evening, after the little girls and the baby had been put to bed, staring out over the little roofs of Chokoloskee and the evening colors of the Gulf beyond.

Martin had come out sometimes, and had known that his father was thinking about his mother, and he'd gone over to sit by him and fling a warm young arm across his father's shoulders. His mother had run off to the mainland with Enoch Jones just a little while after the baby had been born. Secretly, sometimes, he'd cried for his mother, but mostly he'd felt mad and hurt that his father should be so hurt. He wished his father had shouted and sworn the way his uncles did, instead of being so silent. Men ought to shout and swear and carry on, and not stand for things they didn't like. That was the way, Martin had promised himself, he was going to be. He wished his father's shoulders wouldn't be so bowed. Sometimes it made him feel queer, as if he were ashamed of his father, and that was a dreadful feeling. It made him feel all choked and tied up and uncertain. He liked to sit that way in the evening, with his arm over his father's shoulder. His father had liked it, without saying anything, and it had made little Martin feel big and protective.

But this strange man had no business looking like that. His shoulders had no right to look like Martin's father's. Martin gritted his teeth to keep back the tears from his eyes. His father was dead. The funeral was only two weeks ago. His father's chest had been crushed in an automobile accident up at Everglades, and they'd brought him home just barely living. Martin had cried great, racking, terrible sobs into the limp, outstretched palm of his father's hand.

Martin slipped down from the gunwale and stood with his back to the rest of the boat, kicking one toe hard against the deck so that the pain would help him control his childishly contorted face. He bumped his toe harder. He wouldn't care now if everybody died. Everybody could die right off. He wished they would. All these people could die and he wouldn't care. He'd be glad of it. He wouldn't ever be sorry at anything any more. He wouldn't be sorry about those thin, hunched shoulders behind him. He wouldn't think of them.

Before him suddenly, and before that thin questing bow, opened out the broad last reaches of the river. The wide wind of the Gulf beyond glittered on the water and all Martin's misery lifted. He snapped on his engines full speed again. He wanted to yelp and dance and snap his fingers and holler. There was nothing for him in the world but the beauty and power of the boat he controlled and the exultation of his own speed. There wasn't a boat like this in the world. It was the finest thing in the world. The sun glittered on the river water and the white spray hissed backward.

An adult face mouthed words near his ear. He slowed his engines to hear better.

"What do you think you're doing—drowning us?" Mr. Sam was shouting. "This is the wettest boat I ever saw in my life. We're soaked."

Martin looked at him coldly. The man was wet. His shirt was wet and his hair was wet, and wet dripped down his nose. But anybody is a sissy to worry about a little salt water.

"I thought you wanted to get to Everglades in a hurry," Martin said with dignity.

"That's all right, but we don't want to get drowned doing it. What's this town you're taking us to?"

"Everglades, if you want to get a train some place. It's about a three-hour run, fast. Slow, it'll take longer."

"Well"—the man was staring ahead with narrow eyes. He certainly didn't act like a man who'd just lost a valuable boat. Or like a tourist, either. "Well," he said again, "my friend and I have been talking. There isn't much hurry. And now we're here, we think we'd like to cruise around, get a little fishing or something. What about it?"

They weren't interested in fishing. It hadn't been that they had talked about with those curious, still lips. Martin spat over the side with what he hoped was grown-up nonchalance. "I got fish rods," he said. "They'll be a dollar a day extra."

Mr. Sam made a careless gesture of the hand that Martin's eye glinted to see. Three dollars more for him, telling the tale in Chokoloskee. Mr. Sam went on, "We'd like to see more of the country."

He wasn't interested in the country. Not that Martin cared. The open Gulf was before them, the wideness and the cleanness of a world of quiet, greenish water under a bright wind along a bright, great sky. Here and there the brightness of sea and sky was broken by nearer islands, mounds, rounded hillocks, of the constant mangrove, like dark-green haystacks in a meadow. Martin edged the speed up until the engines droned.

On an impulse of pure mischief he turned south instead of north. Any minute he would be spoken to about that. Even the dumbest tourist in the world would know that the town of Everglades lay northward, on the mainland, up beyond Chokoloskee Island, and that southward was only mangrove and more mangrove, to the sand beaches of Northwest Cape and the empty dazzle of the Caribbean. They said nothing. Well, it would cost them a full day's time.

"You wanta still-fish for tarpon," he said, "or do you wanta troll?"

"Tarpon?" Mr. sam said, around his cigar. "What's that—fish?"

Martin glanced at him with a crow of laughter in his throat, which he choked back violently under the icy narrowing of the man's eyes. Could there be in the world anyone who did not know about tarpon, the leap, the fighting silver in the sun?

Mr. Sam called back lazily, "Hey, Julius, there's a thing they call tarpon. It's fish. You fish for it. How's for going back all broke out with tarpon?"

"Good here," Mr. Julius said. "Can you eat it?"

"Can you eat it, kid, he says?"

"No, sir," Martin said. Funny how cold the man's eyes made him. "They're the hardest thing to catch there is. People have their pictures taken with them."

"That's an idear. Ain't that an idear, Julius? Have your picture in the paper with a tarpon."

"That's an idear," Mr. Julius said. The third man sat exactly as he had been sitting. Martin averted his eyes hastily.

"If you wanta still-fish for tarpon," he said to Mr. Sam, "we'll have to run up in the lee of that island there and anchor. Or you could try trolling from this boat as we go along slow."

"Yeh? Well, don't stop the boat any. We want to go around, see? Looking at the country. Just looking at the country. That's right, ain't it, Jule?"

"Yeah, that's right. We might wanta buy it, see? We might wanta buy it ourselves and go into the fish racket."

"Sure," said Mr. Sam. "That's right. Maybe we'll put a race track on it."

"For weasels," Mr. Julius said. Martin had turned around and he was facing forward, and Martin saw him say it. His mouth went one-sided. "A race track for weasels. Hey, Williams, that's a good one. Let 'em run round and round." Neither man laughed. Mr. Julius said suddenly, "Isn't there any land in this God-forsaken country? Isn't there anything but water and these damn trees on stilts? What do you do when you want to get out and walk around?"

"You wanta get out and walk around?"

"Anybody would, wouldn't they?" Mr. Sam said testily. "I'd give ten dollars right now for a sidewalk."

"There's an island out thataway," Martin said, pointing. "It's got a hard sand beach. People go swimming there sometimes. You wanta go there and walk around?"

The glitter of Mr. Sam's eyes fixed on the distant mound of

green. It lay out from the nearer islands, defined against the broad glare of horizon. From there the man turned deliberately and swept his gaze along the intricate lonely mangrove coast to the east.

"See any other boat around here?" he asked.

"No, sir," Martin said. "There were some boats came out for tarpon, and Charlie Davis was going to Rabbit Island, but no boat come as far south as this."

"Where's the nearest boat likely to be?"

"'Bout six miles north there's the clam dredge from Marco."

"Hear that, Jule? What about that island?"

"Oke," said Mr. Julius.

"Good here," said Mr. Sam. "Speed her up, can't you? Let's look at the island."

Martin pushed the gas lever. Mr. Julius came amidships. He and Mr. Sam sat side by side on the gunwale. They hunched their shoulders under the drum of the spray. The third man sat just as he had been sitting in the chair aft. The spray plastered his hair to his skull. Martin gave only one glance aft, hastily.

He pulled around in a wide arc into the glassy water in the lee of Sand Island. There was a cove behind the rampart of mangrove and sea grape and coco plum. Martin snapped off his engines and the boat slid nearer in the immediate silence. He ran forward with a long pole, thrust it into the bottom and held it as the boat leaned against it and stopped. He ran aft with another pole and planted it and lashed it at the stern. The dinghy bumped softly against the boat's motionless side.

It was very quiet. The diminished wind ruffled the tree tops beyond. The thin piping of four yellow-legged sandpipers came clearly. Eastward the sand ran in a long spit, across which the shallows jostled. Vines and grasses ridged the beach. Hundreds of fiddler crabs waved, jerkily, their white claws from a swampy level that reached toward the middle of the island. A fish crow cawed suddenly from the highest trees.

Martin had stayed aft, pulling up the dinghy. He looked forward. Mr. Sam and Mr. Julius had just said something to each other, soundlessly. Martin had just caught the crawl of their lips. Martin looked squarely down at the man in the chair.

The man's face slowly turned to his, as if at last aware of some change in the condition of the boat. His eyes met Martin's with that blank, dull stare. Then, quite slowly and carefully, his lips smiled. Martin's throat twisted with pain. He glanced forward. Their backs were turned. "Look," Martin said, his small, grimy paw hard on the man's shoulder. "What is it? Want me to do something?"

The living flicker came back deep in the eyes. The head shook very slightly.

Mr. Sam had turned his head and was watching them. All he said was, "C'mere, kid. How do we get ashore?"

It took Martin a moment or so to answer. Suddenly the stark terror that lay in that man's look had leaped to his own heart. Terror blanched his world. Terror lay in the quiet light pouring over all their figures and over the boat on the quiet water. Terror ran in the light salt wind, sounded in the ripples along the sand, in the crying of the sandpipers. The tiny, jerking signals of the fiddler crabs meant terror.

He swallowed violently before he could say, "I'll take you in the dinghy, sir."

He stood in it alongside, holding it there, looking up at them mutely. Mr. Sam dropped into the other swivel chair. Mr. Julius stood up with his hands in his coat pockets, glancing sidewise, down at the back of the third man. "Well, Williams," he said, "let's be going."

He had to poke the shoulder with a thick forefinger before there was a response. Then the man got up stiffly, with the bumping awkwardness of someone newly blind, and got into the dinghy. Mr. Julius got in. They both sat down. Martin stared over their heads, poling the small boat across the few feet of shallow water to the beach.

Mr. Julius and the man got out. Mr. Julius stood easily, looking around him with that heavy face in which one eye-socket was pulled lower than the other. He looked quite pleasant. "Just run around, kid," he said, with a gesture toward the sand spit. "Just run around and play if you wanta. I and my friend'll take a little stroll around this other side the island."

Martin stood stock-still, glancing after them doubtfully. The dreadful uncertainty of childhood was on him. The men were walking quickly, arm in arm, away from the beach, up the open space among low bushes that led to the higher growth beyond. Martin felt small and lost in a perilous, adult world. Tears were stinging the back of his eyelids in fear of things he could not understand.

He began moving slowly down the sand spit. When he looked back, Mr. Sam was looking sleepy and comfortable in the boat, his cap over his eyes. The other two had disappeared. And suddenly the island was for Martin just as it always had been, when his father had let him swim here. The white clear light was free of all terror. He ran along the sand, stamping and jumping and throwing handfuls of small stones at the sandpipers, in the vague exaltation of release. He yipped joyfully at the fiddler crabs scuttling for their lives before him.

He saw an empty whisky bottle up the other side of the beach, that was hidden from the boat by the ridge of vines and grasses. He set that up and threw stones at it until it smashed.

A single shot slammed out from among the western trees. He looked up and saw a faint whiff of smoke vanish on the wind. Then his heart began hammering. He remembered everything. One pistol shot. The stick dropped from his opening hand. There was no other shot or outcry or any other sound, except the slush of the little waves at his feet and the sandpipers' crying.

The next moment he was running forward desperately, across the mud flat and through the brush beyond. The pull-and-haul-back vines ripped their hooks through his sneakers, across his bare legs, caught at his short trousers. He shoved his way with elbows and knees among the tangle of bush mangrove and coco plum. His breath came sobbing from the crushing weight of remembered pity and terror.

He had to go more slowly crossing a half swamp, half inlet among black mangroves. His feet slipped on the twisted roots and he pulled and climbed forward. Then the mangroves gave way to the dry white shell ground and he ran through a patch of yellow weed. Coarse grass grew in the white, coarse ground. It was the center of the island, sheltered on all sides from view of the water by the low bushes, which gave off hot green smells under the hot sun. The silence stopped him abruptly. His bright eyes darted here and there alertly, while he listened like a small, wary animal.

He saw the feet on the ground after he had taken another step forward. They were a pair of tan-and-white sport shoes sticking out from the ends of light trousers. The soiled toes were up, a little turned out from the heels. One of the heels had dug more deeply into the shell soil than the other. They were motionless. Martin stood staring at them with a face that was old, that puckered suddenly like a child's.

Behind a screen of little bushes the third man lay. There was no sound.

The man was dead. That was what the shot had been. That was what it was all about. The wind moved softly in the leaves of the little bushes. The shadow of a great, circling bird passed across the white soil. Martin could see, by the torn vines and weeds, the way both men had come and Mr. Julius had walked back. He looked uncertainly at those heavy feet. And then, with a jerking mouth, he turned and ran back the way he had come—the difficult way—through the mangroves, through the snarl of vines and the thorns and the close-woven bush jungle.

On the white sand, hidden by the grassy ridge from the other side of the beach, he stopped and took deep, deliberate breaths, against the choke and hammer of his heart. Then he went on again plodding down the sand, with his jaws and fists clenched. As he walked, lines deepened between the corners of his nostrils and his mouth. His eyes, that had been the bright, darting eyes of a boy, were level-lidded and intent. It was as if something had gone out of him forever—the volatility of childhood, the facile, unrelated thinking. In him now, behind the shut look of his face, burned a new thing, bitter and irrevocable. In this death by violence, with one wrench of a curious agony, his childhood was put away.

With every plodding step now a man's passion deepened in him, a man's slow rage, a man's need for justice. The affair was nothing to him. The third man was nothing. Yet he was everything. Those two in the boat, waiting for him now, were suddenly his own enemies, as if the dead man left lonely in the clearing were his own dead. The boy, without question or comprehension, was suddenly the aroused anger of his world.

They must not know that he knew, or had been aware of the shot, or had seen anything. They would be watching him with those intent and heavy glances. They would have not the slightest scruple against killing him also if they could get along without him or thought it wise. He must seem to them just as he had seemed—a careless and ignorant boy. He cast wildly about in his mind to remember how he had acted, what he had been like. He could not recall it. In his thoughts were only the sound of that shot and the look of those two feet still against the earth.

He crossed the sand spit and moved along the beach toward the dinghy. Mr. Sam had not changed his position in the larger boat. Martin stooped and snatched a handful of stones and flung them heavily at the water. Mr. Julius was sitting on the bow of the dinghy, smoking and watching him.

Mr. Julius said, "My friend decided to stay on the island until tomorrow. He decided he liked it here. He's a nut about camping out. He shot a bird, and he'll shoot some more and camp out. You can come and get him or tell someone to."

Martin said nothing, but bent to shove the dinghy out. Maybe he ought to act surprised or ask questions. But his tongue was cold in his mouth and his eyes avoided that right-hand pocket of Mr. Julius' coat.

"What did you say?" Mr. Julius asked abruptly.

Martin said, quite clearly, "Yes, sir."

The dinghy bumped the side of the boat. Mr. Julius climbed aboard. Mr. Sam did not raise his eyes from their sleepy stare over the water.

Mr. Julius said loudly, "He decided to stay ashore, like he said he wanted to. I told him he was a nut. He shot a bird. He's crazy about shooting birds."

Mr. Sam said, "He always was a nut," and tossed his cigar butt over the side. Both men seemed to be waiting for Martin to say something. But he did not say anything. He went forward and pulled up the pole. When he came aft to pull up the stern pole, their glances flicked across his face. They sat in the swivel chairs and faced him.

He had no idea at all of what he was going to do, or could do, in the long miles of water that stretched between this place and the town of Everglades. He pushed hard against the bottom with the pole, swinging the heavy boat out. They could shoot him any time they thought of it, and he could not stop them.

When the boat was well out in deep water he hesitated, looking at the men aft before he started his engine. Their waiting glances met his with a little shock. And he hated them. He leaned against the starboard gunwale with his hand on the switch, facing them squarely, with his eyes gone quite expressionless and his young mouth set. His hatred, a man's full-bodied hate, poured toward them. They might have been a pair of cotton-mouthed moccasins that had invaded his shipshape cockpit.

He said, "You want to go away and leave Mr. Williams? Has he got any water? Can he get along?"

There was a perceptible relaxing in the leadlike quality of their gaze. Mr. Sam said, "He had a flask and plenty of matches. He'll be all right."

Mr. Julius said, "Get going, kid. I'm getting hungry."

The boat came around in a wide, flying arc and the flung spray hissed and whitened. Martin's gaze fixed itself northward. Roar and stinging salt water were all about him, speed under his heels. He looked ahead steadily at the long hours of wide, quiet water, colored and polished with afternoon.

There was open Gulf all the way. Yet something had to happen between here and Everglades. They would never give him a chance to get to the police there. They could as easily shoot him and drop him overboard as they could run the boat.

The only chance he had—he narrowed his eyes against the spray and tried to squeeze the tremor out of his heart, so that he could think—the only chance he had was to keep them guessing. They had to feel they could not get along without him. But how could he do that? He looked long and searchingly at the blank barrier of the mangrove, a dull bar to the right, all that there was, between soft sky and quiet sea, of land.

After a little time they passed in roaring flight the clam dredge from Marco, on Bonefish Sound. Martin saw the cook leaning on the rail watching him. As if on the watch, Mr. Sam rose and came forward to him, to lean on the deck-house roof just the other side of the instrument board.

Martin said, to his lifted eyebrow, "Clam dredge."

"This town of Everglades, now," Mr. Sam said in a minute. "It's straight ahead north, is it? Is it the only place?"

"Only Chokoloskee."

"What's that?"

"An island. People live there. That's where I live."

"How far is it from there to this place Everglades?"

Martin replied briefly, "Four miles." He hardly heard his own words. He was lost suddenly in a wave of startlingly deep feeling at the sound of that name. He saw it more clearly than he ever had before, there hidden from him by all the distance of the water and by this thing in which he was involved. He felt the pangs of a tenderness like love for the low-roofed frame houses by the ragged shore and for his father's house, lifted above hurricane high water on the mounded middle of the island. He saw the place suddenly small and distant, lost in a world too big for him, too frightening and strange. He saw, in that blinding flash, every leaf, every roof top, every yellow cactus blossom along the sprouted gumbo-limbo fence posts clear edged in the light of his emotion. And he saw himself, as he had been that morning coming along the one grassy roadway across the island, an immature boy shying bits of rock at the nonpareils flitting like jewels among the weed clumps. He remembered, as if it had been a long time ago, his morning's grand ideas about coming home with money and power. Well, that might have to wait. There were more things about life than he had guessed.

He went on speaking as if he had not suddenly widened and deepened his thoughts in that flash. "It's due north. But it's not easy to get from here to there quickly, among the islands. Especially if you want to get to Everglades by traintime tonight. There's only one train a day. Or would you stay awhile in Everglades? There's a right nice hotel."

The man beside him stirred impatiently. "Don't miss that train, hear? . . . Hey! Look out——"

Martin had swung his bow sharp starboard. He had seen what he had been looking for in that distant line of land—three clumps of mangrove standing out above the others, five narrow mangrove islands to port, the leaves of the nearest stained white with pelican guano. From here on he knew every island and channel he passed. Last winter his father and he had come all along here shining for 'coons, their flash lights catching the bright eyes of the animals climbing at low tide for the oysters on the mangrove roots. He could turn and twist and bewilder them in the strange, intricate waterways for as long as he chose.

"It's all right," he said. "This is the short way. Only you have to know where you are. Anybody could get lost who doesn't."

The man beside him moved restlessly, staring at the mangrove leaves sliding by, seeming at every moment to shut them into a brown patch of water no longer than two boat lengths. Yet they always opened out ahead. The brown-and-white boil of the slow wake always trailed steadily along the mud and roots under the bushy branches.

"How does anybody live in this country without going crazy?" Mr. Sam said. "These infernal trees are getting my goat."

"You have to know the country, all right," Martin said.

Ahead, the channel widened into the clear color of a small lake. Mangrove made its banks, walled it in ahead, mangrove like the hundreds and hundreds of acres of other mangrove, with the dark band of high-water mark halfway up the roots.

Three white herons rose and flapped over them. A burst of dull-blue Louisiana herons followed after. The two men behind him did not raise their eyes. They sat and stared heavily at the nearest line of mangrove. Martin had seen women tourists, who did not like fishing or boats, sit and stare like that for hours, at the eternal sliding sameness, as if it did something to them. Well, it could do something to these two any time now, as far as he was concerned.

His engines loafed at half speed. The high light overhead was deepening and lifting into the fine blue of late afternoon. The oily green masses of the mangrove leaves were greener.

"We aren't getting anywhere at all," Mr. Sam said angrily, moving forward again. "Look here, you've got to get on faster than this."

Martin kept his eye on the curving, sinuous channel ahead. "Can't go any faster. Look at the sand bars."

Mr. Sam looked. He was gnawing his cigar ragged.

The water rushed endlessly by the boat's sure bow. On each side the living mangrove slid and rustled.

"Where'd you-all come from, anyway?" Martin asked. "You musta come down from Everglades yourself to get there. Or did you come up from Key West, to south'ard?"

"Yeh. We came from Key West. Cruisin'. Just cruisin' around. My friend wanted a place to camp."

That was some sort of lie. Maybe they came from Matecumbe, on the east coast. He couldn't figure it out. Not that it mattered as long as he had found they didn't know their way around here. Martin glanced sideways at Mr. Sam's hands, lighting another cigar. They shook a very little and the man stood tense, staring at the oncoming ranks of mangrove.

The water widened then into a broad bight. The open Gulf was just beyond a thin screen of mangroves, a straight course northward. But they did not know that. Martin snapped on his engines full speed and grinned into the instant sting of spray. The weight of his fear and anger and uncertainty had lifted considerably. They wouldn't kill him yet, anyway.

Out of pure boy deviltry he ran them around the same island twice, just to see how much they would notice. They noticed nothing, even though for a little while the boat ran in the dappled wash of its own making. The two only sat and stared dully.

They looked almost disheartened. Or so it seemed to the boy's eager desire. At least they were so quiet, seemed for the moment so little frightening, that his mind leaped to all sorts of heroic exploits by which he might dominate them. Suppose he could snatch that gun from Mr. Julius' pocket? Suppose he could attack them with the fish grains? Those would be deeds to impress his uncles. If his Uncle Harvey were along he'd have licked them both already, single-handed. Martin glowed a little, remembering some of Uncle Harvey's stories. Maybe he could act like Uncle Harvey yet. An unquenchable grin creased his brown cheek. The open water was narrowing again to a mere channelway. He glanced back, in a rush of self-satisfaction.

Mr. Julius' glance was there, waiting for his bright one. It was sickeningly as if the heavy-lidded gaze had been there all the time, waiting to catch him. Martin's eyes dulled under that lead-colored glare. He turned to his steering with a cringing chill running down his spine.

Mr. Julius got up heavily for the first time. Martin heard him coming forward clumsily, a man unused to boats. He stood like a cold shadow by Martin's shoulder. The channel turned and curved, deep buried in mangroves.

Mr. Julius' voice was a kind of explosion in the boy's ears. "You're not taking us the straight way," he said. "That was open Gulf back there. You're trying to put something over on us, you little rat. You ain't smart. Don't kid yourself. Take us back out now. That's the only thing you got to do."

Martin waited until his mouth was not quite so sticky. "I can't turn here," he said doggedly. "We'd get stuck and you'd never get out. I got to keep on this way. Honest. You can see. And it is the quick way."

"Aw, tie it up," the man said. His hand on Martin's shoulder tightened cruelly, shaking him until he was sick and dizzy. "Get on to some place we can turn, hear? And cut out the funny stuff. There ain't anything you can do. Get that."

Martin jerked his shoulder out of the burning grasp. His lips were white. He said, "Yes, sir." Mr. Julius stood behind him. The trouble was that it would be a long way now to anything like open water. This last long waterway was really a short cut, short as any. But how would he convince this—this murderer at his shoulder of that?

A dreadful sense of being lost and doomed moved over Martin's mind. Life was too strong for him. It was too harsh, too frightening. He could not imagine why he had thought he could do anything about it. He saw with a damning clearness that, far from being able to bring these two to justice, he would be incredibly lucky to get out of it alive. Even his Uncle Harvey could do nothing now. He remembered vaguely the boom and bluster of his Uncle Harvey's voice. It meant nothing.

There was only the cold clutch of his hands on the rough rudder lines, the automatic necessity of steering, of choosing the deepest water forward, keeping the rushing, knife-edged bow where it should march steadily. He was shivering a little in his wet cotton clothing and his head ached. The endless mangrove endlessly went past. There was nothing in the world that could help him now.

It was strange to him then that he found he was remembering, as if it had always lain deep in him to be remembered, the still look in his father's face. He remembered his slight, bowed shoulders. The feeling of his father's silences warmed him minutely. That man back there, dead on the island, had been like that. Even where you were paralyzed with fright, you could be still and hang on. Maybe all over the world there were men, grown-up men, who were frightened and still and enduring. Martin took a deep, slow breath, deeper than he had taken for a half hour, breathed again, more deeply. The glow warmed in him and his pulse steadied.

There was an immense soap-pink sunset burning unaccountably

overhead. The winding channel was dark and glossy, the mangroves were blackening. Mr. Julius put his hand heavily on Martin's sore shoulder. Martin kept his shoulder steady under it against the too-tight grip. It would be all over in a minute now, when they saw what was coming. He hoped he would not make a sound.

Because ahead, as he had been expecting, opened out the wide water of Chokoloskee Bay, stained with sunset and the night. The dark ranks of the mangroves fell away to the horizons. Ahead, glimmering in the shadows as the boat rushed forward and the sky darkened, was a little low light in a distant shadowy streak and, beyond, the vague roof clusters of Chokoloskee.

Martin looked at it steadily, carrying his heart like a full cup. The other man had come forward. They both stood looming over him and their thoughts were cold weights. Mr. Julius lifted his hand and put it into his coat pocket. Martin felt the movement against his side. He was still and cold, and his lips tightened in a kind of grin.

"What's that there, kid? Everglades? Is that the place we want?"

Martin waited as long as he dared, because he had thought of something. The boat drove forward, but his eyes leaped suddenly ahead of it eagerly, desperately, along the surface of the rose-shadowed water.

"No," he said clearly. "Everglades is four miles more. There's a channel—I'll show you the way—in a minute—as soon as I see—look," he said and pointed suddenly; "it's Chokoloskee."

And in that instant that they looked he ran the finest boat in the Ten Thousand Islands square into the cement barge that had sunk in the last fall blow. There were no markers. All Chokoloskee knew where it lay. He had remembered it and had found it.

The concussion that crashed in the bow and brought the long, lovely boat to one sickening, listing halt, hurled the two men staggering backward into the stern.

Before they could recover themselves, cursing, Martin had leaped from the gunwale and was swimming for long moments under water. He was so busy swimming and breathing he had not time to notice if they shot.

It was a long swim. Up on the gallery of Smallwood's store, under the hanging lantern, with the cavernous depths of the sudden night behind, Martin, dripping and panting and shivering a little, stood at the top of the stairs and saw his Uncle Harvey and Mr. Smallwood and Charlie Lopez and Packy Davis' father and another man. His uncle saw him and opened his mouth with a long roar. Martin walked nearer and stood under the light, dripping and panting and looking at him.

When the roar had subsided, Martin said, "The boat's out there piled up on the cement barge. There's two men in it that I saw kill a man down on Sand Island. You've got to get your guns and take them up to the sheriff at Everglades. I should think maybe there'd be a reward. It's going to be mine."

They stared at him with their mouths open. "They're out there now," he said. "Didn't you hear them shouting? You've got to hurry, or they'll take the dinghy. Their boat's up Lostman's, to be salvaged."

Martin returned gravely the look his Uncle Harvey laid on him. "Go on," he said quietly. "It's so." And in the men's eyes he saw dawning a curious look of belief and of respect, such as he had seen sometimes in their eyes when his father, at rare moments and in the same voice, had spoken.

7

BEES IN THE MANGO BLOOM

A LWAYS, IN THE SIX YEARS in which she had fought passionately to keep these acres of pineland soil which her father had left to her to keep, Penny had had the bees to work with in the hard moments. Now, in the hardest moment of all, she was achieving a portion of the serenity the bees demanded, looking for young queens in the hives under the mango trees. But it was not really any use. She was licked at last. A straggle of bees, drowsy in the cooling light, clung to her short, sun-gilt hair. Her small hands, colored, like her sober young face, a smooth, dull gold with years of Florida sun, moved with the suave, slow gestures of the born bee master. But they could not do anything to help the blankness of her despair.

The muted droning of the hives could not drown out the sound of the piano in the distance and mamma's pouring, golden, triumphant voice. Penny had put the hives here at the lot line years ago, because it was only here that mamma's music, or the uproar of mamma's beautiful voice quarreling with the beautiful voices of Maddanella and Francesca and Elphin and Sylvanus, Penny's beautiful, hero-sized, older brothers and sisters, could be tolerated. Now the family were not here, but mamma's well-preserved cello tones were like salt on the wounds of her failure. Which was failure also to her dead father, and to this beloved earth.

The last bank failure, last summer, had done it. Penny had been scraping along on bottom all fall, hoping her last hope for a warm winter and a good mango crop. But the winter was already setting in, wet and chill. If it kept up that way, there would be no mango bloom.

She would not be able to pay her overdue back taxes and her fertilizer bill. She would lose everything.

And then mamma, who had left her to manage her own affairs for herself, except for a few inopportune invasions, had arrived and had put her foot down.

"My precious baby!" mamma had boomed, exploding from the taxi in which she had bumbled all the thirty-five miles south of Miami, in a shower of untidy hand luggage, stained chiffon scarfs, wadded newspapers, an empty red-satin candy box and two brocaded dolls. "But—but, Penny, you have grown up. And you're lovely! I never dreamed—who would have? All those bones—and in this wilderness. But that's over now. Look, mamma will arrange everything for you."

She could not, of course, pay the back taxes. Mamma never had any money. She had only occasional brilliant concerts, many invitations, past-due bills and great expectations. This time she had more—a talkie contract. She would not help Penny save an inch of earth, but she was going to teach her to use rouge properly and crimson her finger tips and wear clothes instead of those terrible overalls. Add her, in short, to the galaxy of Candace Heston's family prodigies in Hollywood. Penny could be her secretary. Or mamma would get her married. Everything would be prodigious. They would leave in a week.

For Penny, it was even worse than failure. It was annihilation. Yet in all sorts of the best cities of the best continents, numbers of the best people spoke warmly of the wonderful Heston family. Candace Heston's stormy black eyes, the drama of her gestures, the fluted black-and-gray pompadour always a little askew over her majestic brow, her slightly dusty, black satin skirts flowing from her regal hips and dipping a little too much in back, her angry, affectionate ways with managers and audiences and newspapers, were as much part of her tradition as the splendor of her voice.

And the tribal strength of her fiery, brilliant family. They swarmed around her always, tumultuous and beautiful and heroically tall. Whether Elphin was a greater poet than painter; whether Maddanella, all dark fire and ivory, would go on being an actress; whether Sylvanus, with his Greek-marble profile and his eighteenth-century manner, would do greater things with the harp or with architecture; whether the blond-silvery Francesca should keep on with the piano or give up everything for bookbinding—these were only some of the great questions of family drama always coming to a boil about Candace Heston herself. The family was its own best audience, its own intellectual life, its own stimulus.

There were no more than four or five people, when Penny was little, who had ever said to her, "But your father is charming too." Aunt Amanda Heston implied that, buying the Florida place, "For some peace," as she remarked dryly, dying and leaving it to Penny's father. The others were mostly plainish, sensible females at Penny's occasional schools. They had seen Lennox Heston's good profile and the quiet, happy look he had, coming to take Penny to the zoo. They said, "You are like him." It irritated mamma awfully that one of her children had not any of her own great gifts.

In her own inconspicuous way Penny had enjoyed irritating mamma. She had yelled herself black, at the age of three, whenever mamma called her "Penelope" in full. At seven she yawned, fortissimo, in the middle of mamma's most important concert. At ten she had refused to go to any more concerts or to sit up later than nine at   mamma's   chamber-music-and-intellectual-conversation-with-celebrities evenings. Penny could not stand celebrities. She went right on being small, bony, brown, inconspicuous and calm.

So mamma had been glad to let her come south with her father, to the quiet brown house among the rich, flat, sky-wide acres. Even more than he, she loved it instantly with a deep, still passion. It was her country, the white-earthed ridge of pineland at the end of Florida, before the Everglades began, with the long, straight roads among the dark green of groves and the lines of the tomato prairies, rimmed around always by the twisted ranks of the Caribbean pines and, to eastward, the glistering green and sapphire of the sea. The height and intensity of that immense air glittering upward in hot noons, in the long, diamond-lighted summers, carried her funny little heart soaring upward among the utter snow of the clouds. The huge, star-powdery nights were hers, and the whity skies before rain, and the purple blackness of the shadows, and the green-glary moment after storm, and the enormous amazement of sunsets. She breathed under it deeply, with quiet, happy eyes.

The people of it were her people, in all the scattering towns south from Miami, by the railroad and the filling stations, people in the dim interior of packing houses and on the sun-bleached verandas of the little frame shacks, or in the remote schoolhouses or women's clubs, or in the trim houses of the great grapefruit and orange groves, or plunging back from town in battered cars full of white-headed children, or just walking, in worn shoes and overalls and palmetto hats, trudging the lonely distance between the horizons. They came from everywhere, with every sort of accent, but they looked alike, with brown faces and eyes shadowed now with five years of trouble, but mouths that smiled. They were all hers.

They were what was left, after the rich, easy years when the citrus fruit colored goldenly on the rich trees, when the early tomatoes in one good year brought a man a stack of money, and the avocados and the new, great, rosy mangos were just finding the Northern markets. They had come through the boom.

Those were the days, back in 1925, when people suddenly began to act with a kind of madness, as if Florida earth were semiprecious, more valuable than all the crops that could be raised on it. All around here, in the Redland district and at Homestead, where it had spread from Miami, the boom raged. People who lived in little shacks bought expensive automobiles and diamonds, had millions on paper overnight. In this back country people who had homesteaded or developed the early groves—the tomato men and the pepper growers—left their groves and their crops untouched, sold out at unbelievable figures, to join the crowds boiling up in Miami, looking in at store windows with their first-payment checks singeing their pockets.

Everyone down here had been touched by it, it seemed to Penny, except her father. He would not even discuss real estate. The tales of big profits bored him. If he had lived he would have seen the men gradually drift back to their neglected groves, their first-payment checks gone, the other paper in their hands quite worthless. He would have seen the back country fill again with the calmer hopes of working people, with the courage and patience of those who plant trees. But he had died and Penny's grief aged her overnight, and mamma and the family, in a whirlwind of mourning chiffons and arm bands, descended.

Mamma decided to sell everything instantly. There was a tremendous scene with Elphin and Maddanella, who wanted to take the money for a new school of the dance, and mamma, who meant them all to go to Italy and make Penny a great violinist. Penny remembered retreating to Stephen Wilson's first chicken yard, just about here, to get away from the hullabaloo of that. The beautiful, shouting family voices had taken on suddenly a roary, angry booming that had frightened her at first. Until she started running a small blue-overalled streak, yelling for Stephen.

It was Stephen's bees swarming, just as she had warned him they would. The dark funnel of the rising swarm was already booming and swaying in the direction of the mangos in the windbreak. Penny yelled and beat on a pan. After an hour or so, when the swarm hung, a living bag of bees, glistening with slowing wings, Stephen held Penny up so that she could saw off the limb and lift the swarm into a new hive. She did it deftly, as her father had taught her. Stephen's serious, plain brown face looked worried behind his bee veil.

Afterward, sitting on the sunny grass, he grinned at her and said, "You like 'em, don't you, kid? Because, look; you can have that swarm. And the other six hives. I'm sick of getting stung. You've been doing most of the work of them anyway."

Penny's face shone up at him. "You're the most wonderful man," she said. "I love you, Stephen."

The slow red had gone up his face. He had been twenty-two then, and his mother was still alive, in their little frame house on Stephen's five acres. Goodness, she thought now, how could she go away and leave Stephen? How would she tell him she was quitting? He was all mixed up with everything.

Even then he had been. Because, suddenly, when he gave her the bees, she had remembered to tell him that mamma was selling the place and taking her away to be a great violinist, or something. His easy burst of laughter had shocked her.

"Your mamma's seein' things, kid," he'd said. "She can't do that. She hasn't thought about the will yet. But your dad made me an executor. And the place is yours in trust. They can't sell it. So you'll have just to take charge of the bees besides."

It had been one whale of a grand scene, when Penny had walked into the long brown living room and told them that. But she had had one whale of a good time. After the hullabaloo was over she found herself alone, with nice Mrs. Jenkins from Perrine for a housekeeper, mistress of her own acres. The education her father had planned for her—Latin and mathematics with old Mr. Laban down the road, reading lists and a lot of botany—went on. What she really needed to know she must find out for herself, driving the old car around to talk with grove men, with the men at the Government experiment station, with people at packing houses, with visiting horticulturists. She needed to know hundreds of things more than her father had taught her—about fertilizer and scale and spraying and anthracnose on mangos and the future of avocados and the possibilities of raising small fruit in the tropics. Everything, then, had been a stimulus and a challenge to her.

And here she was, she told herself bitterly, not to be twenty-one until next June, and she had come to the end of things. Out of the curious weakness of her despair she turned and looked back across as much of her ten acres as she could see. The rest—leaf and blade and bush and tree, rich earth she had made from the original coarse soil—she knew by heart.

There was the long, low, brown house. She and Mrs. Jenkins had saved that, the night of the big hurricane. It hit suddenly, with the long, yelling shriek of the wind out of the pitchy dark and went on through yelling, inky hours after, when the house was battered under force of the one-hundred-and-fifty-mile wind and the rain cascaded blackly through every cranny. They managed to save the house by piling up all the furniture against the doors and windows. But in the morning the world outside had been a gray devastation. There were only a few stripped trunks of trees standing out of the twisted ruin.

Well, they had got over that. Everybody who was not injured turned to and helped everybody else. Roads were cleared, trees were reset. Food and water and labor were common property. It was a great time to remember. There was that spirit abroad of fine friendliness and a common courage and great hope.

It had been mamma and the family who had been hardest to bear. Mamma had arrived in two weeks, on a milk truck from Miami, in the manner of a South Pole relief expedition, with headlines, all flowing satin skirts, maternal bosom and contralto dramatics. The rest of the family, with their indomitable family feeling, arrived shortly after—Elphin with new riding clothes and six cents in his pocket.

Francesca with two scratched trunks, Maddanella with ideas for a little-theater movement in the back country, and Sylvanus, having read a book on the train about the holiness of tilling the earth, all aglow, behind his eyeglass ribbon, with the holiness of tilling the earth.

If Stephen Wilson's expensive layers had not been so scared by the hurricane that they took to the tall trees and refused to lay a single egg, there would have been hardly enough for the family to eat. But Stephen, to Penny's horror, went simply goofy over Maddanella, and supplied roasting chickens for almost every meal. And mamma was quieted by having the piano fixed, which, having served nobly to keep the French doors from blowing in, was the least bit water-logged. The family, all agog to help their little girl in her great trouble, immediately gave a tremendous concert in the schoolhouse, which Penny had to have cleaned for the purpose. Through which most of the exhausted workers, including Penny, dozed blissfully.

But in the dull months afterward, when the trees were slowly throwing out their fine new green, the family got bored and left. Stephen got over Maddanella by setting himself up in the chicken business. And Penny forgot all of them, looking at the splendid line of mangos growing up again from their own twisted roots.

Her father had planted them for a windbreak and they had grown, were growing again, into thick-thatched, dark-green masses. The fruit her father had harvested casually, more interested as he was in his grapefruit, limes and avocados. There would be no more fruit until next year now—the glorious crimson Haden mangos, the pale yellow Saigons with their smooth, fiberless flesh and subtle flavor.

They were to her the rarest, the most marvelous fruit in the world. Dealers in the North had only just begun asking for them. She began to read the few Government bulletins about mangos. Why shouldn't the mango, which, in all the United States, grew only in this narrow strip of dry Florida pineland between the Everglades and the sea, become the greatest crop the region produced?

She was seventeen that next June, but she felt older than that. There was so much to be done and learned. Life was so adventurous and exciting. This country, coming back with tropic vigor from the hurricane damage, was so fine and courageous and dramatic a place. She remembered that next summer and fall, because Maddanella was

150

married to a very splendid coughdrop manufacturer and sent her two hundred dollars. And Stephen did not seem to mind.

But the following January the frost came suddenly, for the first time in twelve years. There had been no warning of any sort. It must have begun to get chill, cold for South Florida, after midnight. Penny woke suddenly out of an unhappy huddle in her one blanket and ran to the window. The thick starlight fell in motionless points of brightness along the motionless, dark points of the mango leaves. The stars were red and yellow and crackling blue-white. She threw some clothes on and went out. The thermometer stood at twenty-nine under her flashlight, and even as she stared it seemed to creep down a little more.

In the grove not a leaf whispered. The air was dead cold. She wandered up and down the path, wondering if bonfires would help. But there was no wood. After a bit she went back to the thermometer. It was down to twenty-seven. She could hear Mrs. Jenkins snoring in her room.

A light showed suddenly where Stephen's house was, behind the trees. Directly, he bulked big and dark among the shadows. She went to him, swallowing a salty throatful.

"It's down to twenty-seven," she said. "Would it do any good to try brush fires?"

His arm was warm along her shoulders.

"No luck, kid," he said quietly. "This has got 'em."

They walked up and down a little. It was so cold and still they could hear a rooster crowing far away, the long nocturnal quaver of the tropics. It went down to twenty-six. They talked a little, about the funny places, like Siberia, where cold meant forty degrees, sixty degrees, below zero. Then they walked a little more, in silence. It seemed to Penny that everybody in the world but Stephen had frozen up and vanished. There were no sounds in all the wide spaces of the night. But she didn't care as long as his arm was along her shoulders.

Just when the first light was red and sullen in the east, so that they could see more plainly the wideness of the delicate, hoary world, the fine tracery of the frost on the mangos, on the lime trees, on the bent, tiny arches of the grass, Stephen said, "Come on, kid. Make me some coffee. You don't want to watch what's going to happen now." She knew what he meant. When the sunlight touched the first frost-whitened leaf tips everything would start to blacken. Only after days would the real ruin show. They might as well have a good breakfast.

It was only a freak, wedge-shaped strip of country that was affected. But the trees had to be cut back to three-inch wood. They would all bear again, but not for another year. She had her bees and her vegetables, and Stephen's chicken business was getting good. She figured she would be all right with what she had in the bank to tide her over.

That same week the bank in Miami failed. The family, thank fortune, had not heard about that. Elphin's book of poetry was just out and mamma was buzzing around at a lot of fat literary teas for him, and Francesca was going to have an exhibition, and Sylvanus was sailing for London. Penny was eighteen that year. There was a good honey flow and she had fifty colonies of bees. There was always enough to eat. And existence was an exhilarating challenge.

She was nineteen, and she was twenty. The taxes were paid with money from avocados and limes. Once mamma, for no reason at all, sent her sixty dollars.

And in the fall there was an all-day blow that was not quite a hurricane, followed by rains that flooded out all the grove lands, killed the avocados, drowned the early vegetables. After that, the Mediterranean fruit fly hit Florida, and all the Dade County fruit and vegetables were quarantined, although the fly did not affect them. There was still plenty to eat. Mrs. Jenkins patched her overalls and refused her wages. But the taxes could not be paid, or the fertilizer bill. And the spring before she was twenty the heavy spring rains killed the mango blooms. There was also another bank failure in town. That did not affect her, but it wiped out Stephen.

This fall Penny had been counting on the spring mango crop to pull her through. She was beginning to feel that five years like that was too much. She felt tired all the time. That was when mamma descended and the winter set in, chill and damp. It was too much. Penny, sitting on the pile of boards behind Stephen's chicken yard, which was her refuge, stared at the ground as mamma's music rose louder, triumphant and too sweet, from her distant house. Penny knew she was licked. She didn't have any fight left in her. Maybe mamma was right. Maybe she had missed a good deal.

Stephen came suddenly around the corner of the chicken house. She stared up at him. She did not notice at first the bemused, excited look in his good blue eyes. She was aware of the solid lines of his figure, of his matured, understanding, dependable brown face. She would have to tell him she was quitting.

Stephen said, "Kid, I just picked up your brother Sylvanus and your sister Francesca and brought them down from Miami. I'm awfully sorry about it, but one of her trunks got scratched. Gee, she's—she's marvelous."

Penny got to her feet slowly. She might have known the family would start piling up on her. But Stephen? "Oh, my heavens," Penny thought. "Not—not Francesca." She trotted back to the house in her untidy cotton working trousers. They were there, shattering the peace of the worn, airy living room. Sylvanus was unpacking his harp. He was actually portly. He was arguing in his beautiful, fretful drawl with mamma, flopping her pompadour at the piano, shouting and bearing down on the bass. It seemed that somebody's fingering was important, or something. Penny slowly turned her eyes on Francesca.

She was doing her hair by the wall mirror, wearing already a trumpery violet-and-silver negligee yanked from a trunk whose contents were all over the floor. Francesca was lovelier than anyone else in the world, Penny thought. Her hair was thick silver-blond and her black eyes were enormous. Time laid no stain on the smoothness of her face. Her small, reddened mouth never changed its bright petulance, except when she shouted arguments over her shoulder at mamma and Sylvanus. "Pig!" she was shouting. "Pig! Pig! Pig! Pig! Pig!"

Then mamma saw her by the door. "Look, Francesca! Look, Sylvanus! There's my baby—my lovely baby. See how she is all gold-colored and exquisite. Taken away from this dreadful place, with the right clothes—- Think, Sylvanus, in bronze and scarlet and blue, with that dull-gold hair—- I have made up my mind. I shall make something of her yet."

Francesca looked over her shoulder. "But such a savage," she said. "Like a little pig. Why haven't you fallen in love with the Wilson farmer? He's sweet."

Mamma roared out a great, gorgeous scale or two: "Ah, *jeunesse*, ah, *giovanezza*, we go Thursday," she said.

Penny looked at them coldly. She said, "I haven't the slightest intention of going."

Mamma crashed both hands on the keys. "Francesca, play this.... Bad baby, we go Thursday. I have notified the newspapers."

"I shan't go until spring! If then!" Penny shouted at the top of her voice. She had never shouted before in her life. It made her ears ring. "How dare you order me about!"

"Pen-e-lope!" mamma thundered.

"And you can pick up all this junk!" Penny went on shouting. She felt like throwing things. In another minute she would be acting just like mamma. "I will not have my living room made into a—into a pigpen." Penny glared at Francesca.

Mamma stood up, and her eyes were dangerous. But Francesca, trailing to the piano, said, "Oh, your contract doesn't begin until June. You are dreadfully out of practice. So is Sylvanus. And a few months in Florida might be amusing."

Penny bolted to her room, trembling all over. She was going to have to buck up now, sure enough. Well, they would live on fish and grits, all right, if they lived on her.

The next morning early she stared out her bedroom window at the most extraordinary sight she had yet seen in Florida. Francesca, in the trailing violet-and-silver negligee, her hair one silver-gilt glory in the early sun, stood over in Stephen Wilson's chicken yard, holding a pan of chicken feed. And even at that distance Penny could see him, almost looking up at her because of Francesca's heroic height, with the limp hand and rigid head of a man spellbound. Penny's jaw snapped shut so hard that her teeth ached. All right then. All right for Francesca. All right for mamma. All right for Stephen. Her face was smooth, rigid, gold color, but inside she was one seething, red-hot mass of fight.

She paced up and down before the beehives and the long, massed ranks of the mango trees, pulling herself steady. The line of them, close-thatched, with their long leaves like dark jade spears, went all down her boundary line, all around her land. Here and there through the avocados a mango reared its dark bulk. Already a veil of milky cloud, a thin, bright floor, was drawing overhead across the sky. Presently the December day would go white and damp and chill. Penny walked and thought clear, decisive, hard-bitten thoughts. If these mangos could be made to bear as they should, the luscious, vivid fruit would bring her in nearly two thousand dollars. There would be other things, but the mangos could save her.

It was chance that had always governed the mango crop. She remembered the heavy, casual yield in her father's day. He had sprayed a little. All around the countryside every farm had its mango, or its windbreak of mangos, but people did not work at them seriously. If the crop failed, people said, "Oh, it rained this spring. The mangos don't seem to be fruitin' right plentiful."

Yet there had been a growing demand from Northern dealers every year. Was it just because of bad luck, or had anyone really used his brains about them?

Penny stood stock-still. Suppose she made her fight with the mangos, her wits, all that she had learned about tropic fruit, all her ability for hard, thorough work against the fluctuation of chance? It would be worth the gamble.

There were three dangers. The deadly anthracnose came with too much wet. You sprayed for that. People sprayed casually, about five times a winter. Suppose, if the threatened drizzle came, that she sprayed oftener? Suppose she sprayed one tree once a week, another one twice a week, another one every day? She would find out something.

The chill kept the bloom back, so that there were no flowers. It didn't need a bad frost; just a damp, continuous cold. She remembered the night she and Stephen had walked, watching the frost. But suppose she were prepared this time, with brush for fires, with smudge pots? They did that in India and saved their mangos, even when it was colder.

And then the pollination. There was a lot of argument about pollination. You could have mangos without it, but only little, undeveloped fruit. The rain was supposed to wash off all the pollen. But Wilson Popenoe said that the pollen only swelled. It could still be carried. And there was an argument about the wind's carrying it. Penny looked a long time at her trees. Then her glance dropped to the close, white ranks of her beehives. She had almost as many hives as mango trees. She grinned suddenly, a long, slow, surprised, delighted grin. Presently she went to work.

The Heston family—mamma and Sylvanus and Francesca—

enjoyed their winter in Florida with even more of their gusto and tumult. The fact that the climate was being treacherously cool, that the whity-gray light hung wetly over the long green levels of country between them and the hotels of Miami and Miami Beach, did not daunt them. They ran back and forth constantly in borrowed cars. Mamma was taken up by women's clubs and gave a concert. Sylvanus was pursued, to his happiness, by two heiresses, and Francesca came and went in smart, twinkling cars, staying over often for affairs in Palm Beach. Francesca always had a lot of dark-haired, cool-eyed men around her. But she gave an unusual amount of time and attention to Stephen Wilson, who took her, a little dazed, to tea dances and ran up to fetch her from Palm Beach. He passed sandwiches—egg sandwiches, as Penny noticed wickedly—at informal concerts that went on every now and again in Penny's house, moving gingerly, but still bemused, among a crowd of smart, leggy girls and jingly matrons and elderly, brushed gentlemen, all obviously thrilled at this adventure to the hinterlands. More musicians, a few theatrical magnates, visiting popular novelists, Russian princesses looking for jobs, and newspaper men covering fights or politicians for the big papers, came and went, bumping into Stephen staring at Francesca in corners. The egg business suffered. But Francesca preened herself in the light of a fresh and unsophisticated devotion.

Penny didn't have time to look at Stephen much. The poor, dumb egg, she thought often, lowering her lids over the pure green blaze of battle in her eyes. He hadn't any business to suffer like that. But in the meantime the wet, damp, cold, unusual weather went right on.

But Penny had learned things. You must spray mango trees every four days. More than that burns them. Less than that brings the creeping anthracnose. When the sun came out briefly, the great trees stood coated with the fine blue-green of the spray, like amazing blue-green jade, artificial and lovely under the sun. Three water colorists, friends of mamma's, painted them. Penny strode past, seeing only that the sprayers hissed regularly and thoroughly down the grove.

Then it was time for the first hints of spring and the coming of bloom, and the nights were chill. No frost, but just the damp, penetrating chill which keeps the blood sluggish, and the sap, that should be rising. So Penny started her fires and her smudge pots.

156

All night long, in the cool drip of the starlight, the smudge pots glowered down the grove, and the smell of pine wood burning drifted across the long, starlit roads and the piny levels. Penny stayed up, watching them. She had to see that the warmth was even and that the smoke did not get the bees. She had spaced out the line of the hives, so that they stretched out, under every mango tree. The bees were not yet working.

Her hair smelled of pine smoke, and little bluish smudges came under her eyes from lack of sleep. It was lonely, sometimes, in the early chill before dawn, with nobody but Big Jim and one of the other grove hands. Her face grew pale, slipping unnoticed through the continuing uproar that went on in the house.

But sometimes Stephen walked out of the house, dazed with looking at Francesca, and paced with Penny the glowing line of smudge pots. The music behind them, the laughter of Francesca and come of her smart, black-haired, suave-eyed beaus, was muted behind them in the night and the fire-lit leaves. They did not say anything. Stephen did not even seem to wonder what she was doing. He was like the shell of a man, a man walking in uneasy sleep. Sometimes she was so sorry for him Penny could have cried. Except that she was not crying any just now. She was too busy and too mad.

The weather went on, a few days of sun and then the shutting down of the damp chill. Francesca went to Palm Beach for two weeks. Mamma had an at-home.

Stephen looked at Penny suddenly, one day, his forehead wrinkling with a curious trouble.

"Look here, kid. What have you been doing to yourself? You look awful. I don't like it."

"Look at yourself," Penny said hotly. "You look awful. And your place looks awful. You know darn well you're making a fool of yourself about Francesca."

He stiffened. "You're a brat. She's the most beautiful, the most—"

"Aw, nuts," Penny said, and watched Stephen walk away stiffly. Now he would never forgive her.

She couldn't bear it. She could stand anything but Stephen's angry, contemptuous look. She loved him. That was the trouble. It wrenched her with a curious pain, like a stitch that would not go, right under her heart. It was worse than it had ever been with her. She stared after him. The line of his good shoulders, the back of his head, the way he swung his hands, the very back of his legs, was so near, so curiously important, that her very living seemed to depend on them. Yet to Francesca the stricken look in his eyes was only funny.

The season was over. The family was getting very restless. Not so many people came to see them. All Francesca's black-haired beaus went away in their twinkling cars. Mamma practiced scales half the night, and Sylvanus was peevish. Francesca took it out on Stephen. Everything was dreadful. But one day Penny looked out her window on a blue and brilliant morning. On the mangos, the long flower spikes were whitening in the sun, crowded with innumerable tiny blossoms. Only a few of those could come to bearing. But Penny's heart beat suddenly. She had a chance still. For the bees were busy.

Then the rains shut down again, drifting like clouds across the wide, wet distances. Penny escaped the hubbub of the house, and the sprayers hissed regularly. She had hardly any money left. The family were argumentative for hours over beans and fish. Penny was surprised that they still lingered, until she realized that Francesca kept them. Francesca was restless and snappish. But evidently she could not yet spare Stephen's pinched-face adoration.

But presently Penny forgot everybody in her preoccupation with her mango trees. Even her feeling for Stephen retreated to a dim corner of her heart. For here and there, little by little, the mangos were beginning to show fruit. It was only the beginning. The little, hard, green ovals hung on their long strings half concealed by the bluegreen, sprayed leaves. It was too soon to tell if they were pollinated. It was too soon to tell if the anthracnose would spot them. And the wet alternation of the days, here and there sunny, went on. Hope was so strange in Penny that it hurt. It might not be real yet. She was a little afraid of it. Then the spring rains began to thunder in from the distant sea.

Stephen, buying eggs in a dozen grove yards, heard the news first, that went drifting around the country. The mango crop had failed. It must have been the first time that he had thought of it definitely. He came straight to Penny, picking beans in the patch.

"Penny," he said harshly, "I hear the mangos are ruined."

"Did you just hear that?" she said.

"I should have known it before, but I just realized. What will you do, kid?"

"I'll go."

He made a curious, blind gesture toward the earth. "Leave this?"

"I'll have to, if I can't pay my bills and the back taxes. Mamma wants me with her in Hollywood."

She could not quite understand the look in his face. But then she had given up trying to understand him.

"How soon?"

She made a vague little motion. He looked at her once, hard, turned on his heel and walked off. He did not come back to the Heston house for three days.

It was in those three days—balmy, warm days, hot with the good weight of the sun, cool with the wind running clear from the distant sea, humming with insect sounds in the dried saw grass— that mamma delivered her ultimatum. She was sick, sick, sick of all this. She could not stand it a moment longer. They were all to pack. Francesca had nothing to say. They were all to pack instantly—instantly. Send for a taxi. Send for two taxis. Instantly. Penny's face was perfectly still.

She walked down the grove, past the mango trees, once. Then she strolled over the lot line, past Stephen's chicken yards and around the corner of his house. He was sitting on his side steps with his empty hands on his knees. He looked up slowly from her feet to the curious brilliance of her eyes.

"Hello," she said.

He didn't say anything.

Penny said, "Mamma's having everything packed."

He didn't say anything.

She dropped to her knees in front of him, so that he could not escape looking into her eyes.

"If I'm ruined, Stephen," she said, "if I have to lose the place, is there anything you could do, so that I wouldn't have to go?"

He said slowly, "How about marrying me, kid?"

Penny looked at him. "And you nuts about Francesca?"

"I can't let you go away," he said. "You're my little girl. You're mine. You know that. She's had me nuts all winter. But you—nothing must happen to you. Don't you know that? You're the only thing that matters. When will you marry me?"

Penny grinned at him, getting to her feet. "I want to show you something," she said.

He walked down the length of the mangos with her, staring. The trees were heavy with fat, jade-green fruit. Perfect fruit, with no blight on it. And here and there it was coloring slowly. The Saigons were turning a clear, bright yellow, the heavy Hadens their amazing dull scarlet. It would be a good crop.

"Ruined," he said, looking at her with his steady glance— his clear, steady glance. "Ruined. You little devil. Those are the only mangos in the county. You've played me for a sucker. You'll have more money than I'll see for months."

"But you asked me to marry you. Honest you did, Stephen. Honest." She meant to be funny, looking up at him. But somehow her face got twisted and her breath came short. She was crying, wrenched and beaten with sobs. The smudge had worked. The spray had worked. And her secret belief about the dear, foolish bees had come true. Her crop was there. And she was crying like an idiot.

Her head hardly reached to the strong pounding of his heart, but his arms helped. His mouth, when it moved upon hers, stopped everything—time and the world and the beating of her own heart. He loved her. She knew that now. He knew it. And the mangos were ripe.

They did not even notice, at this distance, the renewed tumult of music from the house. Or it may have been only the murmuring of the nearer, and more significant, bees.

8
SEPTEMBER—REMEMBER

*B*EFORE HE WAS AWAKE, the long roaring over the shack had become Jimmy Gowan's oldest nightmare—the faraway roaring of guns searching him out where he lay buried in choking earth. The old trembling shook him half awake. It was not guns; it was trains. And the horror was not the fear of death but the fear of being snatched on and on endlessly, mouth dry with dirt from the floor of the eternal box car, over the remorseless grinding of wheels that would never stop.

With a wrenching effort he pulled himself upright, heart suffocated with that old fear. It was not the planks of a box car. It was a mattress and a cot. The shack was quiet. The roaring outside was wind.

The relief made him shudder more than the unforgettable dreams had done. He put his hands over his worn face to shake himself out of it. The air flowing in the screened opening cooled his dried throat. It was quiet here in the early morning, with two of the cots still empty and only old Butch in the fourth, snoring off his Sunday drunk. Mike and Pie-Eye hadn't come back from Key West yet, then. It was Monday morning.

Rain smacked on the roof, and Jimmy shuffled into his trousers to stare out. Wind. It came roaring out of gray-rolled clouds that yet could not shut out the clarity of the Florida light, smashing down on the huddle of veterans' camp shacks on the rough white ground and beating down the three palm trees and the mangrove scrub beyond. The rain struck a slant like rifle fire, spurting among the whitish lumps of rock. Nobody was stirring yet. There had been a lot of beer about, yesterday, and the cheap whisky the men bought from the houseboat near the bridge. There wouldn't be much road work today, by the look of things. And suddenly Jimmy's relief blazed higher into exultation, as if it had grown up unnoticed through the dulled hopelessness he had known so long. If there were no road work, maybe he could get off by himself again, up the road to the north, where the little white houses of the people who always lived on these Keys stood among palm trees and white sand on the edge of that polished, shallow, glittering sea. There was that man who had begun to talk to him, who was going to pick his limes today. There was a woman who was beginning to be friendly to him, in spite of the silent, suspicious ways of many of the Key people with the men from the camps.

There was no way Jimmy had of expressing to himself, hurrying over to the cook shack, hunched against the stinging drops, how he felt about that place he had found up the road. He had had no words for years to explain how it felt to have nothing, to be nothing, except somehow to cling to breathing and to endure. He never had been smart. He'd only got into the Army, years ago, because he was sound enough to obey orders and use shovels. They hadn't wanted him to fight. He'd been kicked soon enough into a labor battalion, digging latrines and trenches, peeling potatoes and dumping garbage. The explosion that had buried him and cast him into the hospital hadn't really been anywhere near the front lines. It had served only to cast him out later, back home, into the drifting ranks of casual labor that became increasingly not wanted.

There was no place for him or his kind, anyway. His only orders, having been trained humbly to obey orders, were to move on. He was not one of those who could be even articulate about it. The dullness, the sense of drift, had settled into his heart, with no energy even for protest. He had drifted to Washington with the Bonus Army, stood about mutely on curbstones, moved mutely when he was told to. Hunger was something you carried with you, and the blankness that it brought. They had moved hundreds of him and his kind down here, when people saw, finally, that something definite must be done, that you could not shoot men for starving at your doorstep. He had taken this mutely also. There were shacks and cots and food regularly, and a shovel to scrape in the unfamiliar white earth. And there was the sun.

The rain had stopped as abruptly as it had come, when he plunged into the cook shack. Hoofer Kelley, the cook, unshaven and with his eyes bleary, was just making coffee. It smelled great. Jimmy got himself a thick cup of it to hunch over until the grits were cooked, hoping that the sound of the wind had not started Hoofer on one of his long, aimless tirades about second lieutenants. Hoofer was like that—kind of off when he got excited. But he was a good-enough cook, for all the way the men grumbled. You didn't have to listen.

But Hoofer was silent, not yet quite awake, and Jimmy huddled over his coffee with his faded eyes blank, taking into himself with long gulps its hot, reassuring deliciousness. He never could get over eating as if it were a rare luxury, as if this might be the last he'd ever get. It made the absorption of coffee and grits into his spare frame a kind of ecstasy. After that he would think about his hope for the day. It was funny to have plans, hopes, of his own. It made him want to giggle a little, the way the sun did when he was alone in it.

One or two other men drifted in, sour and unkempt. He did not look at them. He did not want to talk to them. He knew everything they had to say, had heard it, over and over and over again—the rambling, wrangling, endless, repetitious talk of the drifter, the misfit, the has-been. A broad patch of sun glared with new brilliance over the table and his twisted hands. He stared at it, knowing his stomach satisfied, feeling rise again in him that curious new surge of—was it happiness? He had no word for that, either. It was something that the sun did to him, that was as good as a quiet bed and food and coffee. Better, if there was anything possibly better than those.

The wind had stopped roaring like a train. The whole broad day outside was brilliant from a sky reft with unbelievable blue. He went out hastily, before anybody could tell him to get a shovel and go to work on the embankment. He meant to go on up the road, no matter what anybody said. It was a long way that he meant to go.

Three men by a shack were arguing about storms when he went by them. There was this hurricane down in the Florida Straits, wherever that was. The one they called Big Lefty—to tell him from Little Lefty, who had had a hand shot off in the Argonne—had been in Key West yesterday. If you had a great big pile of dynamite, he was saying, you could shoot one of these hurricanes all to blazes. Jimmy Gowan didn't notice what they were saying. He'd talked, years and years, like that himself. Now he had something to do.

Nobody paid any attention to his going. The straw boss wasn't in sight. Maybe he hadn't got back from Key West, either. Jimmy took boldly to the one road that ran, a streak of dark metal, all along the backbone of this chain of Keys, by the railroad tracks, a foot or so higher than the tangle of bright green mangrove scrub, of purple, blossoming vines that shut out the sea on both sides. He turned his face to the east, to the sun, and watched for the first glimpse of that marvelous lime-green water reaching clear to the horizon. The sight of it gave him the same sharp sting of pleasure that it always did. The first day he had just stood and stared at it, incredulous. It had been pale blue then—a blinding, misty, polished blue, with the reflection of one enormous cream-colored pillar of cloud reaching almost to his feet. You couldn't believe that anything would be like that in this world. Now another high-pitched gust of that same wind came roaring over to him where he strode. Gray rolls of cloud moved with it, changing that far sea instantly to ruffled plum color, streaked with nearer green. Its roaring did sound a little like a bombardment very far off, or the mutter of a fast freight. But it wrought no fear in him. He liked the feeling of the clean push of air in his face that fairly blew up his lungs with freshness. It made him straighten and walk faster. He did not know that little by little his legs were losing their old shuffle, that he was striding out boldly, as even a labor battalion learns to on inspection parade. When the rain hit him, it wetted him pleasantly. The gray light was pleasant to his faded, brightening glance.

What he wanted, what he hoped, was to get that man to let him help pick his limes. They ought to be picked before this wind got them. He had listened to the man talk about that, sitting on the steps of the little store, still miles to the north. Jimmy had found that if he just sat quiet, the brown-faced, quiet-mouthed men would start talking in their low singsong voices. Maybe they'd forgotten he was there. Or maybe they were getting used to him. That was what he had hoped. They didn't like strangers and they didn't like the men from the veterans' camps. They didn't know what to make of them. Even the lean, bleached-hair children would dodge away from him on their hard little bare feet. So he had just sat, as often as he could, saying nothing, quiet in the sun that made his very bones feel new.

He didn't know exactly why he had taken the long tramp northward so often just for that. At first, it had been to get away from the eternal grumbling, the stale old stories, of the camps. And then somehow he had liked the people. They were different from any people he had seen. They knew how to loaf in the sun. But they knew how to work at the fishing boats, in the queer, ragged patches of tomatoes, in the lime groves planted at what first seemed such lazy haphazard among the unplowed rocks. They weren't all of a sweat all of the time to make money. They took things easy.

But that was sensible too. The glittering sea, the shallows stirring and sparkling behind the Keys to the west were alive with fish. You couldn't plow this rock, no matter how hard you tried. But if you were wise, you stuck a lime seedling into a pocket of leaf mold among the porous rock, and the tiny roots went down cunningly for water and shade and nourishment, and the tough, dark-green leaves spread into a dense tangle, so that the small green fruit hung heavy on every prickly bough. There was plenty of good money in Key limes. And the coconut palms, the tall ancient trees with their swerving fronds high up above the curved flexible boles, stood all along the beaches, over the small white houses, making soft patterns on the hard white sands. You could always eat coconuts. The thing of it was, the whole place, as well as the people, seemed to mean something special just for him.

A car or two passed him, from the north or south, but he hardly noticed them. He had stuck his hand into his pocket and rattled his pennies. There were quite a lot of them. He could buy a soda at the store like anybody. But just one. He had begun deliberately to save money—why, he wasn't quite sure. He thought he wanted a fish line or a cast net. A cast net was expensive. It would be nice to fish. If he could make fifty cents more— He'd done pretty well yesterday. But just now, striding with the gusts in his face, going some place he wanted to go, like a free man, not to beg food or to be moving on, he was a little ashamed of that racket he'd been working Sundays. It wasn't very—well, it wasn't anything to be proud of. He fingered the worn letter in his other pocket doubtfully.

The way he did it, he'd get to talking with some of these people in cars who'd stopped to stare at the camp. He'd answer all the questions they could think of, and then he'd ask if anybody had a stamp, or three cents, maybe, that he could spare. He'd written a letter to his mother, only he couldn't mail it. Well, of course, almost anybody could spare three cents. Generally, it would be a nickel. Nobody would worry about that. The letter was worn and greasy, he'd used it so long. And as for writing to his mother, she'd been dead a long time, the poor old thing! A long time ago, before the war, when he was a boy. He hadn't thought of her for years.

It didn't seem to him, suddenly, that he had thought about anything for years. What was there to think of except food and not slipping down under the wheels when you jumped a box car? Thinking made things worse.

Now he suddenly jerked the letter from his pocket and tore it up, letting the wind take it. It surprised him to realize that he wasn't going to work that racket any more. It was as if, deep down in him, he had a wordless plan that had been forming for a long time. He struck out over a long bridge between the low-lying Keys, over water running, green and gray, fast under the wind from the open sea. He had about ten miles more. It was funny about that sense of plan. That must have been what kept him from going down to Key West, Sundays, or buying more than two bottles of beer and never any whisky. It was as if he were saving up for something that was more than fish lines, something in the future that he wanted. But what did he want? What good were a few dollars to him? There never had been any work anywhere. There was nothing very much that he had learned to do. It hadn't been any good even to expect that there would be work.

And yet that money in his pocket was real and meant something. He puzzled over his own strangeness, watching the white handrail jog by steadily. The wind flattened out again. There was no rain, and suddenly the great sunlight poured heavily upon him from a cleared sky, like a silent blaring of brasses. Heat marched with him, the vibrant living heat of the tropic sun, but the shadow of his old straw hat, the air in his nostrils, was cool. Funny how quickly this whole world changed from gray to sun and back again. He hadn't seen it like this before in all the long, sun-glaring summer.

A car coming up behind him as he left the bridge for the roadway again, stopped beside him with brakes squealing like a rusty hinge. It was a rusty wreck of a car, and the man in it was one of those Key people, a fisherman, hunched over under a shapeless palmetto hat. He had seen him often up at that store.

The man said, "Want a ride?"

Jimmy was astonished. None of those ever offered him rides.

"Barometer's falling," the man said, in his high-pitched voice, over the clattering engine. "Some say that's a bad blow down in the Straits. Don't look quite right to me. You hear anything?"

Jimmy wondered what he was supposed to have heard. He only shook his head. The Key people didn't like talk.

But this man talked. It was as if, suddenly, he had forgotten Jimmy was a stranger. The man said he had to go all the way up to Miami, and he didn't like it. If they was goin' to be a blow, he'd want to be down the Keys, where he'd feel safe. In '26, now, they said that those streets up in the city was just about as dangerous a place as you'd find—things blowin' and all like that.

"That ain't anything. These gusts they seem kind of funny to me. Comin' up from the sou'east. I done tole my son to make the boat fast, bow and stern lines, both. Take no chances. Tide's comin' up. These damn railroad fills. Time was, you could run a boat around in the lee easy. Now you got to go all the way down to No. 5 Channel to get inside. My ole man always says iffen the sea starts comin' up, ain't no way for it to run off into the bay. I dunno, though. It never has."

The excitement of being talked to like a neighbor, the pleasure of riding those last miles in the flowing wind, kept Jimmy oblivious of the man's uneasy tones. At the little store, among the group of frame houses, where a rutty road wandered among lime trees down to the palm-lined beach, Jimmy got out with more real assurance than he had ever had.

A group of men in overalls and dungarees stood about the little porch of the store. Two nodded to him. One called to the driver of the car, "Any news about the blow?"

Jimmy said, "Mr. Bethel begun pickin' his limes yet?" That was the man's name. Mr. Albert Bethel. There were a lot of Bethels.

They stared at him curiously.

"Al done picked his ripe uns yest'day. Says hit was due to be a wind t'day. No sense waitin'. You heard anything about the blow?"

Jimmy was astonished at the weight of his own disappointment. He could have been up here helping when he was working that cheap racket yesterday. And it wasn't just the idea of the money Mr. Bethel might have paid him. It was that other need, deeper. He could have helped, anyway.

The storekeeper came to the door. "Miama just called. The center of the blow's still down the Straits, far's they know. Weather Bureau can't locate it. Goin' nor'west, likely, up the Gulf."

Even Jimmy could tell that they were uneasy. The burned lank jaws were set, but their worn boots creaked the planks. "Glass is still fallin'," someone said.

The sun was once more blotted out by low-rolling gray—gray of doves' wings, pearl-gray, green-gray, steel-gray. The attacks of the wind hissed viciously behind, and all the high shrubs flattened and recoiled as if an invisible weight had passed over. Children were silent in the dooryards. No cars rattled in the roads. No man sat down on the steps. There was only the steady sound of hammers among the houses.

Jimmy did not want to sit in his usual place on the steps, either. For the first time, the tension in their manner drove uneasiness into his centered mood. He fought it off. He had nothing to do with their anxiety. His nerves remembered older fears too much. He refused to take on new ones. Why should he care, when he had nothing, was nothing? It was too much. He could go back and get drunk. Good and drunk. He hadn't been drunk for as long as he could remember, hadn't wanted to. But rather than share in any new anxiety, he could blot it out, let it go by him in an easy oblivion.

Why not? Their concern for boats and houses and lime crops and children was nothing to him.

It was clear to him at once that that was what he would do. Let them do the worrying. The new thing that these months had built up in him—interest, purpose, new hope—was too vague to stand up against his shrinking. He wanted whisky, suddenly, and lots of it, and he wanted it quickly. He would save himself even the fear of fear. He had had all that any man could stand long ago. He'd get a quart of whisky now, catch a ride back, drink himself unconscious. Or there'd be an empty shack around here he could crawl into and save himself even that effort. Two quarts.

It was a little surprising, therefore, that even as he was relaxing all over with the idea of that escape, he should be walking down the weed-grown road to Bethel's. The wind lashed at him savagely with the thousand wires of its rain, but he hardly noticed it. The whisky would be hot in his throat and the blur of feeling would come quickly. It was a great idea.

Mr. Bethel came around the corner of his house, well built of native rock, solid with veranda pillars, in its neat garden. He was carrying a window shutter and a hammer, and nodded to Jimmy moving up the path.

"Catch the end of this, will you?" he said. "I got to get more nails."

The wind shoved hard at their backs as they got that shutter up. The slashing rain made it hard to hold, but the nails went in surely under the loud hammer. Behind them the shallow open sea was piling up in gray and white on the low beach. Far out it was a mistier welter of gray that hid the horizon, and the swift ridges of cloud were the same murk. Jimmy held all the shutters for Mr. Bethel, helped him pull them out from under the house, sometimes drove in the nails. In spite of the wind it was hot and the wet streamed from their hot faces. They worked right around the house, stood back and saw that all was shipshape. The roof wasn't leaking a drop, Mr. Bethel said with satisfaction.

Mrs. Bethel came out on the porch and smiled at Jimmy, as she had before—a brown, spare, energetic woman. "You better come in and have your dinner now, while I got it hot," she said. She meant Jimmy too. He realized it was a long time since breakfast. The fried fish and tomatoes tasted good, even if the shuttered room was stuffy. Bethel's son-in-law and daughter were there, too, and a little girl, and their baby in a crib. They all ate without haste, but quickly, and their preoccupation was not fear. It was only that they seemed to be going over all the details in their minds. The boats had been made fast to the wharf in the lee of the Key. There was plenty of oil for the lamps and the stove, plenty of canned food. All the loose boards and lime crates were stored in the shed. They spoke quietly about the falling barometer. Mr. Bethel had a good one—an aneroid. The thin, wiry hand was unmistakably crawling downward. Sometimes the gusts of wind and rain were so loud that they had to raise their voices.

Somebody recited a jingle about hurricanes: "July—stand by. August—look out you must. September—remember. October—all over." They all seemed to be familiar with it. Hurricanes were familiar. Jimmy glanced at them inquiringly. Bethel grinned at him like a friend. They didn't seem really nervous—that he could tell. But this was September.

Jimmy lingered at the table after the women got up. The lime pie was good, and Mrs. Bethel shoved over another piece to him. He was a little reluctant to go out again. They all stood and listened to Mr. Bethel, calling the Weather Bureau in Miami on the telephone.

"I don't like the looks of it," he said loudly. "This wind ought to be hauling around if it's going off in the Straits.... What?... Sure the barometer's falling here. It's been falling all morning."

Bethel's son-in-law, Charlie Sanders, murmured something in the interval—something about calling Key West. There was somebody else trying to use the line.

"Who is it?" Bethel called irritably. "I'm calling the Weather Bureau. You can listen in.... Who?... Oh, Franklin.... What?... Sure, you can have the line. Did they say they were sending a train?... Well, go ahead. Go ahead." He hung up.

Franklin was the superintendent of the nearest veterans' camp. Jimmy listened, startled a little. "He says he's been trying to get them to send a relief train for the camps," Bethel said. "He can't find out if it's started. If the blow's coming this way"—Bethel looked at them all quietly—"those shacks'll go like match boxes. Those men ought to be getting out right now."

It hadn't occurred to Jimmy to imagine that a hurricane could really be coming, or that the camps, his camp, might be in danger. The idea ripped through the armor of his indifference. A relief train? Then it might be serious? No, no, of course not. It couldn't be. There wasn't anything to worry about. His mind repudiated hotly the immanence of worry. These people didn't really think——

The two women were quietly gathering up the dishes to wash them. The mother of the baby came in with the baby's bottle, sat by it while the little thing sucked and murmured, looking down with that absorption of women in a child's feeding that seems to shut out everything else.

When the men went out on the porch, Jimmy thought that now would be the time to get that whisky and be looking about for a shack. Mr. Bethel went along with him. But halfway to the store a woman ran out to ask them if they thought it was coming nearer. The rain drove through her faded hair and soaked her cotton dress instantly. Her men were out tending to the boats. Mr. Bethel and Jimmy started putting up her shutters for her. She had only two good ones. The other windows of her small frame house they covered with boards nailed close together. Mr. Bethel went back to his own house for nails, and Jimmy broke up a packing case. When that was done, they were soaked through. The rain was driving in steadily, darkening the gray light; heavy sheets of rain that hit in a mist of white along the roofs blew along the wind in masses parallel to the drenched earth.

Jimmy went along to the store, leaning back against the wind, carrying the woman's kerosene can to be filled. Men were not standing in the store porch any longer. They came dashing in with old coats, slickers, burlap sacks over their shoulders. They bought kerosene, or matches and candles, grits, nails, canned goods, hung over the barometer for a moment and ran out again, bent over against the hissing sheets of the rain. The wind was a steady, high, grinding roar.

Although he hardly thought about it, it was past the middle of the afternoon. It took longer to walk between the houses, boring head-down into the wind. Later he stood with Mr. Bethel and watched the relief train work its way south along the railroad embankment.

The coaches came first, streaming with white water, and the engine, reversed, backing it up. The engineer blew the whistle sharply, going by the small station. He'd stop on his way back and pick anybody up who wanted to go. They'd had trouble up the line; trees had fallen across it and a cable had had to be cleared. The faces of a few men peered out at them curiously from the last coach. The water had been high at Barnes Sound, the engineer had shouted.

It did not seem to Jimmy that any of these men were planning to leave on the train when it came back. They spoke only of boats and shutters. The wind must be around fifty, somebody said. Branches were snapping. Leaves littered the roadway, churned up by the rain, blowing with the gusts. When they went back by the store, somebody shouted that the telephone was dead.

Paths were running streams of water as they sloshed back. A lamp or two shone in the shuttered houses. Fewer and fewer figures moved in the paths. The settlement huddled under its streaming eaves, under its rain-beaten roofs, the little houses crouching shapes beside the slashed trees. The few palm trees groaned in long curves, their fronds like bunches of beaten feathers. The aroused sound of the sea was a steady pounding under the roaring wind.

Jimmy went back with Mr. Bethel to his house. It seemed to be taken for granted. As they struggled up the porch they saw that the sea was higher, ridges of white bursting in across the sunken reefs. But he could see only a little way out. Water and rain were a gray fog, and besides, the wind forced the stinging eyes shut, so that he could only peer out under his hand.

Inside the house it was pitch dark, except for one lamp. The roaring seemed louder, shut in by it. All the family was there, sitting around. Jimmy helped Mr. Bethel pack the crack under the door with newspapers. It was stifling hot, and so damp that perspiration stood on the skin in drops before it ran down the body, tickling and uncomfortable.

There was nothing to do now but wait. The barometer was still going down. The baby cried and was hushed, given another bottle.

The little girl played quietly with paper dolls. Jimmy helped her cut pictures out of a magazine with her small blunt scissors. Her hair was pale yellow and smelled clean—the mild, bland smell of a child. Mrs. Bethel knitted.

It had been a long time since Jimmy Gowan had been enclosed like this, close and quiet, with a man's family. They took him for granted, making small murmuring remarks, glancing at him absently as they listened to the attack of some shaking, howling gust outside. The son-in-law and another man, Mr. Bethel's brother George, played cards by a candle. But Mr. Bethel himself smoked and listened, getting up to look at the barometer, glancing at a window fastening. When a line of dark water edged under a window frame, he spoke quietly, and Sanders got up to pack in more newspapers. Bethel was the head of things; you could see that. All these people were a closely knit tribe, looking to him for decisions. There was something good about it to Jimmy. This was the way people ought to be, not batting around lonely, not just a lot of men herded together, but with women knitting and children to have to think about.

Presently, Mrs. Bethel got up and went to the kitchen with her daughter. You couldn't hear ham frying, and eggs, but you could smell them, and a great pot of boiling coffee. The food was good, with slabs of bread, and butter that melted in the saucer. They ate hungrily and heartily, crowded together about the lamp on the table. The little girl wanted to sit by Jimmy. Her name was Anna Lou. It was queer to feel a child's fat hand clutching his knee, bumping with her head against his arm. He had almost forgotten that there were children. The women left the dishes on the table. The uproar outside was louder. The house shook continually under the blows of the wind, as if it had been a pile driver. The sounds of the sea and of the rain were mingled and continuous, and they had to raise their voices to be heard over the uproar. Even the floor shook as if something were tugging and tugging at the supports below them.

It was queer to Jimmy that he was not afraid. If it were a dream, he would have been shaking with horror. But it was real—as real as his senses—and he sat quietly, as they did. Perhaps it was being here with them that made the difference; men and women and children equally sharing in the apprehension of whatever was to come. And besides, he had no decisions to make, nothing to think out. Mr. Bethel would do that. They all looked at him from time to time, and his set square face, with its thoughtful eyes, glanced from one to another of them, watchful, responsible, caring.

"If we have to get out," he said suddenly, speaking loudly, although he was quite near, "remember to keep together, right across the garden, to the storm house. That'll hold. I built it on purpose. Poured concrete and bolted to the rock, with cables from the roof to the ground."

It hadn't occurred to Jimmy that they might have to get out into that. The beginning of a tremor out of his old horror ran in him, but he forced his muscles to stillness. With this child here, pushing up against his knee to put her doll on the table, you couldn't let yourself tremble. Children mustn't know fear, not ever. He felt queer and angry that they might ever have to know. It was too much, it wasn't right, by the Lord Harry. A little thing like that. His curious indignation burned hotly in him, warming and bracing him.

When he followed a fixed glance of Mr. Bethel to the floor under the east window and saw a crack widen and darken, as if something were pulling it apart outside, and a wide ripple of water run in smartly, right across the floor, he felt no fear at all. It was coming, then.

The house shook again with a great, pounding blow from outside. Water, like a flexible black skin, slipped down the walls, and there was a crashing and snapping, as if axes were at work on the corner of the roof. The lamp flame flared and wavered, and salt wet air moved about them as if the wind had found an opening at last.

They were putting on coats, buttoning the baby inside the waist of Charlie Sanders' trench coat. Charlie tightened his belt outside his coat to support the baby's small bulk. Mr. Bethel was trying his flashlight. George Bethel tossed Jimmy a slicker. The women were tied into wraps. Mr. Bethel was making a sheet into a coil of rope. He looked them over carefully. George had the little girl covered with a shawl. The crashing and straining at the house were continuous. They could hardly hear their own voices. Water was chill about their ankles. The floor, unaccountably, sagged. That was the sea, that hissing roar, close outside.

"I'll go first.... Hang on, Mary.... Then you, Bertha... Then you, men.... Hang on to this, all of you, and you, Gowan. Don't get separated. Bunch up. Right across to the other house. Don't let anybody get away."

His voice went out like the light in the assault of the wind. They were a huddle at the door, the children in the middle. Bethel plunged and they followed, caught and shaken like rats in the instant immensity of that black force outside, plowing in water up to their knees, choked with driven water, choked and battered by wind that could have beaten them to rags if they once had let go.

But their hands gripped convulsively, hand to hand, arms rigid, stumbling and plowing through the running weight of the water. Bethel's flashlight glared on the boiling white foam over blackness that caught at them. They bent to it as if they were hauling on a weight, groping after the light that moved steadily before them, clinging more and more convulsively together.

Some floating debris hit Jimmy under the knee, so that he stumbled and almost fell. But the baby's mother caught him about the waist and held him until he could catch at the coiled sheet.

The flashlight suddenly picked out the door in the lee of the storm house, and they could breathe more freely. When Bethel opened it they went in, in the same close huddle, and shut and barred the door behind them.

It was breathlessly stuffy in the small closed space, but nobody

174

minded. There were candles on a shelf, and in the small flame's light they stared gravely at one another. They were as soaked as if they had been submerged for hours, but no one was hurt. The baby emerged, staring a little, from the wet trench coat, but he wasn't crying. They clustered about him, watching his arms begin to jerk gaily and a beginning grin curve his wet toothless mouth. He wasn't hurt at all, his father insisted, shouting against the raging din outside. Stout feller. He was having fun. Little Anna Lou wasn't frightened, either. They hung about both children, set on the one small table, smiling down at them anxiously. Nothing seemed to matter if the children were all right. Nothing, nothing, neither hurt nor cold nor fright, must come to them. Closer than the stout walls or the threat of the rage outside, the adults were drawn together by that single passion.

They sat on a bench or chair, or stood, around the candles and the children, straining to the sounds outside. When Jimmy put a hand on a wall he was startled to feel it quivering steadily like a harp string. The blows of the rising water were continuous, terrifying. The walls that had seemed so stout shook under that force as if they had been thin wood, and the faces turned to Jimmy as he felt it, staring at them, were drawn with understanding. They huddled in a tiny void in a black enormity of night and sea and hurricane, and knew, suddenly, how frail the respite was.

They waited. Only the baby's face was bland and unaware. Little Anna Lou clung to her grandfather soberly, her eyes wide, her mouth pinched shut. Their wet clothing grew warm on their tense bodies. The minutes were interminable.

The quivering of the solid walls was becoming a steady shaking. Water tugged at the door, slipped over the sill. The very sill was heaving. A long crack snapped across the cement floor and white water boiled through. The shaking reached to the roof. When Jimmy looked at the floor again, a whole slab of cement tilted as if a black enormous paw was working it upward.

When Bethel spoke, Jimmy could see by the filled throat, the straining jaw, the veins starting in his forehead, that he was shouting. But none of them heard more than a few high, thin words.

"Get. . .get out!" he was saying. "Stick together. . .lean. . . against wind and tide. . .lean. . .against wind. . .and. . .tide!"

The baby was wrapped again, high on its father's shoulder;

Bethel had Anna Lou. They tied the women together. When the door opened, water was behind them, water raved to meet them, blackness engulfed them and the hurricane screamed its unearthly clamor into their deafened ears.

The racing waves caught them high above their waists. They clung to one another, a small mass of human life, leaning, groping, stumbling for a foothold on the uncertain earth. Water, rain or sea, choked them, smashed at them, dragged them down, battered at their breathless bodies. They could hardly have told if they breathed, or if they made any progress, or if the very body next to any of them was left alive. Only the frantic eye of the flashlight went ahead of them, glaring on the foaming wave tops, glaring on black, perilous, swirling water, racing ahead of them with the dizzying horror of a dream.

There was a little tree, bent in a bow, but standing, thirty feet ahead of them. Its leaves were gone; its bark. Its branches were snapped off even as they stared. But it was rooted fast. It might have been less than thirty feet away, but it was farther than the forgotten rim of the world. They fixed their staring eyes upon it, in that feeble spot of light, as if it were the very outpost of hope. Jumping to breathe clear above the waves that blinded them, they struggled terribly to move toward it, fighting for foothold, straining lungs, straining muscles, drawn and unseen faces. Only the grip of their arms about one another and about the children was real. The blackness screamed and raved and fought them, every step, every inch, every gasp. The tree—and the children—if they had thoughts, those were all they had. Stronger than their hands, that impulse held them together, a single, passionate, painful flesh.

The tree was nearer. They were reaching it. Someone touched it, held on, drew them close. The little girl was thrust into Jimmy's hands. He felt the terrible mute clinging of her arms about his neck. Somebody passed the sheet around the women and the tree. The man with the baby was pinned to the tree by another's arms, so that he could hold the small bundle high. Jimmy felt the shaking tree with one desperate hand. It was no bigger around than a whisky bottle. It was a thread, a nothing, in the midst of the terror. But it held and they drew close around it, feeling the shaking of their bodies and its shaking as one thing. The flashlight picked out their aged and straining faces, one by one. They were all there. In the wave troughs they could gulp wet breaths. Suddenly the light went out. Jimmy felt a body slip down under water by his leg. A vicious thing out of the dark— planks or a door—had hit suddenly. Frantically, Jimmy fended off its leaping charge, felt it move away on another surge of water. He passed the child to another pair of arms, dived, groping and choking. The man down there was a dead weight, moving sluggishly. He brought him up, gasping, fought to keep the face above water. It felt like Bethel himself. He might be dead, for all there was any way to tell. But the head must be held above water at any cost. Hands helped him in the blackness. Other hands clutched him tightly. A voice screamed in his ear, words he could hardly understand. But the tree held, and was holding.

It could not hold long. The water was higher. Breathing was more difficult. The wind increased beyond the ability of the choked heart to withstand. Debris surged about them—planks, pieces of the house. If they were to live at all now, it could not be for long. But the baby—but the child—but the unconscious man—hold on—on— hold on.

The screaming voice was in his ear again. It was words, not the wind. "Look—something"—that was all be could distinguish. He stared, his eyes distended in the dark. A blacker shape was looming nearer them against the wind, against the waves. Eyes that stared at it might have gone blind, might have imagined it. But it was a shape, enormous, uncertain, growing. If it crashed down on the tree, they were gone, broken instantly into gasping and helpless particles. If it searched them out—whatever it was—.

Waves broke against it. It loomed steadily. It was upon them. A despairing voice cried disjointedly. It lurched against the tree, and the humans huddled away from it, not giving up their clasp. The tree shivered with the impact of solidity, of timbers. It floundered there, rested, sucked down firmly, was wedged.

It felt like solid boards. It was a wall. There was an opening like a window. The shout in his ears was a faint cry, but new with hope. Some little shed or shack had been carried down to them by a trick of the waters, and was held solid there for them.

One by one they scrambled, were pulled, climbed up into it. There was a tilting wet floor under their feet. There were frail walls, holding, making a shelter against the storm. Jimmy felt the bulk of some piece of furniture, pushed at it. A wall gave way, fell out. The small shelter shook and staggered. But the other walls were firm.

They could see nothing, hear nothing. Only the sense of touch remained to them, feeling for one another, feeling at the warm faces of the children, feeling the inert body of the man who had been injured. He was still breathing. They braced themselves in strained and awkward attitudes, unseen, against walls or things like old bedsprings or boxes, fumbling to make the children easier, taking in breath painfully, as if they were all wounded, conscious only vaguely of aching arms, bruises, wrenching hearts. If the sea was less, they did not know it. If the wind screamed with diminishing violence, they were not aware of that, either, for a long, long time. The thin gray light that came with morning found them case there, like debris, in a shack little more than debris itself. Their eyes turned from face to face. With a curious wrenching of recognition, they saw they were men and women again, separate, enduring, in a wrecked gray waste of world.

Three days later, Jimmy was cooking canned beans over a tiny oilstove, in the only house left with a roof, by the place where the settlement had been. He had been cooking things out of cans, boiling coffee in a great tin, for nights and days. If his eyes were bleared and his bearded face haggard, he did not know it. He had on the dried wreck of a shirt and somebody's overalls. The cans had been unearthed from the debris of the store. An endless procession of battered people, with hands still shaking and faces yellowed, ate hurriedly at the one table and went out again. They did not say much. There was no stove anywhere else. This was all the food there was. Sometimes, for an hour or two, while Jimmy slept on the floor, Mrs. Bethel kept the coffee going. She worked the rest of the time tearing up rags for bandages, swabbing their scant supply of iodine on an endless procession of cuts and wounds.

Outside, the sun had come out again, blazing from an enormous and peaceful heaven over the mashed heaps that had been houses. Nothing was left. The few bushes still standing were hung with rags that had been clothing, bedding, caught on them in that night and now drying in the soft air. The men and women who came and went looked strange. They had no concern yet for their possessions—

mattresses in trees, a piano wrecked across the road, heaps of indistinguishable shreds of things washed clear into the torn jungle. They were still hunting for wives, husbands, children. The faint reek of flesh already rotting hung in the sun. Nobody knew how many had been washed away, might be floating in the western inlets, might be caught under the torn branches of the mangrove swamps.

Only rumors spoke of the veterans' camps to the southward and the relief train that had not come back. Bridges were down over the waterways between the Keys. Relief could come in only slowly along the washed-out highways. But cars were working their way through. Medical supplies would be there soon, more food, workers to take the place of the exhausted searchers. Jimmy kept on cooking beans.

If he had had any previous existence, he had almost forgotten it. There was no desire left in him but to help these people with whom he had endured that night. Bethel was still unconscious, among the wounded waiting to be moved to a hospital with the first ambulances that could come through. His ribs were broken; there was a concussion of the brain. But the two women, Charlie Sanders, George Bethel—above all, the baby and the little girl—were all right. They all worked, shoulder to shoulder, in the frantic haste of all that was to be done.

So that when relief did really come, and the militia, and cars from the north with food and tents and clothing, they stared incredulously at people with fresh faces and steady hands; people who had not lost everything they had, whose wives and brothers and children were not still missing. The survivors moved stiffly, with voices a little shrill.

There was milk and sugar for the coffee, fresh meat, a man to relieve Jimmy at the kerosene stove. He walked out, unable to sleep, staring at the heaped wreckage. No one had been back to the place where Bethel's house had been.

Jimmy pushed his way there, searching for landmarks. The shack that had saved them stood on drying ground, against the tiny tree. But there were no other houses, only strewn debris. He stood a long time looking out at the sea.

It stretched a shimmering field of exquisite color beyond the wreck-piled beach. There was no wind. The sky was marvelous, an exquisite unmarred blue. Only one cloud head, a high-piled mass of sheer ivory, towered at the horizon, and its reflection stretched across the blue peace of the sea without a ripple, almost to his feet. The flat land was brown and rotting with destruction, but the sea and the sky stood perfect in a serenity, an exaltation of beauty beyond belief.

When he went back again to the crowded relief shack, a man in uniform, with a fresh, ruddy face, glanced at Jimmy sharply. "Look here," he said "Aren't you one of those veterans?"

Jimmy stared at him mutely. The tone was that of forgotten authority. The voice was the same that had said to him before, time after time, "Move on."

He didn't say anything. Mrs. Bethel glanced up at him. Her face was more familiar to him than his own. He knew every line of strain, every mark her suffering had left. It was his suffering too. She waited in her shapeless dress that had belonged to some other woman, her feet in man's shoes, her hair caught up somehow with a borrowed pin. But for the keenness of her eyes, she looked an old, old woman.

"We're rounding up all the veterans left alive," the man went on. "Our orders are to get them out of here as quick as we can to hospitals or to camps up north. We're checking all of them, to see how many there are left. I've seen you down there. There's a car outside. Tell them you're to go as soon as the wounded are cleared out. Hurry up."

He could say nothing. They were moving him on again. But a protest deeper than he had ever felt burned in his throat. He couldn't move on again, he couldn't. It would have been better to have died.

Mrs. Bethel saw his face. "You leave him along," she said to the man sharply. For the first time for three days her voice was full and clear. "You aren't going to take him. With Mr. Bethel still unconscious, he's the oldest man in the family. We need him. You leave him be."

Jimmy returned steadily her long, quiet glance. It was strange to feel so happy with so much sorrow all around. His caught breach relaxed quietly. He was strong and sure.

"You made a mistake, mister," he said, turning his eyes from Mrs. Bethel to the sharpened glance of authority. "You can't send me any place. I got too much to do. And I got no time to argue about it, either. You'll just have to take my word for it. I belong right here."

9
THE ROAD TO THE HORIZON

AFTERWARD, IT SEEMED to the boy, Harvey, his life, his whole adult life, began on the edge of that firelight in the rough sand among palmettos, looking down on that stooping bony back. He'd followed a long way through the pineland. The smell of bacon cooking squeezed his stomach against his sharp, growing bones. But it was the man's eyes that were important, bright with the small flames, turning at him.

"Mister," he said, humbly and wildly, at once, "are you the one fixing to get across the Everglades?"

He began to shake then, less with hunger and tiredness than with the conviction boiling up in him—learned sleeping on wharves, being kicked off boats, working in the slime of the clam house—that he'd got to get clear out of wretchedness it hurt to think of, clear out, across there where almost no white men had ever been, to that other side. It was the only chance he had.

The man's face was long-nosed and dark as a dog's under a flap of black hair and those small, fixed eyes. He forked the bacon popping in the pan and slid in batter. The boy watched the face.

"I've not concealed it," the man said; his voice was mild and a little nasal, but well tuned. "But I haven't made any great noise of it either. Where have you jumped up from to ask me that?"

"Back there," the boy said. "I saw you with your scissors grinder at house doors. They said you were the cra—The man that was going to find out what was in the middle of the Everglades. They said you thought there was a great beautiful island there, beyond the swamps, where the Indians have fine secret towns and fine gardens and all the game anybody could want."

"Do you believe there is?" The bacon fork, the jetty eyes stabbed him as the voice went shrill. "You, boy, do you believe that?"

The boy, Harvey, snuffled and grew more haggard under his sun blisters. His eyes were pale and disconsolate, and he shivered now with plain hunger and fatigue.

"No," he said, "I don't. But it don't matter, if you're going out there. They said nobody but Indians could get through the black mud and the cutting sawgrass. So I come to go with you. I got to get to the other side."

"Why?" the man said, chewing at his bacon and corn bread. "What would there be about that side different from this side?"

"I don't know," the boy said dully, thinking of the broad, slow river to the Gulf, the palms thick about neat quiet houses, the sleepy air, the smells of the fish wharves and the clam cannery, that had seemed to trap him in. "Only it's got to be."

The man nudged the skillet toward him in the sand. "Cook yourself some bacon," he said. "Batter's in the jar. You from Fort Myers?"

"Thereabouts," the boy said, trying to speak politely, eying the heavenly browning food. "Before that—a long time—Tampa. My dad took sick in the Army there and they buried him. Yellow fever. He never did get to go to the war in Cuba, like he wanted. He brought me down to a woman there, so's he could enlist. Afterward, I couldn't make out to stay with her. I tried to get out on a boat. I got put off at Punta Rassa. I couldn't seem to . . . get out. You walk fast, mister. Will we get to the Everglades tomorrow?"

He ate the last delicious crumbs carefully, eying the fragrant grease still in the pan. The face of the man was a long brooding. The eyes slept a little, forgetting him, watching an inward thing. It was the kind of face and eyes that would believe in strange, hidden cities and gardens that never in this world could be there. He wouldn't be thinking about swamps and sawgrass and poisonous snakes and maybe ugly Indians. But if he was crazy, it was no kind of craziness to be afraid of. More like it was a religion to him. The boy looked around him with eyes calmed and sharpened with food and the sense that he'd done, so far, what he'd set out to do.

The man had food and cooking things in a blanket roll, a rifle and a larger canvas pack. It was a lot for one man to carry. Harvey grinned. He had a gunny sack and a fishy piece of tarpaulin he'd found—well, stole, then—and some dry corn bread he was saving, in case he didn't catch up with the man. He had a fish line and some hooks and a pan and this tin and his knife and matches. And ten cents' worth of meal.

The fire dulled and reddened. Stars trailed brilliance beyond black pine tops. The dew-wet wind, from acre after acre of cooling and empty pineland, scuffled the palmettos. Somewhere near, a chuck-willis-widow began abruptly its whistling, echoing, insistent call. When it stopped, the answer came, lonely and far, a whisper, eastward.

The long, Yankee-faced man got up to reach for his blanket and mosquito netting, and nearly stepped on Harvey in the warmed, root-veined sand.

"We'll start before dawn," he said. "I don't know how the two of us will make out with what food there is. But I figure it ought to be only two-three days more before we'll be eating venison and turkey and wild honey and the small sweet vegetables that they have there. Drinks of strange roots they'll give us, in their own country, to make us feel fine. I aim to see the deerskins filled with flowers, and the dance." The man smiled down suddenly into the boy's eyes, his face softly folded. "My name's Abner Petteway," he said. "Maybe you're a sign sent to mean we'll get there sure."

He lay down and went to sleep without turning, with only a long, light sigh. But Harvey sat up, thoughts singing in his head like the late-rising mosquitoes. He felt alive, all over him, as if parts of his mind and body that had lain deaf and drowsing had come completely awake. If ever anybody needed looking after, it was this man. Harvey knew about what lay ahead. He'd listened to men arguing about the unknown wilderness of the Everglades—if there was a watershed, or another lake, or great rivers through the sawgrass where the snakes rustled. There might be streams eastward to the other rim of pine and the sea winds and the wide salt sea. They'd built a railroad to that new town on the Miami, and there would be work and a chance to get North, where his father had come from. That was what he longed for, staring out of his hardening, scrawny boy's face.

But what would happen to this long man when he found there

was nothing there like what he dreamed? For himself, he wasn't worried now. What he had to do he would do when the time came. But it was going to be bad for the man.

The sky was only a little thinner in the darkness, when the man woke him, clinking about among his things.

"We'll go on," he said vaguely. "There ought to be a lake."

Harvey slung his own pack and picked up what else he could carry, trotting after the long legs measuring out the path in the softening light. Birds made light beginning flutings as they came to white sand and a pool of mist, that was misty, root-smelling, sweet water, a little lake like mirror glass as the light thinned and grew crystal and clear pink beyond the new green tops of the trees. They washed mightily and Harvey caught bass with a bit of bacon rind as the breakfast fire crackled on the twigs. The sun was not clear up when they were packed and striding, as the man's compass pointed south, thirty-two east. The man wasn't entirely crazy. They divided the packs before starting again, and Harvey felt the new weight. But there was nothing in the world to keep down the lightness and excitement in his heart.

The man's long legs went striding and swishing before him, in a gait that thrust the miles behind. It was not until the high-blazing midmorning that Harvey got the trick of that, with his second wind, and had not to catch up by running. The pines had been left, the palmettos were thinning in a grassed prairie, with blossoming yellow weeds and clumps of silverleafed shrubs from which the little birds darted. In the blue, enormous sky buzzards sailed like black specks against white clouds, and there was a smell of herbs warmed in the sun. As far as they could see along the level land there was no sign of cultivation except a rusty line of barbed wire going off somewhere. Then there were wide shallow places filled thinly with water, in which the grass grew bright. They had to wade through that. They ate the morning's corn bread and scooped up water as they marched. The afternoon went gray around them and they were damp with fine rain, and that night there was nothing but a sparse clump of willow bushes to camp by, and damp wood and no drinking water. But it did not matter, because they had hardly started, and tomorrow, the man hoped, they would come to the Everglades.

By the next night there were no Everglades either. All day there had been the prairie and the fine grass and the glittering, brilliant, metallic blue sky. Harvey's load had grown so heavy he had thought his back, or his legs, would surely break. Sun blisters were raw on his face, and his feet were bruised and blistered in his worn shoes. But the man's long face seemed unaffected by any fatigue or hope deferred or question. It was curiously cold that night, damp, with a piercing cold wind, as if from great northern spaces.

But the wind was gone in the morning and they stepped out lively enough in the first warmth with hot food in them and Harvey with a sudden new sense of toughness and springupness in his well-used muscles. They saw more deer that day, that flashed white tails and bounced off on their brittle-looking legs. Abner would not shoot them. Deer meat would taste good, Harvey thought wistfully. They mostly ate corn bread now, with bacon grease, hoarding the bacon. They'd have to shoot something or catch something soon, or go hungry.

All day long, the next day, they strode with an equal pace over the fine-grassed prairie, among clumps of scrub oak and willow and denser patches of jungle. Late in the afternoon they came to pineland and moved through the gray-silvered fingers of palmetto and shadier places where the pine needles lay thick and brown and warm-scented, and jay birds scolded at them among the high criss-crossed twigs. They came out on the other side of that, in the east-slanting sunlight, and stood looking out on a mile or two more of prairie.

Beyond that they stared at an enormous level openness to the horizon. Water stood clear and shining in green-brown sedge, and dazzling white cloud shadows were reflected in it, and the blue sky itself, sun-blazing, open and yet misted with an extraordinary sense of distance. Here and there beyond, green islands humped, shaped like whales, solid with dark leaves. Wind came over it from miles of growing stuff, sweet with water smells and blossoming weeds. Harvey looked a long time, his body tingling. That was east.

"That's it, isn't it, Abner? There they are."

The lank-faced man looked soberly. There was such a clear light over those levels, the sun glittered on so many million points of leaf and grass edge and water ripple, the clouds stood so ranked with pure snow, that, staring hard to that far, thin-circling horizon, you could almost see—you could see——

"Everglades," Harvey said, letting his breath out. "Everglades are—Why, I never thought they'd be like that. I thought they were all dark, with trees and moss and hanging snakes——"

The man's face quivered a little, as if he had gone blind. Harvey put his hand on the thin, hard arm, and got him turned around. "Just here in the pineland is a good place to overhaul everything." Abner went with him like a child that has been dreaming and has been waked abruptly.

But he liked the camp Harvey made on the sweet pine needles, and lay down to doze. Harvey was glad to get away with the rifle, west, to the pine edge. It would be fine if he could shoot a turkey. Back on the prairie, in the sunset, he came on two Seminole Indian women walking, balancing on bare feet their flowing, bright-striped skirts. The round-faced young one ducked her chin on her high-piled throat and shoulder beads and veered away from him, frightened. But the other was a raisin-wrinkled old thing, with bright hard eyes for his youth. He got her to speak a few words of English.

He said, "Turkey?" and she shook her head. "Indian men," and she pointed north. "Big cypress—hunt." He said, "Miami, how far?" and she stared and flapped her hands and cackled with her sunken jaws. "Miami, how far?" he persisted, seeing she understood him.

"Hunder' mile," she said suddenly. She could not possibly be right. He said "How many days?" twice before she cackled again and answered him, quite clearly, "Indian, two days. White man, fifteen."

He realized, with dismay, she might know what she was talking about. They were utter fools not to have a boat. But going back among the trees he got three squirrels. Tomorrow, perhaps, he could find more food.

The squirrel meat smelled fine over the fire. Sleep had done Abner a world of good, by the smoothed look of him.

"Gosh, Abner, I don't see how we can get along without a boat."

"Without a boat?" The lank man stared at him. "You think I'm crazy? Of course we've got a boat. We'll set it up tomorrow." He slept again, early.

Harvey lay on his satisfied stomach, staring out at the dark, mysterious reaches to eastward, happier than he had ever been in his life. Now and then a night heron croaked overhead. Spiders' eyes in the grass shone back the last gleam of the fire. Wind came cool across the watery places. Then, louder than bird sounds or insects, he heard a strange, muffled roaring, as if from the depths of the mud. After his skin warmed again he thought what that was. Alligators.

In a fine yellowing dawn, he thought soberly of what the old Indian woman had said. The world was an enormous place. Water, lying over it in long streaks, paled and silvered. Green grew luminous. Birds went up into the lovely airiness of the sky in crying flights, little birds near by skimming and darting, and beyond a lifting burst of blue-and-white herons, and even higher, in a long wavering line whiter than the light-struck cloud, wheeling and soaring, white ibis. The light lifted clearer and higher over the flat-reaching earth. Then he jogged down to the nearest water and washed and drank, and filled the coffee-pot, and came back to find Abner cooking bacon and grits, and eager to start at once. It wouldn't do, Harvey told him soberly. You couldn't just walk down to the edge of that solid land and step off. It made him feel old to be talking to an older man like that. But somebody had to be practical. He sent Abner off with the gun.

There were grits as well as corn meal. Enough, he hoped. And quite a lot of coffee and sugar and bacon. He figured on cooking enough corn bread tonight to carry with them tomorrow. He made two tight bundles of all the food. In an hour Abner was back, triumphant, with a big hunk of deer meat and some of that starchy meal the Indians make from the coontie root, for the mush they call "sofkee." He had found the Indian camp. They roasted the deer meat and cooked corn bread, and lay down early to sleep, although it seemed to the boy that he was too excited to keep his eyes shut.

It was still dark when they swallowed their hot coffee and the corn bread, their eyes turned to the opening east. They set up the clumsy canvas boat at the edge of the Everglades water standing clear over brown tussocks of weeds and rock. It was too shallow to pole the boat, so they loaded it and waded out, ankle deep, shoving the boat ahead.

Under the water, as they splashed forward, the rocks were rough edged, but slimy with growing things, among mudholes into which a leg would slide up to the thigh. The first brown tussocks of sawgrass grew here not quite breast high among the wandering brown water channels. From this level, as the boat scratched and grated among the rocks and hissed in the grass stems, they could not see so far as the horizon, but only the sea of brown and occasional islands of bushes that loomed like trees. The sun went higher, pouring its weight of heat and light upon thin, bent shoulders, so that sweat wet them as much as the water. Once or twice Harvey slipped into mudholes up to his waist. Until he learned to tie them on tightly, mud, a dozen times, sucked off his shoes.

They learned not to clutch at the sawgrass. The stuff was edged by fine teeth, like broken glass, that cut to the bone. Where it was whipped across a face it left a long, bleeding scratch, and their hands and ankles and arms dripped blood. Slowly, the sawgrass was growing taller and more dense, cutting off the wind as they bent to pull at the boat.

But the water, over the mossy, uneven rock, was clear and good. They drank as much as they liked and dashed it in their salt-streaming faces. There was constant reference to the compass, a constant need of getting up higher to look around. Yet even standing up in the boat they could see nothing but sawgrass tops, blossoming brownly here and there, and the nearest island-like clumps of trees. He knew they were only scrub trees, but from their chin-on-the-earth level, they looked like forests.

Standing in water, they ate corn bread and deer meat, and pushed onward at once under the beating noon sun. It was impossible, here, to tell what progress they were making.

The sawgrass grew taller, more level, more completely covering the distance ahead of them with its wind-blown brown. They came to a channel like a creek between abrupt banks, and it was delicious to sit in the small canvas thing and pole, as best they could, against the muck-covered rocks below. The mud on them dried in the hot sun and every sawgrass cut stung like fire, and it was midafternoon.

In another hour, as they began to feel sure their channel was a small river, it ceased abruptly and the sawgrass went on, thick as wheat. But there was a hammock ahead there, with tall trees that meant dry ground, at least. So they jumped out, sinking to the hips, and began again that slow, dragging, difficult crawl.

There were bushes to catch at, and they came up with a rush, pulling the loaded boat as high as they could. It seemed to Harvey, if he could only fall flat on his face he would be perfectly happy never to move again. But there was wood to be cut, and leaves to be piled for beds, and supper. Abner stood staring westward, and Harvey looked as he pointed. The sun was going down there, gilding and reddening the illimitable sea of the sawgrass to north and south, but there, dark before the brightness, were the ranked pine trees on the solid ground they had left that morning. Not more than two miles away.

For a moment the boy tasted despair. It would take months. They couldn't stand it. But he looked at Abner's quiet face and kept his mouth shut. After all, what was there to go back to but the clam cannery? Hot food was fine and the sawgrass cuts did not burn any more. But with the dark, a cloud of dark, soft-bodied, savage mosquitoes blew in on them, covering every inch of exposed skin, biting through wet shirts and trousers, setting them crazy. Stampings and thrashings did no good. Mosquitoes shrilled in their ears and flew into their eyes and mouths. The irritation they set up was so great, it seemed to Harvey, that he could have sat down and burst into tears.

But they built up a fire of damp wood that set up a choking smoke that kept off the pests until they could huddle under the one net. Before Harvey died of exhausted sleep, their strange, thin screaming hung just beyond his nose.

But the morning was clear gray, with a raking north wind that had carried away every sign of mosquitoes from the world, a wind that chilled the light and the flattened sawgrass with great cat licks and rippled the bright water in the water places until the edges of everything glistened in the thin, bright sun. He woke, healed and hungry, to the smell of bacon and grits cooking and Abner's eyes glinting.

The only thing to do, Abner said, blowing on his coffee, was to keep clear of the sawgrass, if they possibly could. If they had to swing due south, as the shape of that water out there indicated, it would be better to try it, always watching for a river or some sort of stream opening eastward. Two miles a day wasn't enough.

They found deep water to float the canoe in, and poled south with that sense of delight that comes with a renewed journey in the fresh day. Poling, Harvey found, wasn't so easy as it looked. His pole stuck in mud, slipped off concealed rocks, sent the shaky craft dipping and careening into mud banks and, more than once, nearly turned them both, and the boatload, irretrievably into the bright brown water. There was no good hurrying or leaning his weight on a thrust.

Sawgrass went by slowly. Turtles flopped into the water ahead. Now and then, a water moccasin, its black head only a dark bud out of water, wavered in a long v-shaped ripple carelessly across their bow. Fishing herons flapped away from them into the wind, tucking their beaks on their rounded breasts. Alligators slid down the mud. And up the branched, aimless-seeming water channels ducks thrashed water white with their squattering, frightened wings. The wide brown mud-and-grass-and-water world was flashing and clacking and boiling with life. They managed to shoot, and retrieve, some ducks and a queer long-necked bird that Abner said was a water turkey. Then the waterway, or channel, or natural ditch, ran out in a threadlike tangle of shallows through which they could neither pole nor push. Abner cut his hand savagely, trying to pull at the high sawgrass. There was nothing for it but to go overside again, down into the scratching, oozing mud, armpit-high, trying at the same time to hold themselves up by the boat and send it forward.

Deeper water was at last there before their sweating faces, a maze of channels among sawgrass. Any one of them might lead anywhere, or narrow again, suddenly, into unending swamp. They waited, resting and eating cold food, trying to decide whether to follow compass bearings or water drift or luck.

Abner grunted. Something round and dark seemed to glide, at a little distance, above the feathery sawgrass tops. A Seminole, brilliant in red-and-yellow-striped skirt and blouse, poled into sight his long cypress canoe, with that slow ease that Harvey knew now was one of the hardest things in the world. His dark face under the black bangs and curious, rolled red turban looked at them without emotion, waiting while Abner spoke. He would show them a place for the night and a way to go in the morning, but he could not guide them farther. He moved on with that easy, deliberate pole and they followed into deeper water, almost southwest. There was an island with a tree in the middle, large enough to climb and stare out from. They had come nearly five miles. After they ate supper the Indian poled off under an enormous rose-and-brass sunset, a brilliant figure against the greeny-brown levels, serene, impenetrable and at home.

But the next day, before half the blistering hot morning was over, the sawgrass closed in about them completely. Harvey climbed up on Abner's shoulders in the unsteady boat to stare about. The wind rippled the cruel greeny-brown grass tops. There was the angry, blazing sky overhead. That was all.

They sat in the muddy boat. They could not go back. There was no forward.

Abner said, "We got to think. Let's eat."

Harvey chewed, watching the bony back, the sunken, patient cheek. He had felt, time and again, that he was the leader of this now incomprehensible attempt. But now his cockiness was gone. Thinking was despair. But slowly he was aware of strength in the older man. Perhaps that was what being older meant—that you had lived longer and endured more, and so were not so quickly vulnerable either to pride or to despair. Perhaps there were deeps of strength that youth alone could not know. For a moment he was eased and comforted.

But what good was it to sit and think?

The man stood up to sweep a long look about.

"Harve, you're lighter," he said. "Hop out and get forward here a little way, straight on our course, like that, and set fire to this eternal stuff."

Harvey found the matches and went overside knee-deep, thigh-deep, in the black muck between the binding grass. Sometimes, he thought, if he hadn't had two legs he would have kept on sinking. But he sat astride upon the grass roots, struggling forward with great heaving pulls, leg by leg. It got firmer shortly, so that he could trample down the tussocks, his hands and cut face bleeding freely. At Abner's shout he trampled a swath of grass, as the black water began to ooze through, and set his flaming match to it.

It was extraordinary how the stuff roared into great flame fringes, yellowing and darkening the sunlight, running like a strong river, crackling and hissing, clouding the sky with greasy smoke. Abner had fired the grass rim between them, and that flame roared up and went out like charred paper. Abner waved at him in plain sight.

"Go on ahead!" he called. "Start another. When it cools, we'll take the boat forward!"

The ground underfoot was black and still smoking, but it was easier to get ahead, except for the low places, where he sank again to his hips and had to go on with that extraordinarily tiring process, drawing out one leg, thrusting it hip-high and forward as far as he could, stepping on it, and so down and down into the oozing, bottomless muck. It was worse than climbing an interminable staircase on his knees. He gained about a mile. Then he came to a lagoon, sat waist-deep in ooze, seeing the fire, under a changing gust of wind, making a swing back toward him from the unfired south. The wind whipped the raging, ragged banners of the flames, so that the sharp crackling, the heat and the smoke poured over him. He plunged into deeper water and ceased to breathe. For a moment the flames roofed him in. They ceased.

He lay there until Abner shouted and pointed southward, and he got up to stare across acres of burned country at the greenness and shade of a small island of trees, glittering in the freshening wind.

It seemed to Harvey that those strange, beautiful cities and gardens could not be lovelier than that mounded green. Or more difficult to get at. If he could forget Abner and the boat and the packs, and crawl toward it flat on his face, now, by himself, it would be enough to ask. Nobody could expect him to do more. He looked back at Abner, stooping to haul at the boat, alone. So he began to go back.

It was useless to lighten the boat by strapping on their packs. The added weight only made them sink lower. There was nothing they could throw away. So they pulled and pushed among the desolate, burned-grass roots and the heavy mud; the boat even then not so difficult to manage as their own crawling and clumsy selves.

It was dark before they pulled themselves to the island. Hour after hour it had stood there, its greenness glittering. It was the only thing that had kept them going—that, and the numbness of their fatigue. They had energy enough left only to light a small cooking fire and boil water for mush. Coated as they were with mud and charred stuff and slime and smoke, they fell down on the tarpaulin and slept.

The next day, all day, was no better. Harvey found he was cooking the last of the bacon. There wasn't much meal left, some of the grits, but almost all the coontie flour. They had killed or caught nothing for the last few days.

It was evident that firing the sawgrass did not help matters much. The black muck was still there. But it did show the hidden, aimless-seeming pools and concentrations of water. The fires were slower to kindle, because of the heavy dewfall, but as the sun rose and dried the shimmering yellow-brown stalks, the orange flames burst up like an explosion and ran away before them. Slowly they followed. It was a wonder that the canvas-boat bottom was not torn to ribbons. They had to use extra care, lifting it over rock outcrops and sharp root ends. When they reached a little channel of water, gleaming blue from the sky and golden brown in the shadows of the grass, they were thankful there was anything left of the boat's bottom to keep the water out. It didn't last long. The shallows went into the sawgrass and became mud. Harvey let the bow hiss among the grasses and waited. Abner had slumped forward, sound asleep.

The boy looked at him with dismay, as if he had not noticed him for a long, long time. His beard was rough and muddied on his streaked face. It was surprisingly white, and there were heavy purplish circles under the closed, sunken eyes. He looked as if he had died, but his scrawny chest moved regularly enough. The boy could not bear to wake him. He had to force his own eyes open, in the utter quiet. A turtle moved beside the boat. Harvey caught it. He caught two more small ones and was cheered. The Indians roasted them in their shells. Presently Abner stirred, and they got out into the muck and struggled on.

In the late-afternoon light they came on a tiny island, no more than a hump of rock and a few stunted trees. It was a miserable place, and at first they thought they would be forced to it. But from up in the tree Abner saw a cypress hammock not too far away. A cottonmouth moccasin was coiled darkly beyond the tree, its open jaws like a white flower. Another curved toward them. They went on.

As the light cooled and afterglow bloomed in vast roses on the eastern clouds, they saw streamers of great white birds sailing low under the wind, to turn and drop downward into whitened treetops. The squawking and complaining and deep guttural notes of the rookery were a growing clamor. White wings lifted and flapped, birds leaped and veered off with a confusion of crying as they pushed under the bushes. The fuzzy-white young ibis inched away from them on their stick nests.

The drier land under the trees was whitened with feathers and rank with guano. But they got a fire lighted and killed off a few bird-hunting snakes and ate roast turtle and roast young ibis, which was fishy and tough, but at least food. In the morning they cooked enough more for the day. It was another day of sawgrass and black muck and tantalizing, curving, short channels of water. There were no openings in the grass and no watercourses going anywhere at all.

In the afternoon they saw grass fires in the northeast, as if the Indians were driving game. Or even, as Harvey thought, through that numbness that had encased him for days—or was it weeks?—perhaps they were burning it because they hated it, as he did, like something persistent and devilish and eternal.

Then it grew cold, with a wind arrowy from the north, chilling their bones, graying the sky, making a dismal wilderness out of the strange, unending, level country. By dark, they had found no islands at all, only a slightly drier place among the sawgrass. Harvey managed to cut down enough to put the tarpaulin on, and to boil water. They slept, chilled and dazed and cramped with wet. They were not warmed until the sun rose high. Then they went on, their minds dazed and queer, a little detached from their numbed bodies. Harvey was conscious, not so much of hunger as of the weakness of hunger. The lank man's color, Harvey thought, was like bad cheese. With every difficult step they took, he went more slowly, gasping a little. That day they could hardly have gone a mile. There was a dry spot for the night.

But in the morning—things were always better in the morning— they found what seemed like a little river, sparkling and deep, rough with fish. They waited for Harvey to catch a good string before they went on, and it seemed to him Abner spoke more cheerfully. Tomorrow, he said, they would certainly get there. This stream must go on, deepening clear to the east.

But around the next curve there was the sawgrass. Abner sat staring for a long time and Harvey thought that everything of intelligence drained from his haggard face. Alternately the boy dragged the boat and moved Abner forward and went back for the boat. He had no particular hope of anything ever being different. All he had in his head was that they must go on.

He slept that night on sawgrass in the ooze. Abner hunched as he could in the boat. There was half-cooked mush for breakfast. He thought he would never rouse Abner or, when he had, that he would never be able to keep him from falling face down in the muck and staying there. After an hour he got Abner into the boat and went on by himself, looking in desperation for what might not be anywhere.

194

He found it. Bushes and the wreck of a Seminole hut, bits of thatch on a rotting plank platform by a half-dried pool. He brought Abner up to it by late afternoon, although he thought many times it would be better for them both just to lie down and let the muck cover them, and free themselves of the horror of effort. Abner's face was a blotch of fever as he lay on the platform, his eyes vacant in his head. At least, the boy thought,they were above the mud. He caught two turtles before dark. Then the mosquitoes screamed in, and he covered them both with the net and seemed to die.

Abner was obviously worse next morning. He must have lost twenty pounds. Now only his ribs seemed to show under the blanket. Harvey made soup of the turtles, but the older man could swallow only a little.

From the ridgepole of the thatch, Harvey thought he could see a dark line of trees eastward, and a thread of smoke. He had to get there.

It would be a strange thing ever again to walk lightly on a hard road. Yet without the boat or Abner, it seemed to him he floundered forward more quickly. In several places, actually, he sank only above his ankles.

The trees were tall cypress, ancient with moss, young with new leaves, in shadowy water he had to swim to get across. But a long canoe was tied to a plank on the other side, and he scrambled up, dripping, to find thatched huts on littered, worn ground, kettles about a cooking fire, and brown babies who howled and ran in fright, and round-faced, peeping women. Now he had a word or two of Seminole for them. There was a half-grown boy who had a little English. As usual, the few old women were more curious than frightened.

The Miami, the boy said, pointing in an unexpected direction, was a good twenty-five miles away. It seemed incredible. He could not think how long it had been. He made them understand there was a sick man back there, and the boy took him in the canoe, in a winding sort of circle that brought them quite near the abandoned camp, so that presently they got Abner into the canoe by lifting and carrying him about fifty feet. He wasn't so much to carry, and did not open his eyes.

A tall old woman looked at him and took charge. The younger women had lost their shyness and skimmed around on their bare feet, in their gay, billowing skirts and ruffled berthas, bright-eyed and gigling. He ate broiled alligator tail and sofkee and palm cabbage that night and slept like a baby. In the morning, the boy had told him, maybeso one of the men would be back from the hunt with alligator skins and aigrettes to sell in Miami. Maybeso, he would take him.

Abner was conscious in the morning, but so weak he could hardly lift his eyelids. Whatever the squaws had given him had been good, but it was obvious he could stand no more for a while. Harvey began to be anxious to get on and see about a job. He could send money to Abner later.

"Fine. You go," Abner whispered. He had the rifle and cooking things he could give to the Seminoles for their care of him.

That afternoon, the man, Billy Tiger, came in from the north-west as Harvey was taking the steam bath they showed him in the bath hut by the stream. He threw water on red-hot stones as long as he could bear the steam, and then ran out to swim and duck among the lily pads, cleaner, newer than he had ever been in his life.

The sense of cleanness and release and freshness leaped to pure exhilaration in the dusk before dawn. The long canoe slipped shadowlike on dark water, the man standing on the inclined stern moving his pole imperceptibly, like a shadow. Even the sound of water dripping from the pole end was muted with the last shadow of the night. The light blossomed vastly. It seemed to the boy's cool eyes that he had never seen the world before.

He sat at his ease, watching the browning sawgrass, the blossoming sedge, the cattails, the mats of purple morning-glories slip past. Alligators slid. Fish flapped wetly. Night herons startled from the mud. As the light brightened, the thread of channel widened among broad water flats, stained luminous rose by the moment before the sun. The Indian seemed to slow his deliberate pole, for, acre after acre, the birds began to lift.

The airy, enormous reaches of sky were filled, horizon to horizon, with the flashing whiteness of wings. Blue-and-white herons, egrets shining with plumes, great white ibis, green herons, delicate blue-gray herons, but higher than all, wood ibis, wheeling and soaring; thousands after thousands of birds, flashing and turning and lifting. Their cool, faint crying was a mist of sound, their whiteness whiter than cloud or salt-white foam. Cloud-remote, free-soaring, moving and free——

"Look—look! Ah, look!" he kept gasping to the dark Indian face lifted also to the living marvel of the sky.

The Indian said nothing. The canoe slipped on. Birds lifted away from the gray prow, piping and whirling into the wind to float with those wheeling high circles against the clouds, and settled in the whitened water meadows behind as the sun blazed out and color and solidness came back to the morning world.

He could not believe it was all behind him. The canoe fled down the foam-swirling rapids of the Miami, past six miles of slowly curving banks, live oaks and cabbage palmettos and palm trees and glimpses of meadow, to shove its gray nose up the sand of the Indian's landing. Beyond leaning great coco palms, the river spread into the wide-shining bay, with wind that came large from the casting sea. There were an old thick-walled barracks and a new huge yellow-and-white hotel in a garden. The sound of hammering came over the glaring white dust of the streets, where men walked quickly between new houses in the sun.

He had come through, as he meant, Harvey thought. But there was no time for gawking. He must get a job. First he carried bundles of shingles up, and then he sat on a ridgepole himself, hammering hard, with his mouth tasting of nails.

Once he stopped pounding to stare out westward, over the curved river and the sails, to the pine-feathered prairie. Beyond that the Everglades lay in the misty remoteness of a great dream.

It had been Abner's dream, not his. He'd had only the urge to go forward. "What would there be about that side different from this side?" Abner had asked. He looked around. The pines were thin and queer and different. The wind was different, stronger from the sea. There was a livelier air here. Everybody worked under the same sun. But it wasn't that.

He looked down at his scarred hands, his long hard thighs. Bones were longer, muscle tough. Even his mind seemed whetted with new power. What was it the frightened sickliness of childhood had driven him forward to meet? It was himself.

He could not think again those unworded thoughts. He missed

now, not so much Abner as the long man's fantastic, unswerving hope. He'd never believed, yet because of it he'd got through.

Perhaps he wouldn't even see Abner again. He sat idle a moment longer, chilled in the glare of sun, curiously alone.

Must a man be half cracked to keep going in the bewildering world? Nothing like Abner's idea could ever come out of his own head. He was the one that would get things done. But what? Without that, one was empty.

He wished he could talk to Abner. Maybe Billy Tiger would wait and take him back Saturday with the money. But no sawgrass. He'd go not a step through that again, for a dozen of Abner's ideas. Not till they built a road.

He had lifted his hammer. Build a road. Someday someone would build a road through all that—the mud and the sawgrass and water—a road like a bridge from horizon to horizon. It could be bedded on rock. Rock was there. There'd have to be places where the water could run on its imperceptible drift southwestward. He saw it. There was gooseflesh all over him. It was a crazier idea than Abner's. He was crazier than Abner. Because he was the one. He'd have to build the road.

He fell to work, hammering furiously, to drive the quivers from his arms. He'd need more money. This week's was Abner's. Next week—or it would be better to get a job on the railroad, start getting somewhere where they could teach him all of the things that he'd have to learn. He didn't know anything. He didn't have anything. Only this crazy idea. But emptiness was gone. Crazy ideas were good things sometimes. He saw that now. They carried you on.